Angel's Eyes,
Blindfold Chess

By RW Richard
Aka The Romantic Novelist

Angel's Eyes

Published by WEB Press, Carlsbad, San Diego, California.

E-mail your request(s) to rwrichard@ymail.com. Visit the author's blog at http://romancetheguyspov.blogspot.com. The author thanks you for purchasing *Angel's Eyes* and wants to hear from you, either by email, review or blog comment.

WORKS by RW Richard
NOVELS:
Neanderthals and the Garden of Eden, **A unique take on human and wolf pre-history.**
Double Happiness, **Loosely based on Shakespeare's *Comedy of Errors*.**
Autumn Breeze, **Amazon Books of the Year Award. About the aftermath of 9/11, a fourteen year-old genius must avoid deportation by putting a spy and a detective together. Carlos Series, Book 1.**
Angel's Eyes, **A blind colonel is kicked out of the Army. She must now cope with men and disability. Carlos Series, Book 2.**
A More Perfect Union, **Amazon Books of the Year Award, San Diego Book Award Finalist. About the Republican and Democratic nominees for President falling in love. Carlos Series, Book 3.**
NOVELLA:
The Wolves of Sherwood Forest, **A young Robin and Marian save England.**
SHORTS, etc.:
Wings by Christmas **and other short stories and homages.**
BOOK ON WRITING:
101 Tips, Primarily on Writing Male Characters

TABLE OF CONTENTS

Angel's Eyes

Chapter 1

The Role of the Queen and King in Chess

Edan, Edanistan, Sunday May 4th, 1204 hours

The Lioness of Edanistan, Colonel Rebekah Carthage, made a habit of decimating the enemy, until today. She spat out grit and rubbed her nose from the stench and heat of baking road and debris from the city's armpit. On this intolerable day her intuition whispered death, hers.

Ever since she was a little girl, she knew things, could see with her eyes closed. She was some kind of freak, but her premonitions helped save her men's lives. She just couldn't conjure a way to save her own.

Her engineering team pounded computer keys at a cracked coffee table in a roofless home with stucco and shambled walls accented by a looming chimney.

"Deciphered chatter, Colonel. A message from one of Zachari's men."

She jumped over crumpled milk cartons and up onto the foundation with her second-in-command, Major Hollister, following behind her.

The screen translation read, *Today the witch dies. Allah be praised.*

Since there was only one so-called witch in Edan, her stomach turned once again. Perhaps, being armed with knowledge and acting carefully would save her from disaster. But how?

"Which witch?" Major Hollister asked, tapping her helmet.

This six-foot five, hayseed haired, blue-eyed Louisiana farmer's son was easy on her eyes but… But she wanted to rise through the ranks of double standard Army and he felt more like a big brother, a too big brother. "Stay focused, Hollister," she whispered, bopping his breastplate.

Hollister put on his all-too-obvious lovesick pout.

"Pull yourself together, Major."

"Yes, ma'am."

She took a swig from her water bottle. Jack Daniels would have been better.

Drenched-in-sweat, aggravated by an insufferable flack suit, she leaned against the sooty, brick chimney and surveyed the next cratered street and its one abandoned office building. That sixth sense returned to her for something positive. "Sniper, nine-o-clock, second-story, check the blown-out window."

Hollister adjusted his telescopic lens on his slide-down goggles and shrugged. "Don't see him."

They never did see what she saw.

"He sees us."

She barked assignments to the engineers while Hollister's counter-sniper team did their thing. A thin crow fluttered to roost, clasping the twisted iron grate on top of the chimney. The bird peeked down—sun splayed through its outstretched wings—offering the illusion of a pretty peacock.

Squawk.

Her South African and Shoshone blood recalled a simpler time and ancient superstitions. *Fly away brother. Thanks for your warning. I'll not die today.* The raven whitened the chimney while fluttering away—little doubt—an opinion on architecture and not of her demise.

She heard one muffled shot and ping. Pictured the sniper, whipping his scarred, pimpled head around, surprised by a bullet. Once again, she'd want to see for herself if his face matched her imagination. Nearly always had.

Hollister jogged back, proud-of-her jaw jutting. "The street is clear. I'll take point today, Colonel."

"Stand aside."

"Yes, ma'am." He hesitated and then grabbed her shoulders. "We can't lose you."

How did he know how uncertain she was? She twisted violently to break his grip. "Duly noted." She resisted saying, *you lovesick schmuck.*

"Ten minutes, ETA."

"Let's roll, Major." She jogged ahead of her combat team. Yes, unusual for a full Colonel in charge of a brigade to lead her soldiers into battle, but there was no one better.

The team slipped into a once-upscale residential neighborhood of bullet speckled stuccoed-walled and flat-roofed homes. She held up her hand, keeping her men at least ten paces back. She approached the target's front door alone and paused, picturing the home packed with explosives.

"Fall back, now," she ordered. Running, she watched the slowest soldier flop over the courtyard wall three strides ahead of her. She crossed herself, looked up at the glaring sun for a hint of God's mercy. At least, the Army would never forget the Lioness of Edanistan.

She didn't hear the explosion. Pieces of flying house pounded her armored suit. *No pain. Eyesight: gone. Feelings in hands, feet: gone. The metallic taste of blood dribbled from her eyes. Death?* A pure black curtain guillotined in her mind's eye. With one last desperate grab at brain function, she imagined two dilated brown eyes within a white blur. Someone or some creature was trapped in the just blown-up home. The black overwhelmed her…

Monday May 5th, 12:04 Noon, New York City

Physics Professor Jay Boone left his co-op to teach NYU's most popular class, Unexplained Phenomena, a subject, for the sake of academic argument, in which his peers considered him one of the world's leading authorities. However, he humbly and with humor refuted every irrational theory or ill-informed argument offered by his wide-eyed students. If they couldn't prove it, it hadn't happened.

Yet, on this sunny, invigorating day he'd felt a sense of foreboding as if someone was reaching out to him. His stomach ached, his thinking blurred. Today, although an ex-champion swimmer and in great shape, he lost balance, swooning over a smelly subway grate at Spring and Lafayette. A piece of his soul had slipped through the grates into the dark. How would he get that back? Since he shot down unexplained phenomena, he would not treat himself differently than his colleagues and students. His being out of sorts had nothing to do with the unexplained and everything to do with… Not enough coffee.

He arrived at NYU and taught his last class of the spring semester. With the lecture portion finished, he exited the back of the hall to raucous applause, leaving the final exam prep to his TAs.

Jay got some exercise by running down the faculty hallway clutching his ripped leather briefcase. He stepped into his office, locked the door and dropped the bag. Papers flew into the middle of what the janitor had called a giant trashcan office. Okay, he knew where everything was. He found his computer's headphones tucked between the third stack of grad papers and the second row of Quantum notes, next to Basic Chess Endings. The screen fired up.

News bullets burned his imagination:

• Senator Daniel Carthage now presumptive nominee Democratic Party.

• Senator Carthage's daughter, Colonel Rebekah Carthage critically injured in battle. *No detailed reports yet.*

He gripped his desk and peered at the ceiling, pissed. For many years, he had followed the exceptional career of her senator father, but rarely thought of her anymore. The *her* of his life. Rebekah was on his high school chess team. He had loved her, well *crushed* on her, well it was real love, but she hadn't given him a second glance or first, probably because he had been short, pimply and stinky. He held a hand up to his mouth. At least bad breath no longer plagued him.

He then read every word of the sketchy news about Rebekah, Bekah, but nothing could be learned. Pressed for time, he'd click and read more in depth reports later. That uncertain queasy feeling, which had shimmied through his body over the subway grate, returned. Damn it, the sensation had to have been for her, and still for her, now. But, he, a scientist recognized this *magic stuff* would always end up debunked and in this case by him. Still?

Even though he had 'rejected himself' on her behalf in prep school, never uttering a romantic word to her, his heart still twisted if only a little. He assumed they were still friends even though separated since the summer after their senior year at Bishop Eustace prep school. They left for college pledging to be BFFs but neither did anything to keep it going. They sorely needed to catch up and might have a good laugh over their laziness. She needed to recover.

He pushed away the strange paradox of his physical discomfort that occurred before he read about her. His odd feelings had to have been a coincidence. Merely indigestion.

Her being in the military was probably why he hadn't thought of her much, until today. He hated the war, not the troops, not her. But she was the most decorated soldier in a tremendous if probably futile American effort. The good-ole USA had dug into another ill-advised war. The two of them, if they met, probably wouldn't be able to avoid a discussion concerning war and peace, but they had always been frank about everything except dating. *Bring it on.*

He clicked ABC on-line, pushed away all other thoughts and watched a catch-up episode of his favorite show. If he dared try watching *The Bachelor* at home, there wouldn't be a moment's peace.

"It's trite, staged and abnormal," his girlfriend had often said.

He sighed. There was no explaining it to the unbeliever. When Brenda was right—well—she was always right. The show was a fine mix of strategy and tactics, which suited his mind. The prize, unlike checkmate in chess or solving a physics problem, was a bond for life if the couple overcame quite a few post-show and real life obstacles.

The Bachelor program over, he left his hideaway, satiated by the complexities of a love double hex-angle or whatever twelve girls dating one guy was. He meandered in the general direction of Macy's on a bright warm day to buy his mom a birthday present. For the first time, he noticed an Army recruiting poster at the corner of 29th and Broadway.

Jay's cell phone chirped.

"Yo." He knew who it was, but he wanted his mom to think he was answering a student.

"What are you doing?"

"Oh… Hey, hi Mom. Nothing really."

No response.

She often called whenever he was up to something that he'd prefer to keep secret. Perhaps because she called nearly every day. Perhaps because he drummed up too many secrets of the don't-scandalize-your-mom kind. As always, he corrected his flippancy, this time with, "Well, I wanted to stretch my legs and mull over a grant proposal. It's a toasty day here. How 'bout you, Mom?"

"I'm fine, weather fine. Why aren't you married?"

"Mom."

"Did you hear about Senator Carthage's daughter?" Oh now he saw where she was going.

"Yeah, terrible."

His mom always seemed to know what was on his mind. Thinking about Bekah brought back a flood of high school memories. "She's expected to survive, right?"

"I don't know, son."

"I'll see what I can find out."

"Yes, do that but you should go to church and say a novena too." She suggested.

Mom always expected creative and spiritual action from her son. His preeminence in Physics wasn't enough, nor his peace activism, she required he connect with the eternal. He excelled for the first two and realized his mom's encouragement initially helped him. After he became a self-starter, she couldn't quite let go of her role of life coach.

"I will." He wouldn't. Maybe he'd have a word with the Creator. Even as an altar boy, his private prayers had bordered on creative. "Trade Ya a skateboard for two good works, God."

"Isn't she that pretty chess player you had a crush on at Bishop Eustace Prep?"

"I did *not* have a crush on her, Mom."

No response.

Although he loved his mom, she was forever nosy. Bekah, the girl, hadn't a clue about his crush, so how'd this get out? He'd choose another time to interrogate dear old mom. "When's your birthday party?"

"Sunday at 1 PM, I'm having the animal rights people over. So dress up."

The last time he'd visited his mom was on Easter. He'd worn torn jeans. She'd worn a wide-brimmed straw hat and pink dress.

"I'd prefer if you didn't bring Brenda this time. You know she wears fur."

In May? He gave up trying to understand his mother, who had the habit of mixing family, friends, business associates and occasions, as if preparing a stew, but had no trouble excluding Brenda.

"She won't come. I'll dress up. Love you."

"You don't have to buy me anything."

Oh, that's a trap, Mom. "It will be something pretty, just like you. It's time you date again, speaking of marriage."

"I'm much too busy with my canine research. You know they shoot wolves from airplanes in Alaska?"

"I know, Mom. Love you. Gotta go now." His mom needed a man but her wolf research consumed her.

"I love you too, son."

He absentmindedly stared at his phone smiling at the thoughts engendered by his complicated mom. The call dropped. Phew.

Jay's love life had been worse than non-existent in prep school. Predictably, with no overbearing mother to hawk-eye him in college and his increase in height and handsomeness; he became a collector of young women. If she wore a skirt or tight jeans, he'd help her out of them.

While he'd balanced studies with trysts, Bekah, if press reports were correct, had avoided a love life to advance her career. He wouldn't mind volunteering to educate her.

Still, he had mellowed a bit since college. She was his friend, even if unproven over time. He'd bite his lip and treat her like the royal highness he'd considered her to be in prep school. He blinked at the sky. The injured sometimes came home. She had an enormous intellect. She'd adjust. She could work in Washington or for her father in some capacity. With that brain of hers, she could do anything.

Once upon a high school she was a sassy, cheeky and smart girl. Whom would he meet now? A woman as tough as a Navy Seal with no sex appeal left to share. She'd always have that gorgeous face and figure. But what of her heart?

Chapter 2

Set up the board. Let's play again.

Army doctor, Captain Max Fielding, was very good at taking Bekah's abuse. For three insufferable days, probably for both of them, Bekah was very much under the influence of narcotics and in and out of consciousness. She screamed, taunted and cajoled the doctor in an effort to get back administering her brigade. She felt like the witch her enemies thought she was.

At least she experienced very little pain from the doctor's efforts to subdue her. Yes, she recognized he was helping her heal.

Her eyeless world was like the interior of the Jimi Hendrix song as a video, *The Star-Spangled Banner,* psychedelic and pissed-off patriotic.

"You do know you are wearing eye bandages?" Doctor Max asked.

She had just told him about the color of the pen in his pocket, his gray hairs, the yellow and cracked walls, but he wasn't listening. "Somehow, I can see you, Captain Fielding and you or somebody should be able to tell me why."

"It's impossible. I'm sorry, Colonel Carthage, you just have a vivid imagination and a great memory."

She had never seen the doctor before, except from afar and then she wasn't sure it had been him. She needed answers. She didn't want to hear impossible. She didn't want flippant remarks. Nothing was impossible. Nothing couldn't be solved. "I want an explanation, today by thirteen hundred. I want to serve. I want out of here. Trim your nose hairs."

"You're just guessing."

"Answers, Captain. Answers. Keep your uninformed opinions to yourself."

"Most of my patients love me."

"I need off this fuckin' drip. I can take the pain."

"A couple more tests. This afternoon I'll be back with the results and I promise you some research into whatever it is that makes you think you can see."

She knew she had lost her eyesight, but her imagination was sometimes so right on, so vivid, she'd pass an eye-chart test. The problem was, sometimes her vision felt like she had buried her head in a bowl of oatmeal, therefore she couldn't lead her team with oatmeal eyes. *Until I become whole…*

"Let Major Hollister visit."

* * *

"Don't just sit there looking like some love-struck puppy, Hollister. Come closer." Bekah sat up. "Captain Fielding was going to remove these tubes and must have forgotten." She started pulling them out. "Don't you stop me. That's an order."

"No… Yes, ma'am."

"Let your hair down, southern boy. Too, too polite." She slipped out of bed.

"I'm going to pee. Don't stop me. Don't help me. And don't look at my ass."

"Yes, sir."

"Now that's funny, Hollister, very fuckin' funny." Her head hurt as if she was delivering a baby out her nose, not that she had ever been pregnant, or delivered anything out her nose except snot.

She tried the exit from the room instead of the bathroom door. Splat. She walked into something about the size of Hulk Hogan, with the smell of talc around his breast pocket. Hulk, the orderly coached her back to her bed with a firm side-by-side hold.

She pulled up her sheets. "You didn't see anything, did you, Hollister?"

"I'm afraid that's top secret, ma'am."

"Your mama never taught you to lie, did she?"

He got close. His hot, French-fried breath made her want to bite him. He whispered. "Your bottom ought to be in a museum next to the bust of Nefertiti."

She raised her hand and cupped his pretty-boy face. "You say the sweetest things." Then she slapped him. Gently.

"A little like fishin' off the dock on a peaceful Louisiana day."

"I'm sorry, Hollister, I don't think I get your meaning. Drugs, must be the residual drugs."

"I'm just saying, Bekah, without eyesight, the Army will give you the boot. I want a wife. I want that gal to be you."

"Better work on your analogies. Unwrap my head please." Hulk, the orderly, came beside her, stuck in a needle and soon it was lights out.

* * *

Max went through a series of tests in which she answered mostly correctly about all her surroundings. The trouble was she knew she wasn't seeing exactly. What she saw, was something like a mix of reality and dreamscape where colors bled and shapes shifted. Well at least her nose worked. The icky smell of antiseptic mixed with tons of fragrant flowers blew her away.

"Well, Colonel, apparently you are one of those gifted human beings who have a picture perfect memory. What you're doing while coming off drugs is having hallucinations mixed with your fine understanding of where everything is, or should be, probably based on your military prowess. I'm going to wait until tonight when the drugs should be out of your system. Then, we'll analyze this more. If the pain becomes too unbearable, just squeeze this paddle. Our experiments can wait."

Doctor Max stood on a mountain of knowledge without enough oxygen.

A little later, after he examined her blackened eyes she said forlornly, "I have beautiful violet eyes, like Elizabeth Taylor's." A girl was allowed a little vanity.

"Your eyes are intact, but will likely be entirely a deep red-black for a couple more weeks." He rewrapped her eyes.

"Like some zombie."

"You're still every service man's pin-up…" He gave her a sedative.

"Thanks, doc, for the compliment. Please call Major Hollister for after my nap."

"Yes, Colonel. Sleep, Rebekah. It's the fastest way to recover."

"These bandages are so itchy."

"Not yet. You'll feel better soon." He made a fast exit.

* * *

Three of her men, including the inept and green, private O'Reilly, clustered around her, spreading their adulations, love, tears and hopes she'd miraculously recover her sight and lead them into battle again. She had saved their asses every time, so why would they want it any other way? Hollister explained that the brass was having a problem with her notoriety. The enemy wanted her dead. Their base was at risk, more now than ever before.

She understood the threats, but her talents would trump the risk.

Anyway, it was just regs, she knew. You're blind; you go home. Hell, regs, got her here. Her perpetually running-for-president-father—after 9/11—jammed through the Senate, a bill eliminating sex and age discrimination in the Army. The U.S., in a life and death struggle, hadn't had the luxury of not promoting the best. So the argument went. So had she and others proven. The reality for most women was still get-to-the-back-of-the-bus unless you're pretty and then sit on some boy's lap. She didn't need or want a man, period.

Why wasn't her father here by her side, now? Just because she had screamed at him for marrying an ugly bimbo after mom had died. Just because she ignored his calls. Even though the bimbo divorced him as soon as she could grab some of his fortune. He being a bleeding-heart liberal was not the point, just a small aggravation for Bekah.

Some fried plantain and bitter melon aromas from Filipina cooking wafted out from the nurses' station. Her stomach contracted. Remembrances of helping her mom prepare Filipina dishes came flooding back. Sweet times.

She'd wait for this food, if she could bum some. She'd wait to serve. Wait. Wait. Wait.

"Attention." Her small contingent of men scuffled and snapped their feet. She loved that.

"O'Reilly, tuck in your shirt, stop picking your nose."

"She can see, Captain Fielding. I mean, Colonel Carthage, you can see even through your bandages."

"It's a parlor trick, son," Doctor Max said. "Tuck in your shirt, private."

9

"Okay, Okay, I admit, men, I'm a little groggy, but I believe I have something that makes me see in some way. But before I was nearly killed, I wasn't on morphine and I saw something in my imagination that has been bothering me. You all know how good my hunches are. So, Major Hollister, you're acting commander?"

"Yes, Colonel Carthage."

"I want you to form a sweep team and go through the rubble of what's left of the building. You'll be looking for an oven."

"Good news, Colonel. We found an American Eskimo pup in an oven, badly needing medical. It's with the town vet. A local boy has been there wanting to adopt the pup when it's well enough to leave, so the pup has a chance at a good home."

"Thank you. I need some time with the major now. Dismissed—except O'Reilly—and thank you again for the flowers and chocolates, men." The men said their adoring goodbyes and left. "O'Reilly, wait at the nurses station until the major gets you."

"Yes, Colonel Carthage."

* * *

"How does an American breed get lost in Edanistan?" Hollister asked, rhetorically.

"Yeah and with that fur and this heat? Listen, Hollister, I have an assignment. It may be nothing, but my hunch and logic tells me the boy put her in the oven because his father wouldn't let him bring the dog along, because it might bark their location. I'd guess the father had something to do with the explosion. And yes, find out how an American dog got here. Transfer O'Reilly to mess, before he kills himself and others on the battlefield, but before that, make his assignment to guard me official, because of the threat against me and because I need you to do more important things than sit here moon-faced."

A Filipina nurse stuck her nose in the door. "It's time for the Colonel to get some rest."

"Will there be anything else, Colonel?"

Hollister had a hint of hesitation in his voice.

"Consider one of the beautiful nurses here, Major. I am not much of a woman now or before." She felt sure that would paint the major's face red and with a little luck get him off her tail. Bekah was half Filipina and part South African, Shoshone, white. Perhaps Hollister would be interested in the nurse corps, if her golden skin and long black hair was what turned him on.

Besides, she felt when the time was right for her, if ever, there would be someone, someone else appearing. The time was never right in the military unless she made general. At that point, she'd call the shots. In today's Army, in spite of the equality laws, a woman of lower rank only need make one slip, one flirt, one wink and her serious career was damn well over.

"Yes, Colonel Carthage." On his way out he said, "I'll always be there for you, if you change your mind. I hope you think on it."

"Another thing, Hollister. Start a local rumor that I'm not expected to recover."

"Yes, ma'am." Hollister was handsome, smart and quick to grasp her meaning. This six-foot five, hayseed-haired hick often surprised her intellectually. He knew Zachari's men would blow up the hospital to get rid of her, if they could, but they couldn't. The combat team had already found and destroyed the tunnel she'd predicted the enemy was constructing under their camp.

"Oh, a personal favor, call my dad and sister on their secure lines, give them a heads'-up on the misinformation and ask them to visit ASAP."

Handsome, hopeless Hollister probably left her room with tail between his legs but with his patriot's heart pounding strong. His love for her was little doubt surpassed by his love for the USA.

* * *

Private O'Reilly kept her company but seemed more interested in flirting with the nurses. Awful bodyguard, awful soldier, awesome cook but she had plans for him. He'd help her get out of here, tomorrow.

If she were forced out of the military, perhaps she'd need a more permanent companion. Not since Bishop Eustace Prep School had she been remotely interested in a guy, and then a boy at that. The skinny, short nerd she liked only knew how to play chess and be a gentle-boy. He had had a crush on her, but was so unsure of himself, he could hardly say boo. His verbal repertoire included variations of, "I resign. Good game, Rebekah," usually accompanied with trembling while he shook her hand. What was James Ripisi up to these days? Perhaps, if they kicked her out of the Army, she'd find him. He was probably married by now, with six chess-playing kids.

Chapter 3

Only a friendly game

Wednesday Noon, May 7th, New York City

Professor Jay Boone had watched another back-episode of *The Bachelor*, read more about the colonel and left his NYU office for the park. He heartily inhaled the spring air and crossed over to Washington Square. He was drawn, for no rational reason, to and lingered outside the dog pen. He liked dogs. Having nothing better to do yet, he turned on his perpetually overactive imagination and grinned. He could almost hear an English bulldog and shepherd-mix thinking.

Mind if I sniff your rear?

Not at all, you first.

I insist, be my guest.

Let's do it at the same time.

Right oh, old chap.

To his right, students carrying open-faced coffins, with military uniformed actors inside, marched with grim intent. One of his Quantum Mechanics students planted himself on a soapbox.

"Join us, Prof," the student boomed over the gathering crowd.

"Next time." Jay pointed toward the chess tables. "Chess, you know."

Most knew of his lunchtime passion. He thought how he must look to the students. Shoulder length sandy-brown waves, faded jeans, John Lennon sun-specs. His tight-fitting tie-died shirt with an American Sign Language translation below the words, "Peace Now" served to show off his politics and incidentally a physique honed by the hundred-meter butterfly. At least these pecs kept the co-eds awake in class. He looked like a hippy of yesteryear or a hip professor. The students thought he was all that. And he was, in a geeky, nerdy, jocky way.

He squinted at the late noontime sun and untucked his shirt for a swirl of air. He bought an expensive soft pretzel with deli mustard and munched his way over to a bowed-out concrete promenade, made so, for the chess tables. He plunked down on a bench at the end table, which backed up to the long bowed-out black chained fence. He readied the chess pieces for his friend, Carlos Petrovich.

Although Carlos had his Russian father's last name, his mother was a Basque from Spain's Pyrenees. Carlos grew up in cold war Moscow and seemed never to leave the past entirely.

Waiting, he noticed Anatoly. The ragged, elderly Russian émigré hustled chess for $2 a game. Although his eyelids and sockets resembled layers of mud pies, his vision on the chessboard remained dagger sharp.

The local toughs likely took a piece of Anatoly's action, what little there was. Most of the students couldn't afford him always winning. Strangers wanted to spend time chatting. Some locals made lame excuses not to pay. The gang and Anatoly had some sort of arrangement in which the poor sucked the poorer dry. Jay remained curious and had asked Anatoly what was going on, but Anatoly shooed him off with a grandfatherly smile. If he called the police, Anatoly might find it difficult to play chess here. Where would he sleep if the kids had arranged a flophouse for him?

Again, something altogether different from Anatoly tugged at his soul. Bekah. Jay took a deep breath.

His attention shifted to the hotshots on the other side of the concrete court. The pounding clock of a speed game between the New York City twenty-one-and-under champion, and some sloe-eyed doll—who looked to be holding her own—excited the gathering crowd. Most of the time, the kids would be playing their own games. *But no, a slinky-eyed girl shows up and they surround the table.* These young men paid little attention to their appearance, which could be described as mixed and unmatched. The only girls who'd date this group of mostly NYU undergrads had to love chess. The boys would have to get lucky, very lucky.

Then he recognized the girl, from a recent Chess Life cover, the first board of the Chinese Student Chess Team. *I wonder if they know. If not, they will soon.* The dual-faced clocks banged on to the inevitable finish. Girl on top. Jay stood and clapped. He lamented the lack of popularity for chess. He teased his imagination listening to an Olympic stadium crowd roar.

You're never late. Where are you, Carlos? Antsy, he worried about challenges and having to fend off fish, the ever-present amateurs with fervor for the game only exceeded by their lack of skill. Maybe he should walk over to Anatoly. But he seemed preoccupied with an unusually hard game, so Jay waved instead and the Russian nodded back half-smiling. Meanwhile some of the park regulars meandered toward Jay.

Colonel Carlos Petrovich always walked up from Soho, but today he came from the north side of the park, surprising Jay.

Carlos saluted and said in his halting Russian accent. "Ready to lose?" He seemed stressed.

Jay mocked, "Could you find some other girl for me? Brenda's driving me nuts."
"You do not like my matchmaking?"

Carlos missed the intended irony, as if Jay really needed help with affairs of the heart.

Just because I lose my girlfriends, doesn't mean I'm a loser. I'm just overworked. I've got a closetful of old girlfriends, just waiting to tumble out and on me when Brenda leaves. Carlos had brought the two of them together, suggesting Brenda move in. They laughed at him, but she moved in.

"She has her qualities, if you like the domineering type."

"You don't have to marry girl. A little shtupping is good for soul," Carlos said, raising his shaggy eyebrows and doing something obscene with his bishop and hand.

He ignored his friend's teasing. "Let's play. Take White, today," Jay said. On the chessboard, Professor Jay Boone rarely met his match. The Chinese girl, after her win, stood at full cat-stretch and gaped at Jay from across the way. *What a puckish pose. Did she want a game? Kibitz? Or me?* On the board, the girl would be deci-mated. On a mattress, she would be satisfied. How liberated were Chinese women these days? Both the girl and Carlos were chess masters, but Jay was one notch above with two titles: International and U.S. Senior Master. These titles were about as far as you'd climb without becoming a full time professional. Still, tricky Carlos gave Jay a good game and the girl was a bit too young to fool with.

Carlos seemed to drop his anxiety and jumped into the moment. "Jay, you surprise me, accepting my King's Gambit." They spoke about the game in technical terms not for each other, but for the gathering groupie-gawkers.

Jay pressed against the long bench, dropped his head back and let the dancing sunlight push through the tawny maple leaves, tease the spring sparrows swirl on his face and make imaginary moves on the chessboard. The sparrows showed no concern for the messed-up lives of Brenda and Jay.

"Brenda is a control freak. She won't let me watch a certain show. I accepted your gambit to finish you off quickly."

From the corner of his eye, Jay caught Carlos twisting his king's bishop onto the c4 square initiating the King's Bishop's Gambit, a sharp variation meant to cause mayhem.

Carlos stood and faced the onlookers, "Gentlemen and lady, today the Professor and I have personal matters to discuss. So, I ask you to move on to another table, before I embarrass my friend. The squirrel can stay." People didn't mess with the burly Carlos, who could snap any of them like twigs. They left wishing Jay luck with his girl problems. The girl slinked off for more five-minute games with the NYU students.

After a while Carlos said, "Today, I think you will get far more than you bargained for. Get your head out of clouds. This isn't blindfold simul. So, what is this TV show?"

Jay closed his eyes, leaned back to take in the dancing sun, and winced. "It's *The Bachelor*. You see I like the strategy, tactics…" *Uh, oh. Blundered this time. Never tell another guy, especially your best friend, you like The Bachelor. Checkmate.*

Carlos interrupted. He had the bad habit of finishing Jay's sentences, anyway. Jay was used to it. "I like show too. Chess players are logical; use tactics and strategy. The guy should eliminate the girls who show disrespect to the other contestants."

"That's a good show," said one remaining onlooker. Carlos stood again and the skinny fellow took off after an exaggerated bow.

"Exactly, Carlos, a girl with a caring soul. No disrespect to you. It's just...she's a headache." He leaned his head back again, this time exhausted by the end of the school year and hopefully the end of a relationship with Brenda. "Please move my queen to check you."

"Okay, Jay, I slide my king to f1. How would you like to get away for a while, hide from Brenda, start a whole new adventure, maybe whole new life?"

Carlos was the head of a U.S. agency associated with spying who had hired Jay as a once-in-a-while consultant. "You know you still owe me for a consult, back seven years ago."

"Here is bank account with your name on it and $8,787,646.23 and counting, in it. No string attached." Carlos loved numbers and made *little joke about accruing interest, yes*?

"That does not compute. I think my bill was around $5,000. What are you up to?"

"I resigned as Director of OTTS. I've nominated you to replace me."

Carlos had explained years ago how OTTS was the nickname President Eisenhower had given for the start-up agency the president created, which was devoted to taking advantage of unexplained phenomena for purposes of war and peace. John Foster Dulles had quoted the president as having said there was nothing stranger than an "Over The Top Secret." It stuck. However, no references could be found in the congressional budget.

"Pawn to f3, okay?" Jay snapped his head and focused on the board. "Don't move my pawn. It's a blunder. You go knight takes, I take..."

Carlos interrupted again, "You take king's pawn. I sacrifice bishop with check. If you eat, knight forks queen and king, caput. Jay, your mind is not on game. I have different war you will like. Let us make draw. Leave pieces, act like we are playing."

Jay rearranged the position to something more befitting his prowess. Jay hadn't blundered like that since Rebekah totaled him at the chessboard in high school. Something was afloat, tasting like grit, but it was a clear day with a dose of a hair-jostling Atlantic Ocean breeze. His stomach knotted, again. Bekah.

"Okay, shoot, but I'm not moving to Washington and yours or anybody else's house of mirrors."

"Nyet, you will stay here. Tell me if anyone approaches. After new administration took over years ago, I had to start cutting down to volunteer field operatives, close those offices and keep small staff. The President does not believe in razz-ma-tazz. Called it a magic circus. Then, in August of 2001, one of my ops spotted a terrorist team in Vegas and warned about an imminent attack. After report was ignored and word spread, I lost almost all of my people. The money in your new bank account is now funneled from anonymous VIPs and a small government residual budget. Your main donor is Dennis Kucnarich. He's got this thing for aliens."

"Our administration is a bit unpopular," Jay said.

"They all are at some point. You will meet President Unpopular tomorrow. His GAO has your consult fee, which is precisely $4821 and they have an ever changing formula for interest."

"I'm not qualified for OTTS."

"Actually, you will do better than me. Your background as leading physicist in area of paranormal, grounds you. You are also expert on unexplained phenomena. You lecture worldwide. You are healthy skeptic, which trumps my spy background. Listen to me. Before President destroyed OTTS, I just hired anyone who claimed to have special powers. Pretty fortune-tellers were my worst mistake. The only thing they foretold correctly was the blow-jobs they gave me."

"I see— I like NYU, lunch in the park, maybe a new girlfriend. I don't know."

"You will."

What did he mean by, you will? You will get a new girlfriend, continue here, or like his new job, or all of the above.

Carlos pulled a sparkling black pearl laptop bordering on notebook out of his valise. "This little honey comes from the NSA geeks. It is not what it seems. Well, you will see."

Jay was intrigued. It looked like a computer; had to be one. Perhaps it did dishes.

"This foxy box has my recommendations, a tentative to do list and your first prospect."

So what's the big deal, that thing was a computer. "And who might that be?"

"Colonel Rebekah Carthage, about to be *Newsweek* and *Stars & Stripes* cover girl."

"You mean that foul-mouthed, overrated, born with a golden spoon up her ass, tomboy, Zena-wannabe?" Carlos could probably see right through his defense mechanisms. Jay's objection to Bekah wasn't just the war. He felt abandoned by her, not that he was a catch. He was irrational about love and would have to invest in introspection to get to the bottom of his feelings.

"You know her?" Something told Jay, his friend knew a lot more than he let on.

"Yes, actually I do." Yes, the Colonel's story kept splattering the media and Jay had dug into older stories. He caught up on her career. She amazed him for being the fastest promoted, most decorated officer in history, except for field promotions in the world wars. Yes, there remained reactionary elements both military and civilian to a woman in combat. For those, who would open their eyes, they'd surmise General Patton could have learned from Colonel Rebekah Carthage. Although Jay was a pacifist, he respected the soldier, a pretty one at that.

Her link to unexplained phenomena had to have some rational explanation. Perhaps this was what tugged at his soul, not just his unrequited passion or , let's call it love. This incited him to take the position Carlos offered. "In high school, we were on the same chess team. She always beat me, and she was real good at letting me know it…"

Jay's mind wondered.

…Bishop Eustace Prep Library, Sophomore Year.

Jay, that is James, lugged the chessboard, pieces, clock and his short pimply self to slaughter again. His way too pretty executioner dispatched him in thirteen moves, but he didn't mind.

"Thank you, Rebekah, for the lesson. You played great." Playing the New Jersey Junior Champ felt more like a lesson than a game.

"Shhh." The librarian lingered over them like the grim reaper's sister.

"You don't have enough fight in you, James, nor enough knowledge."

He leaned across the table for the traditional handshake.

"See you." She rose and swiveled, showing off a cheeky Lacrosse outfit, which barely covered her cute bottom. She tapped rubber cleats across linoleum squares and glancing back flashed a metallic cat smile.

"Good bye, Rebekah." He trembled, just above a whisper.

"Shhh," from the librarian.

The princess never gets a shhh. Why am I so lucky?

He wasn't the evil student who stuck chewing gum under this maple table or sprinkled salt in the librarian's coffee…

Carlos interrupted Jay's remembrances. "Her press has distorted the lady to legendary proportions."

"Maybe." Jay said.

"No, not maybe, it is so. The troops want a heroine, a Joan of Arc. Anyway, you will discover this for yourself. She is very fair-minded, mature. Foul-mouthed around her men and a princess with superiors. Did you know she is the current armed forces chess champ?"

Hoping for insight, Jay decided confession was the best approach even if Carlos already knew. "I know. In high school, she picked on me. I had pimples; I was skinny, short for a while, bad breath. You name it. I had a crush. She was so cute. Big beautiful smile, even with braces."

"She might not recognize this magnificent lady-killer before me, if you do not want her to know you were that pimple boy."

Ignore him. Boone was Jay's mother's maiden name. In high school, he was named James Ripisi, super nerd, his runaway father's last name. He had grown and changed from ugly duckling to a six foot two college campus hunk. Rebekah would not likely know him immediately.

"You aren't trying to set me up again, are you Carlos?" Carlos displayed his poker face, a bit too easily.

"I think she's a good start for OTTS, nothing more. You would think $8,787,646.23 and counting, is too much date money, even for best friend?"

Bullshit of the highest luster. Jay was curious. Colonel Carlos Petrovich, ex-KGB, then ex-CIA, always had a plan. "You're too young to retire."

"I talked my way into a job as strategist/tactician for the Carthage campaign. It's like chess."

"Carlos, you dog. Mazel tov. The Senator could use a man of your unusual skills." Jay wondered if Carlos would use his "gifts." He was a brilliant strategist and tactician in chess and a notorious spy. Would it carry over to politics? Would Jay see the Senator, since he'd be working with Rebekah? Perhaps the four would enjoy a victory tea party in the White House, on fine colonial china.

Carlos prodded, "So accept already, you do not have to marry the girl."

Marry Rebekah. I don't think so. I'm waiting for my soul mate, not a drill sergeant.

Jay found the job challenge, status and chance to affect change, irresistible.

"I'm blown away. Resurrect an agency. Of course, I accept, but if your stint with Carthage is temporary, you can have the agency back." Jay's mind continued down a wholly different path. *Get to see her again, wow. Maybe, I'll teach her a few chess lessons.* Jay's heart raced. He felt like that sweaty, uncertain boy again.

"Listen schmuck, you recruit Rebekah because she is going to be kicked out of Army. She has lost her sight, but she claims she can see and I know she can."

"Which is where we come in, right?" Jay tried to act nonchalant, but his friend would see right through him. Well thank God she was alive. His heart went out to the girl he had loved, and yes, probably still did. At least, he'll be her truest friend; give her a chance at productivity. They'd make a great team. *Lovers? She'd need to overcome her negative image of me from prep, if I were her type or what she wants anyway.*

"Don't believe press on her, she is not dying. Keep everything I tell you, secret. She is great opportunity. She is phenom. I know you alone can harness her special abilities and help her get well."

Indeed, he would, beyond her yet unformed dreams, one would hope.

Carlos stood up. "Oh… Get rid of Brenda as soon as you can."

"When you worked for the KGB, were you an assassin?"

Carlos started walking away, surveyed the crowd and said, "Study up with your new toy and later I will toss you some old bones. Oh, do not kill Brenda or anybody else. That is my job."

Carlos disappeared into the crowd like a ghost. *The usual cryptic finish to a Carlos encounter.* Jay leaned back again and handed a bit of pretzel to his favorite squirrel, who had watched the game with his usual intensity. He put the small laptop into the valise. With a slight alteration, he could slip this equipment into a business suit breast pocket.

The Chinese girl leaned with her hip against the metal fence post, munching on a hero sandwich, licking her lips suggestively and just ogling him as if sex-starved. He waved, pushed his palms skyward, pointed at the school, shrugged and finished with a smile. To say he didn't want to take her right here, right now, would discredit all men everywhere. Ah, propriety. Anyway, Jay was a one-girl-at-a-time sort of guy. There remained the small matter of Brenda, his one girl. She got the point and turned back without emotion to watch a game. So inscrutable, so feminine.

He headed for his last exam conference for quite a while, while he planned a new life.

* * *

Leaving Washington Square for a few stops on Sixth Avenue, Jay heard a muffled female voice coming from his valise. It sounded like a plea from someone with her mouth, taped shut. *Entirely too dramatic.* He dropped onto the steps of Saint Joseph's and opened the valise.

"Phue, thank you, it's stuffy in here," said a voice sounding a lot like his all-time favorite bygone actress, Audrey Hepburn. How did the engineers who programmed this voice know he had idolized Audrey? Carlos. He took out the laptop and flipped it open. *No keys, no ports, no sockets.* Jay, the Physicist, imagined formulas, circuit diagrams, satellites and cell towers, but couldn't put it together just yet. The lack of an obvious power source more than anything else blew his fuse.

"Talk to me," His voice rose in boyish wonder.

"Professor, your Dean is on the 4th floor of the library right now, flirting with the rare books librarian, named Gertrude. Don't you think you should see him?"

Jay stuck his nose between the laptop flaps. "Are you in there, Carlos?" His eyes peeked over the top and swept the street. A priest, rabbi and minister walked down the steps and smiled while they passed.

"Hey, nice toy," the minister said.

"Use it in good health," the rabbi said.

"May the Lord be with you on your journey," the priest said. The men shook their heads like bobbing Chihuahua dolls and seemed amused over their comments. They smiled more at each other than Jay.

"You rang?" Carlos said, speaking over the priest.

"Nice, real nice, Carlos. What do I do with it? Have a nice day, ah, men of the cloth." The threesome waved goodbye already halfway across the street.

Carlos said, "She will not bite you. She is there to serve. You like puzzles, so I'll see you later."

"Yo Carlos. Carlos," sang Jay.

"Yes, Jay."

"That was too close. A priest noticed the laptop."

"Oh, come on. The device does not look that much different, especially with no close inspection."

"Father wished me a good journey."

"*Getting paranoid?*" Carlos stretched the two words. "Don't be vershugana. My Rabbi says same thing. It's the way they talk. Same kitchen, same soup. Chicken soup."

What Jay really wanted was some instruction in how to be a spy. He realized how odd he might look, having a conversation with a laptop, although it happens when people

Skype. Before cell phones, talking to yourself was considered a sign of insanity. Today people look up, as if talking to the sky, or forward and vacant, like Zombies. He might say something to compromise the mission.

Carlos continued, "Jay, I am disappointed. I thought you figure her out with that genius head of yours."

"Maybe, I shouldn't panic and just contemplate it."

Carlos spoke using a rare fatherly tone. "Watch her feelings. She is not an it. I can assure you. I am sure you could figure her out. Here is head start on spying. Vary the volume of your voice, turn your head, scratch your face or cover your mouth from time to time, pause every three or four words. Ahh, be a little cryptic, then no one will understand you, not even lip readers. By the way, friend, I do not understand you, never did. Must leave."

The computer surface displayed, Carlos is not here now.

Jay whispered to the laptop. "What should I call you?"

"Your strumpet if you prefer or call me positively delightful. Or, how's Elisa, Holly, Sabrina, any name you like, dearest, just not Audrey. She's an angel *now*, you know… Oh, do hurry. When you meet your Dean, say it's a private family matter. They are the magic words, my dear boy."

"I'll stick to your plan, for now. Since we're in Manhattan and you're goofy, I'll call you Holly. I'll leave the zipper slightly open."

"Oh pu-lease don't get arrested." She emoted and joked back with a hearty and anything but go-lightly laugh. Her laugh drew his imagination into the bizarre world of Cat and Holly in the classic *Breakfast at Tiffany's*.

He snapped out of it, found the Dean, made arrangements, made easier since the spring classes had just ended. Then he helped a student who found Bessel functions of the third kind incomprehensible. He bypassed the gym, skipped WAD, a group of very-off-Broadway writers, actors and directors. He treated his replacement professors, the Dean and teaching assistants, to a nice Italian dinner. The only item of prolonged discussion involved which wine went best with a sabbatical. They decided any red would do, although there was a fight to declare Merlot the winner.

He walked home, not ready to confront Brenda, flabbergasted with no obvious strategy to say goodbye. *The girl must go.* She wasn't really, what he wanted for the long run. Why live a shallow existence? It was unfair to both of them. Sure, it was good in a pragmatic sort of way. They were friends who happened to share hot sex. Now, the situation was different. He needed privacy. It was a matter of national security. *Just how to break the news?* Simon's *Fifty Ways to Leave Your Lover* rambled through Jay's brain until he arrived at his co-op, still uncertain. The master of the chessboard was without a move.

* * *

Later that evening, Jay retired to the bathroom claiming constipation. He showered and got ready for bed. He decided to defer his decision to ask Brenda to leave until the right moment, whenever that was. Besides, he could use the comfort of her lovemaking, even if for the last time. He needed someone to share his joy, even if he couldn't tell her anything. He paced naked while studying his laptop friend. He realized he could voice activate anything he needed and get into almost any secret world he chose. Holly seemed to anticipate his needs, considering he hardly had to speak or whisper. After a short time, he devised plans for Colonel Rebekah Carthage and his meeting with the President.

"Oh Jay, could you please open the window? It's just too warm in here," Holly said. "More. A little more."

Jay pushed the window as far as it would go. Candlelight flickers from the window directly across the courtyard caught his eye. A woman in an orange see-thru nightie, breasts visible, ducked. Jay heard a dish plop, then wobble. He grabbed a towel. Wisps of candle smoke rose. One after another extinguished, leaving the woman's apartment dark. Jay heard giggles.

"The two women across from you are watching, Jay. They're arguing about how big your penis is. Keep your towel on, if you want, big boy," Holly said.

"Thanks," Jay whispered. "Did you hear all that?"

"After you're confirmed as Director, I'll explain."

"I'm just a normal guy. Why do they waste their time?" Jay knew he was a handsome devil, but never understood peeking, although he had been thoughtless, prancing around naked. At least, he never had the time and therefore, the inclination to peek at anyone.

"Even two girls having a candlelit party can appreciate your male form. They're just having some fun. Peeking is one of those underreported pastimes in Gotham. Did you know last week 186 binoculars sold in all of New York City? You, you're gorgeous. Six pack, a face like some leading man. Agent, oh oh my."

"Can you see me?"

"I see, but not in the way you would suppose."

"There go a few amendments to the constitution." He didn't really care whether a computer liked his body. He did care about doing his job in an ethical and legal way. He withheld judgment until, Holly had said, he was confirmed Director of OTTS. Only then, the sprite inside the black pearl laptop would get a grilling. He poked his head out the window, towel in place, enjoyed the fresh air under a stream of moonbeams, the rush of oak branches, the transience of life in motion, all shadows of beauty, shadows hiding beauties.

A different and very loud female voice came out of the laptop. "Oh God, Jay, you'rrre fuckin' great. I'm almost there, ye, uwe, ah. Don't stop. Faster, faster." The voice screamed in ecstasy. Jay peered across at the dark window, worried if they heard. More giggles. He was confused as hell.

He heard the hinge breaking entry of Brenda bursting through the bathroom door. He banged his head on the window's top and ran his belly over the heater's relief valve.

The towel dropped. *Maybe she'll spank me.* He wondered if his derriere would mollify Brenda. Not likely. She raced to the window, stuck her head out next to Jay and they followed some sounds up to someone climbing two flights up. Jay contended with more giggles from across the way, a seething Brenda, *foaming at the mouth*, and a girl climbing the fire escape.

How odd. What a sight I must be. Look all you want, girls. I have worse problems. The long-legged girl in dark panties or no panties under her mini skirt, stopped on the second landing. *What is going on in this co-op? All these years, I've had a circus out my rear window.*

The girl stuck her head in a window, about to crawl in. Holly threw her other voice, or there was a speaker outside somewhere. "Thank you so much, Jay. Let's do it again and again," she panted. "Oh God, you *are* good."

Brenda thought up a few choice words for him while she packed. She threw the carved fertility goddess against the wall and shouted, "You can watch *The Bachelor* all you want now. And a bachelor you'll stay. Bastard." The door slammed shut; another hinge to fix? He stooped to pick up the carving, then collapsed into the sofa and giggled like a boy who just put a gold fish down a girl's blouse.

"Brilliant."

"I'm a good girl, I am."

"You sure are."

What a lifesaver Holly was.

It hit him; Brenda's objections to *The Bachelor* might have been more personal than he had thought. She'd wanted him to tell her how he'd choose her over any other girl. How they'd marry someday. Instead, he treated her like a beer buddy, talking strategy and tactics, instead of cuddling and saying sweet nothings. *Oh, beware all ye who watch The Bachelor, taketh care of thy damsel.* She wasn't that domineering, just yearning for love, his love.

What fate would have befallen him if he'd opened his heart to her? They were just too different. She liked Fox TV news, full-fat ice cream and scary movies. He liked National Public Radio, healthier foods and romantic movies. She was almost his height and built like a siliconed centerfold. He liked a slender but fit and less tall type. Someone to have and hold. Oh, she was cute and as a lover, a complete Amazon.

Alas, they could never be soul mates. *Who knew?*

Chapter 4

Gambit

Thursday, Edan

Rebekah had roamed the hospital halls with O'Reilly to get him used to walking her. Just part of her therapy. He had grown on her like one of the brigade's rescued dogs. Good, because he'd, unwittingly, soon spring her from her bondage.

Major Hollister had persistently visited with chocolates and flowers, but always finished second to none-of-the-above. Filling her boots, as acting commander, kept him busy and mostly out of her hair.

The room was full of bouquets from nearly every team and rank right up to General Birchmont's aide, who had promised the General would see her soon. Her head still twisted, she hoped when this meeting occurred, she'd be in good enough condition to offer him an argument on why he should keep her in some productive way. After all, it was her well-trained mind, her ability to envision with superb accuracy, enemy placements that apparently remained undiminished. Plus, she was a good administrator. If a desk job was all he'd offer, she might take it.

She continued to wonder how she could serve and when. She still had headaches from drug withdrawal and intracranial swelling. The pain had diminished down to the mere scream level. She would never let anyone know. She wanted to get-to-the-bottom of her visions. The doctors, men and women of science, issued their latest theory. They told her in so many words, *you have pressure, which traumatizes your brain, which in turn causes hallucinations and, oh yes, because you're good at battle placements, tactics and strategy you take the same approach when you claim you are seeing.*

She entertained calls from her sis and dad. They were trying to get to Edanistan as soon as possible. Her dad had secret service concerns and her sister had babysitting problems, plus her usual black-ops terrorist investigations. The mixture of physical and emotional pain caused Rebekah to act before General Birchmont lowered the boom.

"O'Reilly?"

"Yes, ma'am."

"We're leaving the hospital."

"No, ma'am. The doctor said…"

"Who's your CO?"

"Well, ah."

"No permanent orders yet. That makes me, still in command." A little fib. No one had thought to restrict her to the hospital.

"Yes, ma'am."

"Gather my things. Put them in your duffel and leave the duffel on a bench near an exit and come right back. We are going to take one of our walks. This time, we're not coming back."

After they ambled, arm-in-arm, close to an exit and picked up the duffel, they ducked into a locker room. Due to a lack of time, she decided to enlist O'Reilly in helping her finish off dressing. It was the bra, she couldn't find. He balked at touching it. Well, wherever it was she didn't need it. She was perky.

"Darn it, O'Reilly. I give you permission to look for my bra. That's an order. We must get out of here, fast." She rewarded his sweet, obedient, 24/7-doting company. Yet, wasn't she really rewarding herself? Emotion swelled inside her. Sensual thoughts were the ticking time bomb in her new life, if she had to have a new life. This bomb would destroy her. All these years she had avoided men to advance her education and then career. She might have to change. She'd have to learn what to do with men other than leading them. But did she really want a man? She had grown accustomed to being alone, to excelling alone. A man would just slow her down.

Perhaps her subconscious already knew she had to evac Edanistan. Well, if so, she'd leave with a puppy. Maybe she should reconsider and take a chance with handsome Hollister. At least they'd start-off best friends, a friendship honed by battle. She'd never design or lead another battle. Her career was likely shot. She had to get that dog, maybe or maybe not a man.

Her body was revolting, her mind knew better. Her arousal was for a new life she'd avoid if possible, not for O'Reilly or any other hunk. Liberation was out that hospital door. Damnit, she felt a tingle. She also felt O'Reilly's stares. She had asked him to avert his eyes as best he could while she dressed, put on her newfound bra, but he was a guy, after all. She might as well learn the truth about her tiny boobs and then go kill herself for insubordination to her higher self.

"Are my breasts too small?"

"Wasn't lookin'."

"Come on soldier. I promise, no punishment, no stockade. I really need your opinion. I'm ugly, aren't I?"

"I just peeked for a moment, ma'am, couldn't help it, cause' I was helping you dress."

"I don't blame you. You can tell me the truth. Hurry."

"Well, they are like half grapefruits with Bing cherries on top, delicately accented around the tips with cherry glaze. You are a beautiful woman, ma'am."

The bra snapped. The girl blushed. *Delicately accented? It had to be a food analogy with this guy. Getting hungry again. He's got to be crazy. Sure in high school most the girls were small. His grapefruit analogy was too generous. I guess I forgot to water mine.*

She was more like a side order of cherries, hold the grapefruit. She took what compliments she could get and stowed the somewhat erotic experience. With a lot of luck and prayer, she'd land a man if she had to. Flip-flop, flip-flop, on the man issue. This mermaid didn't take kindly to any hooks.

On the other hand, this imaginary man, better have balls bigger than mine. In the end, who would take on the constant responsibility of caring for a handicapped person with small tits, really?

Without ceremony, she said, "Thank you for your dishonesty. Let's get that Eskimo dog. Then, we'll join up with the brigade."

They unwound her bandages. She shut up his protests, tucked her long hair into her cap, pushed the visor low and snuck out arm-in-arm as if they were grieving. Nobody stops a Colonel anywhere, anytime, anyway. They waved at the guards.

"I'd like to drive."

"*Colonel Carthage*. No, ma'am. I may be stupid. But even if you have sight, there is still the drugs. You ask too much."

"Calm down, Private." She wasn't going to press the point, being unsure of herself. In the future, with the right expert and under controlled conditions she'd test her ability to drive.

They were navigating the streets of Edan without a call on O'Reilly's cell, no one the wiser. Her cell had been destroyed and not yet replaced. Bureaucracy.

"I thought this vet was one block away," she said.

"No, ma'am. That one got blown up. It's just a couple blocks more west in a rich neighborhood."

"We can't go. It's too dangerous. Let's go to the brigade."

"It's one block from a shop I visit all the time. We'll be okay, ma'am."

"I want that dog. Much longer?"

"We're here, Colonel."

They should have been guarded. She now felt guilty for putting one of her men in jeopardy. She also felt like an idiot. Although she was still recovering, her mind felt sharp. *If I had half a mind.* Bekah figured she had seven senses. Her normal eyesight wasn't working which left her with six out of seven. One sense was her ability to see in some paranormal way and that worked, more or less, depending on her focus. This weird sense had more or less deserted her ever since they had loaded her up with drugs. Another sense, she had had a feel for danger, like now. As soon as her head cleared from the severe pain and the drugs were basically gone from her system, she'd be ready to show her usefulness.

The girl who always won, blundered today. She didn't much worry about herself anymore, since she cheated death. Figured the reaper would show again, sooner than later. It was the doting loving O'Reilly, who worried her. What man would shampoo and brush her long hair and jump to satisfy her every need? *If there's an act two, it will be hard to follow the boy O'Reilly's love train with a man of my unexpected and still unlikely dreams.*

They had become the best of friends over the past two days, in spite of the differences in educational backgrounds and rank. He was indeed the brother she never had.

"O'Reilly, how's the street?"

"It's a good looking one, Mercedes, full of beautiful homes…"

"I mean, does it look safe?" She smelled roses, heard a baby carriage trundle by, mother cooing. A teenager argued with her mother, just houses away. The mother responded in a barely audible reassuring tone.

"It's quiet, ma'am. We'll be fine. I came to that shop near here to trade Hershey's for garlic. They give me a pass. They teased me by saying they would remove my head, if I stopped bringing chocolate."

"Can't they buy their own?"

"Shortages and my price, ma'am."

"Did you bring chocolates?"

"No, ma'am."

"Oh my." More appropriate words popped into her head. She reaffirmed that O'Reilly was not fit for combat and now she knew she was not fit for command. He'd be a cook and she'd likely be a pregnant civilian.

O'Reilly brought Rebekah in and sat her down next to a boy, also waiting. He smelled of roses.

"I'm Ahmed." He handed her a rose. Little doubt he expropriated it from the house next door. She let her nose and fingers slide down the stem, to see if a knife was used. No knife, he had ripped it off.

"I'm Rebekah. Thank you, Ahmed. Do you give roses to all the ladies you meet?"

"I'm here for the white dog. I was going to give the flower to the doctor's helper, but she's not here."

"We came for our dog too." She'd play along. This might be the boy she asked Hollister to investigate. So far, they had turned up nothing, but it had only been a day since her orders.

"There's nobody here, Miss Rebekah, just the doctor."

"Come with me." She stood, took the boy's hand, then O'Reilly's and walked to what she felt was a door. "Open it." The door creaked open and they stepped inside.

"Doctor, this boy is here for his dog and we're here to pick up the American Eskimo pup the American soldiers rescued."

The doctor hesitated. "I only have one dog. I have a cat. A Siamese, very nice temperament, striking really."

She sensed something going wrong fast, because the doctor used the word "really." It implied what she had already surmised: she and the boy were here for the same dog. Also, the doctor was beginning to sell the cat to one of them. Now her sense of danger became overwhelming. O'Reilly and she needed to evac pronto or call for reinforcements. She temporized, hoping for a quick resolution, "Where did you get the dog?" She grabbed O'Reilly's belt buckle as if for balance, found his cell and pushed the send button twice.

"What happened to your eyes, Colonel?" the doctor asked.

"I was injured. I'll be alright."

"You're Colonel Rebekah, yes?"

"Colonel Rebekah, yes I am."

"Well, you see," he hesitated a bit too long. "This boy is here to claim the dog your men brought in."

She couldn't help one last push for a quick adoption and a quicker exit. She needed the little white fur ball for her new life. Besides, the pup had somehow transferred a vision of herself to Bekah. It was God's work, no matter the consequences. "Ahmed, do you really want to have a dog in a place where everything is blowing up? I promise to take good care of him."

"It's not a him, she's a girl dog and she is a pretty white, like snow. I've never seen snow." Her head was still not functioning at one-hundred percent. She now remembered Hollister telling her the pup's sex.

The doctor excused himself to go to another backroom and get the puppy and cat.

The boy wrapped his arms around her waist.

Maternal instincts took over. Hugging the boy, she said, "I know, sweetie. What if I get you and your family out of here someday to visit some snow? Big piles of it."

"All I have is my dad."

"Oh, you and your dad. I'm sorry you lost your family."

"They are in paradise. I want my dog."

The doctor brought over the white puppy and the cat and placed them between the legs of the boy and Rebekah, who were sitting next to each other on the bench again. The puppy jumped for her and climbed to her face. *Smothered with kisses.* She felt thick silky fur, triangular ears and curled tail. The pup decided the abrasions around her eyes needed a thorough washing. *This little bandit has already stolen my heart.*

"Are you trying to cure me, or just lovin' it up?" She nestled the pup to her bosom, perplexed whether licking could cause an infection or help the facial cuts heal or both. She recalled stories of wounded tribal warriors of various cultures being healed by canine kisses.

Hollister had filled her in on how the dog got here. "Son, this dog belonged to an Italian couple. They shouldn't have come here. It wasn't their fault. They just wanted peace. We all do."

"Maybe, they are in paradise. So, I can still have this dog, Miss Rebekah?"

"You can, but this pup is a northern dog. Dogs with big fur die fast in Edanistan, because Allah made this part of the world hot. Allah would be displeased to see her suffer. It would be a sin."

"Italy is hot too, isn't it, Miss Rebekah?"

"Italy has many snowy mountains, too. Do you know their name, Ahmed?"

"The Italian Alps, Miss Rebekah."

"You could be on Smarter than a Fifth Grader," O'Reilly said.

"I am a fifth grader."

She smiled. "This dog will love snow. I can see her now, pretending to be a lump of snow. Can you see that?"

"I can see her rolling and jumping."

"Good." Not once did the boy comment about her eyes. *Guess he's seen it all; well at least, he's a gentleman.*

The boy sighed. "Can I visit her someday? Can I have the cat?" The cat flicked Rebekah's arm with her tail and the puppy nudged closer. She felt the pup's fur fluff-up and press into her as though to say to the cat, *No sharing, please, Siamese.*

"Oh honey, I guarantee it." She embraced the boy while listening to O'Reilly bawling. A tear of her own formed, surprising her. Not so much because she could cry, she cried less than her men, but because her eyes were strafed, ripped with some fusion or scars, on and around the lids. She speculated her tear ducks were now working or leaking. It was probable this boy's father was an enemy. Because of this, the boy would not likely live long. She figured the young Italian couple had lost their heads and the boy saw it or knew it happened.

She said, "You know Ahmed, we are all God's or Allah's children. As a child of God, I promise you I will never forget you. All you need to do is send me an e-mail when you and your father are ready to visit. I'll pay for the trip." The puppy started barking which led her to conclude people were near the doors. It didn't take a dysfunctional seventh sense to figure they were likely about to be attacked.

She decided it unwise to reach for her pistol and raised her voice. "O'Reilly, stand down."

It happened fast. Some doors banged opened at once. Locals shouted, "Freeze." The cat hissed and the puppy continued barking. O'Reilly groaned from what sounded like a Taser. Her heart broke for her adopted brother. Someone arm-locked her neck and yanked her away from the boy. She managed to cling to the dog.

An Edanistani with a cultured British accent spoke. "Ahmed's father is ready to visit now."

Being frightened for O'Reilly, collapsed her visuals from so-so to murky. She tried to "see" where the Edanistanis stood. *How many were there? Eight. My chances? Zilch. O'Reilly's condition? Okay. Location? The floor. The boy? With his dad. Checkmate. I'm a royal screw-up.*

Ahmed's father screamed into her face as if she were deaf, "You are responsible for the death of many fine men. Some say you use witchcraft from Hell's belly to murder the freedom fighters of Edanistan. Some say you dishonor all women with same sex acts."

Apparently, her false reputation extended beyond U.S. Army gossip. She started diminishing his arguments in an offhand way; realizing confrontation might get her throat slit on the spot. "I only like men. No one will have me now, the way I look."

Ahmed's father knocked her cap off, grabbed her trundling hair and pulled her head back and to the side. He whispered into her ear. "It could be worse, Colonel. Around here, there are all sorts of sordid types, ruffians really. These nasty lots would consider your head a trophy worthy of a little sweat. These types would blow up buildings to see you to hell"

She assumed Ahmed's father wanted something or she'd be dead already.

Chapter 5

Studying variations

Thursday, Washington D.C.

Jay hopped on the early morning Acela Express to Washington. Then nursed a strong coffee while reviewing various scenarios for dealing with the most powerful man on the planet. OTTS was ready for war or peace. The President would choose. The train stopped. He tucked all his moves away, determined to enjoy the intermezzo provided by a long walk.

On the way to the White House, the Capitol Mall, monuments, museums and cherry blossoms provided calm, wonder and a sense of excitement. Perhaps he'd choose to visit the American Indian Museum after his appointment, considering Bekah's heritage.

Yes, appointment to Director, OTTS, thank you very much, Sir. He stopped for a moment, daydreaming again, no—aching for a better day, a much better day for America and the world. A mirage of Reverend Martin Luther King stood far off at the Lincoln Memorial; Jay surrendered by a sea of people in adulation. "I have a dream." *I too, Martin.* Jay raised his hand to his heart and then patted an imaginary shoulder. He reminded himself of all the questions he wanted, no—needed answered by that silly sprite inside his computer.

Holly anticipated his concerns, "I know you'll do what is right or they'll put you in the hoosegow. You're going to be a spy, James. Get used to it. Get the job and we'll talk. Do I have your permission to lighten up?"

"Go for it." *And another thing, just how do you know or guess what I'm thinking?*

"Later, James." She started playing the opening beats of the James Bond movies. Jay cracked a smile.

"What?"

"Say it, James."

"The name's Boone, James Boone. At your service," Jay said, somewhat subdued by the presence of a young family walking by. The father pushed his carriage a bit away from Jay, but gave him a thumb up and a confused smile. *Must think I'm nuts.* Jay blushed

"Now go see the President. The country needs you," Holly said.

A little later and through the maze of hallways and a haze of thoughts, he found himself ushered into the Oval Office and announced.

"Mister President, may I present Doctor and Professor James Nicholas Boone." Jay was invited to take a seat across the desk from the President, who swiveled around to focus on him. Jay knew this President was famous for bounding around his desk to meet and greet. *Possibly, he has some knotty problem to solve or he doesn't relish meeting an NYU professor, active in the peace movement. Maybe…*

"You go by Jay, right?" The President stood up, dipped and extended his hand for a shake.

Pretty good start. "Yes, sir."

"That Carlos was too spooky for me. He claims his psychic powers killed Andropov, you know the ex-Soviet Premier. Crazy, huh? As we say in Texas, that dog don't hunt. You'll do a better job, but no more spoon benders, no budget."

The President is sharing classified info, a good sign. "I thought the spoon benders were ridiculous, sir." What did the President mean by no budget? Jay worried and awaited events.

"Yeah, a waste of good silverware. Good, so what's your plan? Skip the hocus-pocus."

Jay relaxed. The agency was going to live. Maybe. He had planned a bit of a chess game with the President revolving around lost intelligence opportunities, especially the channel secret report from Vegas, August 2001 and how it would be important today to tap every source for the defense of the country. He decided to take a non-confrontational tact and in the process, show some true emotion. He suspected the President would have checked his political affiliation and realized the professor was a straight shooter.

"Mr. President, first, I want to thank you for the early Secret Service details you authorized, encouraged and expanded for Senator Carthage. Second, I want you to know that I look for scientific explanations for anything unexplained, as best as God gave me the talent to ascertain."

"Amen and thank you. Daniel is a good man. To be honest, put yourself in my shoes. You've made some mistakes, maybe, hum? You'd do whatever you could to keep him safe. Right? Get my drift?" The President pushed some papers aside, uncovering an envelope. He sat on the side of the desk, with one leg bent forward. He was engaged in the process.

"I agree sir. Bravo. I would like to get to Edanistan as quickly as possible and recruit Colonel Rebekah Carthage." The President started smiling. Jay continued, "I'm ready to initiate a disinformation campaign to explain away the dog incident and her insipid lesbian gossip. She'll be engaged to me, for starters. The chatter on the street, over the net and on cells has placed her in grave danger. Therefore, her combat team too. I have Newsweek, Time, Stars & Stripes and the rest on hold and all are ready for amendments. I need your permission for a quick start." Now the President was snickering and Jay was losing his bearings. "I need your permission and authority to hire her. All I ask are two salaries and the normal expenses. You won't be bothered for anything else."

"Son, my helicopter awaits you, Senator Carthage, his daughter, Rebekah's sister, Sissy, she prefers, will meet you on the plane at Andrews. You got the job, but keep it to two people, until they kick me out of here. She can choose to join OTTS. Protect her with your life. Bring her to me safe and sound. I want to pin the Lioness. I'm appointing you chief negotiator, with full authority to act on my behalf and all that jazz. General Birchmont will take personal control until you arrive. Should be a piece of cake." The President pushed an envelope over to Jay. "Apparently, we owed you a little money. I rounded it up, interest and all, to $10,000. Sign here. All crisp cash. Printed it myself in the basement. Sorry about the mix-up."

There's that smile again. Negotiate what? "Thank you. Did I miss something, Mister President?"

Chapter 6

A team competition

The President filled Jay in on Rebekah's capture. He also explained his snickering. "The last thing I want to do is send a Democrat off to get killed. They multiply, you know. Stomp on one and ten pop up. I was laughing to myself; you and I were set to solve a problem named Rebekah, our common ground. I know you're a strong negotiator for the Professors' union…and this situation will practically solve itself. We've got them surrounded. No way out and they are not martyrs. I'm sure the Colonel is doing a number on them, as we speak. Maybe they'll walk out singing cumbiya before you get there. You'd better run. Check the latest intel as soon as you get on board the copter. Meeting over—go, go, go. May the Lord be with you on your journey," he shouted down the hallway. The last hearty bellow blew Jay's mind: priests, ministers, rabbis and presidents. *The same soup.* He and an armed Marine ran through the halls. Jay got an idea. Holly was in the valise. He flipped open his cell. "Command, call Holly." *"Acting," as John Lovett, the comedian, would have said.*

His phone vibrated, the phone number showed as restricted, "Jay," Holly said.

"Hi, I was just calling you. Get me exec summaries on Sissy and the people with Rebekah. Oh, and a little on you, for now. Also, why wasn't I told about this situation Rebekah's in?" Jay was hustled into the copter.

"When you're strapped in, open me up. The reports will show."

The pilot, Jay and armed Marines blew off the White House grounds and revved toward Andrews Air Force Base.

Still on his cell, Jay asked, "But, why wasn't I told?" Jay was miffed.

The outside of the laptop flashed, "Open me." Intrigued by that little trick he opened the laptop. The screen displayed, **"The news was breaking just minutes before you walked into the Oval Office. Do you think you're the only one with a "special" laptop? You wouldn't want to steal the President's thunder, would you?"**

"What voice is in his laptop?"

"His mother's," the screen wrote.

"Bring up Sissy's background and then the other two reports, thank you."

The cell rang, "Just listen. You are just too passive. I bet if you were trying to win a last round game or solve some equation, you'd knock it out-of-the-park. I'll give you credit for figuring out you could use the cell phone. Power up that beautiful mind of yours before you get yourself killed. Also, Rebekah is quite a challenge. Once you get her to go with you, if you can convince her, you may get down on your knees and beg for Brenda… There's something you don't know about me. Well many things. What's the one thing you wish you had? Actually, you have it. It's staring you in the face." Holly hung up.

Jay puzzled it out. He wasn't a chess master and physics professor for nothing. Logic was his game. He realized he must be suffering from some sort of culture shock and it was inhibiting his ability to reason and live in a world of espionage, in which he was a principle player. *Oh, I'm no Carlos, but maybe Carlos is no Jay. New set of balls, please. Those that go clang in the night.* Holly was important to him. *No, indispensable.* He knew she was right. Start thinking, start being pro-active.

There was a bunch of unanswered questions about Holly. For instance her power supply, type of intelligence, human, artificial or both, how she sees and hears, how she grabs any printer she wants, and phones, etc. All of these items were of interest to Jay, but in the end, he could do little with the information, except marvel. No, his only wished for improvement would be a keyboard. Therefore, she had to have one. Since the laptop appeared black pearl inside and out, a gorgeous thing really, maybe the keyboard would come up just as the screens did. Jay started typing on the screen area. Eureka. A keyboard showed up and the screen area became smaller to accommodate it. He closed the laptop and started typing on the case. A keyboard displayed, along with one screen, which said, "well done." Jay turned the laptop sideways, upside down and diagonally. Every position worked. He felt like kissing the thing. Too weird. The Marines might jump ship. He opened the laptop and waited for the report.

EXEC REPORT ON SISSY, FOR YOUR EYES ONLY:
- Joani Locksley; maiden name, Carthage, also known as Sissy. Older sister to Rebekah. Retired Navy Captain - Naval Intelligence, area 51, others—more info on a need to know basis.
- 3 year old son, 1-year-old daughter.
- 6' 3" tall, Martial arts master. Don't challenge her to a match.
- Full time mom, part time consultant to intelligence community, works at home.

Jay typed, "Good intel, Holly. Maybe I'll employ another Carthage after the election."

"Better times are ahead," the screen read.

"Intel summary report for Edanistanis holding Rebekah, please. I'll study their full dossiers on the plane."

Primary source: INTERPOL.
- The leader's name is Jamaal Mustafa Ali, lawyer, educated at Cambridge.

- Secularist, wants to forge alliance of all Edanistani groups to remove all foreigners and take their country back. Attends Sunni and Shia mosques irregularly, refuses to declare his leanings (or lack of faith) for the sake of making a unity point.

- Solves problems using pragmatism. Will sell out any foreigner to extremist groups for the sake of building his political network. Extremely dangerous.

- National celebrity.

- Not a martyr.

- Paranoid about suicide bombers and other supposed and real threats to his life.

- Seven men with him, no data yet. Assume they are loyal and likely unquestioning.

Jay realized his life could come to a very abrupt end. Out of a sense of guilt, he pictured Anatoly smiling. The Russian émigré in the park pushed his chess pieces aside, stood up and saluted him. *It's time I act, act like a man.* Jay resolved to try to help Anatoly when he got back to New York even if Anatoly offered resistance. Jay felt sure he could help in some way.

Although ridiculously irrational, anything could happen when he met the captors. If he had to die, at least it would be for someone who kicked his hormonal clock all those years ago. *A girl, I admit, gives me pause even now.* The boy in him sweated. His stomach in knots. He felt like that kid in the corner of the high school dance, peeking, by his friends' arms, at the most gorgeous girl, Bekah, swirling by in billowing chiffon, happy, laughing. He had no chance. Not scrawny, minuscule James Ripisi. Now, he was desirable.

Why am I thinking about romance with a woman who orders men around for a living? Get real. She's changed. I've changed. Soldiering is her game and she plays it like a champ. Ah, life and death. Saving a friend's life. Does she even know I'm a friend? Not some secret agent sent to rescue her. What does it matter? She'll know what to do. That girl with braces still twists my heart and likely will kick my butt.

Jay noticed the airport fast approaching and typed. "Holly, quick, there's little time. Tell me about you."

Exec report, hold as channel secret (for your eyes only): Holly, NSA prototype (a total of eight in existence).

- I'm petite, more like a notebook. I've tried to keep my weight down.

- Power supply: I absorb power from everything around me and the rest is classified. If I told you…

- I am a conscious sentient being. Whether I'm human, a bunch of humans, machine, or whatever, it is held secret. If I told you, I'd have to kill you. P.s., although I was born yesterday, I'm no pushover.

- I see* and hear acutely at short ranges. *About seeing, I matrix at short range a full spectrum of energy from all wave and particle motion, i.e., heat, light, liquid, electrical, magnetic, nuclear, example: neuron firings, and combine these with GPS and similar external forces, when available. The methods are classified and way beyond physics as you understand it. Better, you do not know, for now.

- • Unclassified: Did you know—when you and others think (often in English)—you form tiny vibrations in your ear and/or larynx that some humans pick up subliminally? I pick them up consciously. I hear the words and translate some abstractions at a short range.

- • My function is to be your friend and helper.

- • A note on your concerns: You are not abridging anyone's civil rights. Take the case of the two girls across from your co-op. You could have easily surmised what they were thinking and doing, had you been using that brain of yours. We are using the executive powers entrusted you by and for all the people of the United States of America.

"Got to go to black. We're ready to disembark. Love you. Don't be a stranger, ding-a-ling me."

Jay typed, "My little sprite, you're not my type. Love you too." Holly didn't go to black like any normal self-respecting sprite. Both screens filled with a jungle at sunset. He could smell the mist. Little creatures scampered, a toucan's beak fenced with the sun. There she preened in tight greens, pirouetting on a branch in the forest canopy.

The nymph waved. The sun set.

Later, the helicopter brushed down, creating very little dust. The blades whirled while the Marine guard and Jay ducked, without needing to. They ran to a huge, non-reflective, cocoa colored plane. The stealthy craft resembled a bat. The guard saluted Jay at the craft's stairs and ran back to the President's helicopter. Wide eyed like a boy in a model shop, Jay scanned the silver planes nearby. With an odd mix of worry over Rebekah and excitement for meeting her father churning his stomach, Jay entered the bat plane's belly.

He was anxious to meet the Senator and his other daughter, Sissy. But they were not yet visible. What was visible and surprised him were the interiors. He was expecting little more than an oxygen mask, straps and a hull to lean on. Instead, he was ushered by posh conference rooms, smaller one-on-one rooms, a bar, bedrooms, bathrooms with showers, toothpaste, sealed toothbrushes, hairbrushes, spare clothing, disguises. His escort said, "the works."

A spy plane or a plane for spies?

Farther down the hall were private, Plexiglas encased computer rooms. In the first room, a guy hunched over, his white shirttails out, working on some electronics at a furious pace. There were sixteen screens stacked in four columns of four, looming over him and his leather chair. The tech was barking orders, grabbing some stuff from one screen and as if by magic, putting it on another screen. He swiveled about and waved, as if he knew Jay. Jay had seen his type before—replete with the required pocket protector—this time holding an NSA top-secret badge. He had coke-bottle glasses, curly black hair and a Roman nose, a Sicilian nerd. His name was embroidered above the ten or so multi-colored pens displayed in order of spectral frequencies. Odd. Little doubt his mama did the embroidering and he, the ordering of pens. The name read Bud.

Bud pushed the slider open, stood, wiped donut powder off his chin, held out his hand and said while chewing, "Jay, want a cherry filled donut? No trans-fat and *noooh* saturated-fat. They're amazing, healthy. Have grape, too." He had a large box of them with *secret stuff* written across the side. He didn't stop talking. "These donuts keep me in shape." He ballooned his belly. "I need a dead celebrity. Got to be dead, damn lawyers. What do you think, Rock Hudson? No time. Cary Grant or I don't know? I'll decide. No time. You've got to get in your state room, until we're cruisin'. Pilot's a cowboy." Jay grasped the cherry filled donut Bud placed in his palm. He stuffed a napkin into Jay's suit pocket, and shooed him down the hallway.

Rock Hudson, Cary Grant, whaaaat? These techies are all cut from the same cloth. Jay cautioned himself. *At NYU, the techs tell you there's not much difference between them and the professors. Or less politely, the professors don't know their waste disposal orifice from a black hole in space.*

It hit the ever so logical and now thinking on all cylinders, Jay. Bud was making a laptop for Rebekah with the voice of some dead movie star. *Must be a legal problem.* Jay mocked his confused love-hate feelings about Rebekah by letting himself indulge in an alien feeling, a little jealously. *Oh God, not Cary Grant. Judy, Judy, Judy. Oh, come on, Jay, if you can have Audrey, she can have Cary.* He smirked.

Bud shouted down the hall. "I'm the NSA's chief engineer, numb nuts." He laughed, then smiled, completely disarming Jay. He bit into another donut. Grape filling oozed out and embarrassment seeped in.

"Okay, catch you later." Jay flashed the peace sign. Bud held up his powder-infested hand and returned the symbol. Jay realized he had made two mistakes: he assumed Bud was a tech and projected it in some way. He whipped through his relationships with the NYU techs and absolved himself of all sins. In fact, he enjoyed equal and friendship based relationships with them. *Assumptions can get you killed. For now on, I'm playing my best game, with every bit of skill God gave me.* Jay added to his goodbye for now with, "Think GPS and echo location for the Colonel's sight problem."

A flash of brilliance consumed Jay. It would help Bekah get about with more than a white cane, seeing-eye dog, or some sort of unreliable sixth sense, which likely didn't exist. His brain filled with logic diagrams; translating bat physiology and other echolocation systems and integrated other communications ideas, like GPS voice recognition programs. He could get a grant to do it, but it would take months, maybe years. Here he was with Holly. Focusing on her, he guessed half the problem had already been solved. She seemed to know where they were on the planet, down to the tiniest detail. He didn't need to know how she worked, nor invent anything on his own. He had the NSA's resources at his disposal and a creative monster named Bud. The girl with the outrageous smile would get the very best.

Somehow, Bud responded to Jay's idea. His eyebrows arched, showing pleasant surprise, Bud said, "I've been working on that, plus some. See you later."

Tabling the mystery of Bud's apparent mind reading, Jay drafted an idea. *What does he mean "plus some," hum? Maybe an electronic work around for her basically melted optic nerves. Fantastic thought, if that's what it is.*

The pilot pinged the PA system. "Knock, knock. ...We're goin' high over the Atlantic and then the Mediterranean; maybe scrape a satellite or two. Two hours and twenty-seven minutes to Edan, hold on to your hats and strap down your asses. Yeeha."

Jay scratched his head, calculated accelerations and decided it was at least Mach 4 at top speed, wow. He perused the stateroom. He needed a shower, needed everything on board, except the bed. With adrenalin pumping, research and appointments, there was no way he'd sleep.

A Mongolian or northern Chinese girl wearing white terry cloth shorts and matching bare midriff top stood at the doorway. "I do massages. Can I strap down with you?"

Holy Mother. Jay looked at the Top Secret badge hanging from her bosom wrap and scanned the room to make sure there was more than one seat belt, "Okay, sorry, I have no time for a massage, but thank you."

She said, "Everybody so busy on these short flights. I give 100% satisfaction gaulenteed massage. Safe, theraapuding, dreamy." He had no trouble understanding this.

"That's pretty hard to refuse. I'm focused on rescuing the woman I love." *Okay, that was a small lie.* Yes, he cared about Bekah once upon a time. Jay noticed the masseuse was struggling to form some sort of response. Probably to shoot down his, 'I'm in love' argument with 'what does that have to do with getting a massage, safe, theraapuding?' Jay imagined a most improbable but humorous finishing sentence for the young lady. 'What does that have to do with the price of rice in Mongolia?' He raised his hand to stop her struggle to speak. "I know your massage is no doubt great, and millions of people enjoy massages."

She interrupted, "my hands are the best." She made what looked like an obscene gesture with her hand, but he wasn't sure she did it on purpose, it was so quick and since her hand ended up flicking her hair.

He stammered, "It's just...I have trouble with strange women touching my body. It's just me, sorry."

"I not strange," she said, face pouting.

"You should have a badge for your shorts, it say bottom secret too." She laughed. *She's a good girl,* Jay decided, while scanning her wholesome freckled face. He refused to dwell on how a masseuse came to work for or with the NSA. *So many things in life are mysterious and some are not worth the time to figure out. If I told you, I'd have to kill you.*

They made small talk until the all clear, but Jay's mind was somewhere in Edan, in spite of her long legs, super slink eyes and inscrutable Mongol face.

After the all-clear-to-move-about, Jay peered up and down the hallway. He had asked for two meetings: a private one with the Senator. Next, with the Senator and his other daughter, Sissy. A girl meeting Sissy's description from her dossier—who else could it be—waved from outside a computer room.

She stood about six-three, an inch taller than Jay. She had half the beauty and twice the figure of her much smaller and younger sister, if you like the voluptuous Brenda type. Her full dossier mentioned brown eyes, matching her hair. The lovely hair flopped to her waist. She, like her sister, inherited a gorgeous and creamy smooth golden skin, which was a textured mix of her father and mostly Filipina mother. The Senator was a blend of black, white and American Indian.

Sissy waved again from the entrance to one of the computer rooms. She mouthed and signed, "Catch you later." She pointed to one of the one-on-one conference rooms. "He's in there." She signed. Sissy may have been doing some homework of her own, studying Jay's dossier. It would say he learned American Sign Language from a deaf college roommate.

Jay could barely compose himself. He entered the conference room. There standing before him was an imposing man. The former college 6' 6" All-American basketball forward, now in his fifties, was still trim. He had game. His square-jawed, hawk-nosed face contrasted with sympathetic eyes and slightly upturned corners on his lips, to present the impression of empathy, wisdom and wit. White sleeves rolled up, he was ready for work. They eyed each other in a friendly, inquisitive way, shook hands and sat. Somehow, Jay would stumble through, star-struck. The ever-present secret service stood outside the Plexi-slider, reminding Jay of the complex web spun for *We The People.*

Jay went over what he knew of Rebekah's captors, and his plan to free her. The plan required the captors not know Jay was now Director of OTTS, or in any way a government plant. The agency didn't exist as far as the public was concerned, anyway.

All anyone, especially the captors knew, Jay was an accomplished professor from NYU, active in the peace movement, now traveling Europe and therefore able to get there quickly, connected to editors at Newsweek, etc., skilled enough in negotiations.

But, more important than all that, he was there to convince a very stubborn girl to come home with him. All of it true with one omission. The Edan veterinarian's office where she was held had a computer attached to the internet and the internet had all the 'right' information in it. The best clue for the captors was Jay's and Rebekah's chess abilities, if they found that useful. Jamaal knew the game enough to ascertain a real master from a fake. Even if Jay wasn't whom he said he was, the captors were surrounded and had no choice but to cut a deal.

They were checkmated and at the mercy of General Birchmont. Holly's report showed the General wanting to cultivate diverse Edanistani groups to band together and focus on eliminating all foreign fighters, which, in theory, would allow the last foreign fighters, that is, Americans to leave. Even though the General could push for their arrests with let's say light sentences, he had no strategic or tactical interest. The General could also order a low-risk tactical assault, but was unwilling to take a chance. Taking or killing these men by force would work against him.

In an odd way, Jamaal and the General wanted much the same thing for Edanistan. At the behest of the President and because Birchmont had decided, before her loss of sight, to groom Rebekah as his possible successor, the General decided to handle the situation himself. So far, they all waited for the professor.

Jay said, "…and so to sum up, Rebekah and I are engaged to be married, as far as the rest of the world is concerned. This counters the lesbian gossip and gives another reason for us to extract her from Edanistan, which is what they want. The first reason being, she's on the top of everybody's…hit list. Also, about the dog, the disinformation campaign states, she heard the dog barking right before the building exploded. She has no sixth or seventh sense. Forced by the hands of fate and the good of her soldiers, she's retiring to marry me. They need to believe she was just a very talented soldier, no more, no less. Do you agree, Senator?"

"Oh yes, great plan, just call me Dan. The family calls her Bekah. Call her Bekah. She's a tad feisty, but I know she'll play along. Super sharp, baby." His eyes welled. He raised his index finger as if to ward off tears and make a point. "Gets it from her mother."

"My prayers are with you, Dan. You must miss your wife badly."

"She was the love of my life, Jay. If ever you find your soul mate. Are you looking for a soul mate, looking to get married?"

The Senator was known to be a quick study, but this was ridiculous. Okay, Jay and Bekah would have to spend tons of time together. They would have to stay engaged until the threats neutralized. *Maybe, he sees it in my eyes. Do fathers just know when a man cares?* "Yes sir, not married and am looking."

"You'll know the feeling I have. It wells up, fills your being. I hurt. I hurt every day. I wanted her mother to walk this path with me some day, to be First Lady." Jay could see the strain on the Senator's face and the sadness in his eyes. No doubt, he was lovesick after all these years. Little doubt he launched a heat-seeking missile aimed at Jay's heart.

"She's with you, Dan."

Dropping his eyes from the ceiling, he focused on Jay, and said, "Take care of my baby. You know I can't go where you're going. I can't say what you'll say… Although, I feel certain my plan for complete withdrawal would meet with their approval." Dan puffed out his chest, as if ready for a debate.

Jay said, "There's a little technical difficulty with my plan." Jay was relishing this moment for two reasons now; the Senator's spirits needed lifting and Jay wanted permission to do something he had dreamed of, what some fifteen years ago. He leaned toward the Senator for emphasis.

"Ye-ah," Dan said with an upbeat in his voice.

Jay raised his palms and smiled, "What is the first thing an engaged couple does when they meet after being separated for a long time?"

Dan started laughing, leaned across the Plexi cocktail table and patted Jay on the shoulder, "Have you tried wrestling alligators, bull fighting, charming a cobra?"

"Is it that bad?" Jay pictured himself head-locked and flipped by the Lioness of Edanistan.

"Let me tell you a story. Elsie—that's her mom's name—Bekah and I were very close. When Bekah was a teenager, she would visit first with her mother, then me, with reports about her boyfriend of the moment. Elsie got the fuller report. I caught up at night. Not one of her boyfriends lasted more than a week. Well one was three weeks and one day. But that's besides the point. We had a vacation at the time. Kissing was sometimes fine with her, but the moment they tried to feel her up or do anything else, they were dumped. She's a bit of a one-eyed Jacqueline... Sorry, baby."

Dan inspected the ceiling. He seemed embarrassed by his choice of words and his baby's blindness. Jay felt it was best to treat a very proud woman, or for that matter, anyone with a handicap, in a completely normal manner. "Not only did her mom's Catholicism stick with her, but my lectures on AIDS and other ugly diseases sealed her fate. The girl was also a tomboy and sports enthusiast. She wanted to stay healthy and die old. I hardly have room for all her trophies. Anyway, I believe her virginity continued in college. She still confided in me. So, she's a bit adolescent. Stuck in high school purgatory."

Jay marveled at the closeness Bekah's mom and dad had with her. He wished someday he would be so lucky, and vowed to ask at the right moment for his secrets on parenting.

Dan continued, "She was hell bent on being the best at whatever interested her. No boy would stand between her and the goal. She once told me, she would know when the right man came along. That man would treat her as an equal and with complete respect. Since she never told me to the contrary, my backup spy, her mother, died her senior year of high school." His voice slowed and trailed off a bit. "Fifteen years next week." The strength of his voice returned. "I think she may have no experience. That is, she's probably still a virgin. Oh, I said that already." Dan leaned back and smiled broadly, no doubt a challenge and a plea doubly stressed.

Jay said, "Well, I, ah, I promise you I will never take advantage of your daughter. I'm sure once she finds out her "fiancé" has come to take her home, save her life, she'll play along." Jay formulated an idea. "She's about five foot seven inches right?"

"Yep, between seven and eight inches."

"Good, I'll tuck the top of her head under my chin and give her the, I miss you so much hug."

"Should work." Dan appeared concerned and said, "Look..."

Jay didn't like the new solemn tone and where the forlorn father might be heading. He interrupted. "I have a secret to share with you, Dan."

Dan dropped his head slightly forward and leveled his eyes on Jay by peering through black curly brows. The stare reminded Jay of a basketball player planning a juke.

"Go for it."

"I care about your daughter, sir. I have since, Prep. I wasn't lucky enough to be one of her boyfriends. From what you've said, I guess it was a good thing, because I don't know what I would have done with her up close. Although I was raised Catholic, I was clueless until college. You know what I mean? I mean, I didn't start dating until college anyway."

"Thank you for making me feel a little better, but why didn't you get in line and ask her out if you had a crush on her?"

At that moment, the Mongolian masseuse stuck her round head between the broad shoulders of the two secret service agents blocking the door. She wrapped her arms around their biceps. Both the Senator and professor waved and then, in unison, shook their heads no, as if they were dashboard spring-doll heads, taking a hairpin turn. Both men smiled.

Jay said, "I was an acne faced, not-tall, chess player with no self-esteem."

"You're a G.Q. kind of guy in a counterculture sort of way," referring to Jay's long hair, little doubt. Dan tapped Jay's knee. "You would have had her mother's blessing and you have mine, not because you're good looking, but because you have a good heart." Jay felt Dan was either applying parenting skills, as if he were a son, or just being gracious. It seemed both of them realized the ruse of marriage was fertile and slippery ground for a couple attempting a tantalizing tango.

"Just be honest with her about yourself and your motivations. She's a straight shooter and once she finds herself, she'll continue to contribute to society."

Like lightning, Jay thought through another knotty problem. "If she goes along with my plan, I'd like her to join me as co-director of my agency." It dawned on Jay, Bekah's assets, experience and organizational skills would make a perfect fit for him. *A perfect fit.* He didn't want to lose her and he wasted no time making an executive decision. "I'm sure the current President—and for that matter—the future President wouldn't stand in our way."

"So ordered," the presumptive nominee for President teased.

"I'll treat her with respect, always, Dan."

Holly, who lay flat and quiet on the coffee table interrupted, "Senator? Jay? They just released O'Reilly, the boy and doctor. Hey and hurray for our side. It wasn't an equal trade. The base had to deliver 20 kilos of Hersheys. That's all." She went quiet.

"Yo, that sounded like Audrey Hepburn. Where'd you buy that?"

"It was custom made. You like her voice?"

"One of my favorites. I had a huge crush on her."

"Can't have her. She's mine… Just kidding. I'll talk to the engineer."

They continued their conversation. Jay filled him in on OTTS's charter. Dan was very curious; especially about the possibility, his daughter had special talents. He seemed to be hiding something, maybe some secret about his daughter. Jay vowed to get to the bottom of it, when the time was right.

A little later Holly interrupted again. "Oh, just breaking, the cat and dog have been released. Just some kibble there."

"That is one hilarious piece of equipment."

"You have *no* idea." Jay rolled his eyes and stroked the black pearl case. Holly purred.

"No tickling, Jay, please." Jay ignored the sprite.

Dan leaned forward and ran his finger up and down her barely visible seam.

"Oh, Senator, you do know how to get a girl's attention."

Dan had his little boy's face on, full of wonderment. His eyes crinkled and his voice cracked, "That's no ordinary voice recognition program. She seems alive."

"Makes you wonder. Hey, you'll get one when you're President. You'll have to pick a voice, or voices. I guess."

"I'll think on it."

Holly started playing Hail to the Chief. The two secret service agents peeked over their shoulders, flashing amused grins.

The meeting broke and Jay dug into his thoughts. Only the President, the Senator and General Birchmont were privy to the plan. All signed off. Next was a meeting with Sissy alone, since Dan had some business to attend to.

Sissy sat there slack jawed. Apparently, she thought Jay a great match, with his chess, looks and kind heart. She voiced disappointment over her sister keeping the news from her. Likely the two girls were close, like their mom and dad. Jay considered telling her the truth after her sister was out of Edanistan safe, provided no threat remained and Jay thought it wise. *After all, she worked and sometimes works in the intelligence arena. But, at this time, she doesn't have a need to know.*

Sissy finished the meeting with a reveal, "You may not know my background; you'd need a channel secret or top secret clearance with a need to know." His cover and agency didn't show to her on the DOD computers, good. "I'm an expert in Judo and other arts, ex-military. I want you to know, I'd be glad to give you lessons if you like. But, if you break my little sister's heart or in any way harm her, I'll teach you a lesson you'll never forget."

Jay got the sense she felt like wrestling on the spot, only dissuaded by all the furniture, electronics, insignia coffee cups about them and the size of the room. "I'm a gentleman, Sissy, and have a true heart. Engagements are for discovering each other. We'll also take the engagement encounters offered at my parish. If we split, I'm sure it will be for mutual reasons. Right now, I'm crazy about her, she's my soul mate. She'll tell you the same, I hope."

She gave him a bear hug and kissed his cheek. She cocked her head and flashed that Carthage smile. This mannerism was all girl sees boy and likes, very primitive, very sexy. Jay enjoyed the texture of her cheek on his lips when he returned the kiss. Although she wasn't by any stretch, beautiful by his standards, she showed the same enthusiasm, charm and devilish mix of tomboy and flamboyant female her kid sister exuded, as he remembered her. Sissy would have been an intriguing woman to know, had they been on a desert island and not married or engaged, *chasing each other naked, wrestling on the sand... Stop it, Jay. You are not engaged. What's this thing you have for Carthage girls? Get over it.*

Chapter 7

Sacrificial lines

Rebekah's main captor, Jamaal, was a pain in the ass.

The trained to be unemotional soldier pushed herself into a fighting mood, a natural and preferred state. However, she was stymied with a few other problems to solve. She tried to weigh them with military precision. Instead, she had to combat her own injured brain, which sometimes played like her three-year old nephew's meandering phone reports.

After the dog and cat left, her inner vision wavered. Coincidence? The doctor had said the pain and confusion would disappear completely, when she healed. With her head barely out of diapers, she pressed on.

There was her soon to appear rescuer to consider, but her most outstanding problem was personal. Before her visions diminished, she pictured her chief captor Jamaal as a gargoyle. He claimed to be the most handsome middle-eastern man she could have imagined. She suppressed a laugh. He was rapidly developing affection for her and didn't mind telling her *all* about it. She did nothing to encourage this. She was merely doing her job, being diplomatic and trying to solve their common problem, as trained. Rebekah knew none of this would have happened, had she not punched O'Reilly's cell phone call button.

Just two minutes after her capture, she had heard the rumble of heavy trucks down the residential streets. Troops and snipers, no doubt surrounded the vet's place, evac-ed the locals, as per procedure. The loud speaker began with the theme of negotiation as a preference to bloodshed. Communications were set up. The General was taking personal control, to insure the safety of her and the eight enemy men with her. Without the surround, Jamaal may have handed her over to some radical group, for his own selfish political gain. She cheated death once again. Without the Jamaal-General phone connection, O'Reilly, the boy, doctor, cat and dog might not have been released.

The lesser problem of being somewhat sightless, preyed on her mind. Rebekah mourned the veil of partial blackness and hoped she could go back to being "weird," that is, seeing without eyes. Most of the color had drained from what she could see or imagine at the moment.

She vowed not to think of herself as handicapped. God had blessed her with many gifts and she'd always use her available gifts. So she worked on sensitizing her hearing— a gift to the "blind,"—during slack time with her captors.

She'd remain whole, one way or another. Regain her military command, if she could force the issue. Her persistent headaches from eye injuries, coma and drug withdrawal may have had some influence on her ability to "see." She shelved an exploration of her abilities for a better time and focused on Jamaal.

Rebekah likened her main captor to the Wizard of Oz with his band of munchkins, noise behind a curtain, all ego, no follow through, at least, not this time. Like the Wizard, Jamaal demonstrated chinks in his armor. She was determined to skewer through. She had a ton of human psychology under her belt, whether ivory tower or commanding troops or working with the generals. Jamaal, although educated, was a piece of cake. Simple really, he just wanted all foreigners out of Edanistan. *Now there's some common ground.* The General had planned a big tent, if possible, if they were Edanistani. If they weren't, it too was simple, blow-em' to hell.

Unfortunately, Jamaal was Edanistani so Rebekah buried her warrior instincts. It was a shallow grave. She wouldn't have minded taking three or four out, before she'd meet the grim reaper stalking her. They seemed at ease around a poor defenseless blind girl, almost protective. Yeah, so blind she felt she knew where some of their weapons were, by the scraping and rubbing sounds, limited vision and their own tactical pronouncements helped her stay ready to rumble.

The stiletto strapped to Jamaal's belt, slit his throat. Grab the M60 from the jerk with BO sitting next to her, butt his head and circular spray the room, a chance she'd get them all. Less than 15 seconds for the entire exercise. Her men would take out the guards at the doors in a split-second. General Birchmont however had other plans. Being a good soldier, she had tacked to being a sociable comrade and ad hoc negotiator. However, she remained vigilant.

My captors must be fascinated that a woman could be so strong and command men, which will pay dividends. I should relax a tad and play up my aura.

Rebekah convinced her captors to remain close to her, because her men might be trigger-happy. "They love me so much," she said. There was also the near certainty her captors were visible through heat signatures, microwaves and other spectral analyzers. This would make a surprise attack by her combat team, quick and lethal.

Jamaal liked her ideas so much he forced her to sit on his lap after a sham argument.

Fuck you, asshole, she had wanted to say. Jamaal was petting her hair again. *Darn it all.* That was beyond annoying, it was just shampooed. She didn't care how good looking he claimed to be, nor his taut chest and muscular thighs. Thank his Allah, he either let his stump slump between his legs or it was a tiny one. Her acclaimed derriere could not detect any lumps. After she sprayed the men with bullets, she'd cut his thing off, walk out the door, hold it up and throw it to her men. What a morale booster, LOL.

"Why didn't you tell me, you had a fiancé?" Jamaal said, using a ridiculous lovesick, high-toned voice. His men must have smiled or perhaps they thought him weak. Chink.

Rebekah had to think quickly. Something she was very good at, in spite of the headaches. Adrenalin rushed and her thought processes straightened out, somewhat. First, no reaction except hope and longing for her fiancé should show on her face. Second, share as little info as possible. She figured the CIA or Army Intelligence was up to their usual tricks. Thank God the general had insisted to be on speaker phone to check on her wellbeing. He talked about her "fiancé's" pending arrival and shared a little of Professor Jay Boone's background. On the surface, he sought Jamaal's agreement. Hopefully, it was all she needed to know.

Answer Jamaal and switch subjects. "We kept our engagement a secret because I wanted my men focused and I thought I might not ever leave Edanistan, alive."

"Very nearly dead, and twice over, I might add," he interjected with an apologetic tone.

"Jamaal, I'm sorry you lost your wife. This war has caused too much misery." She rested her head back on his chest. "I know you want us out and I hope we'll leave, once someone like you can bring order to this country." She placed her hand on his chest.

He pushed upright. "Really? You just don't get it. You Americans like setting up welfare states. Then you wonder why people cheat, take little initiative and in the end, destroy themselves. The Edanistanis are a proud people. We don't like to be treated like children. We are not your children."

"You really ought to run for office, Jamaal."

"Speaking about offices, if your father is elected, I have little doubt the U.S. will leave our country to stand on its own two feet… This guy, Professor Jay Boone must be very special to merit a jewel like you." More petting and a kiss on her forehead served to keep her focused, *on ripping his heart out.*

Jamaal seemed just as interested with the woman on his lap as with world politics or interrogation. *Headaches, darn headaches, don't show the pain.* She couldn't remember just yet from where she had first heard Jay's name. The CIA or possibly the Green Berets' political arm, FID, would have been careful, when assuming an identity, to employ a look alike. Maybe, they recruited the real McCoy. But, what did he look like? Her dossier would provide the answer, revealing the body type she liked. He would be tall, good looking and in great shape. But, what hair color? *This is impossible. Think, Rebekah, think. Maybe blonde or brown, it doesn't matter. Eyes, any color. Maybe, I'll be color-blind. No silly, women aren't color-blind. Are they? Oh God, let's not go there. Do not ask me this, Jamaal.*

On a lark, she tried telepathic persuasion, hoping to discover yet another talent. "Jay is like you, respectful and in full agreement with your ideas. I believe women and men are equal. How are you going to handle the fundamentalists?"

"There is no other way to keep all my country's factions together. There is only so much bloodshed before the people wake up, after we get rid of irritants, like you. You may not know this. America was the main catalyst for violence in my country, just like a chemical reaction. You started it. The sooner you leave, the better off we will be. The combustion will slowly come to a halt."

"I understand." She was a soldier following orders to be diplomatic. But? Edanistanis had asked for help to break their ruler's binds. The king had allowed troops to fire at demonstrators for democracy. He also arrested people who then disappeared. The allies responded to the people's cries, nothing insidious.

How ungrateful.

She wouldn't let on, she had to maintain a reasonable relationship with Jamaal or they would all leave in boxes. Besides, many of her superiors thought of the war as fucked up beyond all recognition, FUBAR. Edanistan's government was gaining strength, hopefully making all this moot soon.

"I don't think you agree with me. It's written all over your still lovely face. Give it time, Colonel. Give it time and you will see the light." Jamaal's cell rang. "Okay, maybe fifteen, twenty minutes, alright, send him in with the food. He must wear no shirt, just underpants and sandals, no electronics... Yeah, Whoppers for six, no mayo, three falafels, Cokes, three Sprites, that's right...oh French fries, ketchup. Yes, you'll have the pancit ready...good...later." He hung up, placed what felt like a finger and thumb on Rebekah's shoulder and lightly pinched. "What is this pancit?"

Rebekah had to ignore the pinch for now. "A Filipino rice noodle dish, in this case made by the hospital's nurses. Thanks for asking. It's sometimes with pork, but the nurses probably cooked chicken, or shrimp so you can try it."

"Your General is very accommodating and your fiancé is going to deliver in his undershorts. I didn't think you'd mind?"

Jamaal was a well-known paranoid so no surprise on his underpants request. This question of whether she'd mind was easy to answer. Her government dossier will have shown her sexual experience and philosophy, since she offered the information under a polygraph to get her Top Secret clearance. Therefore, her rescuer would treat her with care and she had better prepare Jamaal for a rather modest reunion.

"I'm a virgin, Jamaal." She used any tactic she could, but her immediately vibe from Jamaal was of irritation. Nonetheless, she continued being true to herself. To act otherwise, would really make Jamaal suspicious. "I know it's rare these days. But, I must admit, I'm looking forward to our honeymoon. How do you say it, I'm horny, for my man only. Do you mind me asking how you feel about this subject?"

"I don't care. Whatever you do or don't do. Just do it in America if you would be so kind. Yes."

He apparently loved to hear himself speak and her virgin gambit worked, somewhat, by keeping him away from talking about her 'fiancé.'

"Just stop screwing the Edanistani people. Why don't you invade Canada, if you're feeling lucky?" Jamaal's chest heaved, finishing his words with a sigh. This man would soon seek out a wife, she speculated. His son, Ahmed sorely needed a woman's influence. *Maybe I'm not that ugly or maybe Jamaal hasn't had a woman this close since his wife died.*

One of Jamaal's men asked her for a chess lesson. He had constructed a set out of the vet's medicines on an examination table. Rebekah, still held on Jamaal's lap, busied herself barking out a little chess with fervor so earnest, it drowned out any more questions about her so-called fiancé.

While she was talking chess, she was thinking about Professor Jay Boone, nothing yet on his identity popped into her consciousness. She was also thinking about how she was going to greet a "fiancé" in his briefs or boxers: *Should be boxers, it's healthier if we're going to have babies, more sperm. How many babies? Two, like my sister. A home for my pup?*

Oh my God, Wake up, Rebekah, stay focused. I guess I won't mind being hugged by a hunk, I'm sure. He'll probably kiss me. Yuck. Maybe yum. A Green Beret's body, another yum. A James Bond type, yummer. Bond, Boone, Jay, James. I get the joke. He's a spook. It's the CIA… Maybe.

They had better send someone clean. Dear General Jeffery, no herpes please. I like 'em germ free, washed up and scrubbed down, teeth brushed, hair combed. Hair. What color hair? Where is my vision, when I need it? She pictured the professor in recon van, undressing, but couldn't see his face. *Come back to me, oh phantom. I want my puppy. Get ready kid, your knight in skivvies is coming to rescue you. God bless America.*

* * *

Jay leaned against the black command truck in his comfortable light gray suit. How different he was than the men and women scurrying about in full-flack uniforms, gear and gunnery. He could count more rifles glinting off moonbeams than mosquitoes in a Jersey inlet.

He was immune from enemy fire because of a protective trim of tall vehicles separating the command truck from the target building, plus the target home/vet office's court wall. If the Edanistanis tried a breakout, they'd be mowed down like Butch Cassidy and Sundance. If they harmed Bekah, there'd likely be a crater where this fine upscale home once stood. He realized most Edanistanis evacuated this beautiful neighborhood because the lights were off, up and down the block. Only one brave Edanistani woman peered out her second story window, light on. She was accompanied by a U.S. soldier. The neighborhood was secure and considering Bekah's infamy and importance, it was likely the adjoining neighborhoods were, as well.

This neighborhood, although upscale was showing signs of neglect; whether it be the weariness of war or that, half the population fled to other countries out of fear for their lives. The earth tone stuccos on court and home walls were cracked here and there; some exterior trim lights were blown. A small thing really, in comparison to the wrecked or cratered homes, which speckled nearly all the neighborhoods in Edanistan and compared to the hundreds of thousands dead. A tear formed for *all* those who died in this absurd war.

Jay got antsy. He could do nothing to save Bekah if it weren't for this assembled horde of warriors, so he waited while his draft contract for Bekah's release was approved by the General and delivered. He wanted to play his part, a part fate treasured for him.

It was about 7 or 8 PM he figured. The soldiers told him the sun set sometime before 1800, which meant 6 PM. His flight was just a couple of hours, he left in the morning. Edan was 7 hours ahead of Washington. He pushed his jacket sleeve back to fix his watch and discovered it had already been changed: 7:57PM. Holly became suspect numero uno. How that little sprite changed his watch intrigued him.

It had cooled quickly with the late desert winds, likely in the high seventies. He imagined how these soldiers must feel dressed like walking bears.

His spirits peaked by the adulation of the military and civilian personnel running the surround and surveillance. Although treated like a VIP, he knew his part was simple. Present the deal, get it signed and walk out with Bekah. Cumbiya. All in a day's work for Boone, James Boone. Although he was excited beyond anything ever experienced in his life, he remained focused on his goal. Seeing her again would trump seeing the President and the Senator combined. He closed his eyes and found himself at the high school gym again, cowering in a corner. Cyndi Lauper's ballad, *True Colors,* lavished his heart. *Why couldn't it be me? Well, in less than a half-hour, I'll have my slow dance, my high school competitors are all gone now: married, kids, baseball.* The doll with the blissful smile swirled her orange, red and yellow chiffon dress. Her glimmering dress fired his heart. Today, he would step out of the shadows, no longer a boy. The man stood like a groom at the altar, waiting to catch a glimpse of the most gorgeous creature God had ever created. A creature wounded and maimed by battle.

Like the phoenix though, she would rise again.

Jay peeked inside the truck at a large screen to check the overlapped thermal, microwave and other blurred images of the captors and Bekah. She was sitting on Jamaal's lap. Above each figure was an arrow with the name of the person on it. One of the techs or engineers turned to Jay, "We have a 96% chance of rescuing the Colonel without harm to her, sir." The tech seemed pissed.

"Not today soldier. The General, President and her fiancé find value in a political alliance with Jamaal. We'll go only on harm to the Colonel."

"But, I think he's tickling her." The tech said this, half in jest, and half, deadly earnest.

"When I get inside, I'll punch him in the nose." The truck rocked with guffaws. Fear of pending disaster and total focus on a successful outcome made the marginally funny, a five-star howler. These men and women wanted their commander back. For some, he was sure the only thing holding them back from a surprise attack was the General's insistence on diplomacy.

The captors and Bekah were likely listening to every strange sound: the captors measuring their breaths, Bekah "seeing" troop placements and scenarios. Jay figured out what Jamaal was doing by keeping her close, but he didn't appreciate his attempts at familiarity. Jamaal had lost his wife and he must know the Lioness of Edanistan would sooner see him dead.

There you go again, you jealous goof. Jay believed jealousy a defect, therefore he absolved himself by starting the sign of the cross. He stopped when noticing the personnel in the truck glued to his every move. He finished the cross with a flair, playing to his audience. He had them. They were with him. But God, they wanted Jamaal dead; not a bad idea in principle.

Jay reviewed his feelings and they were merely protective. Bekah wouldn't live long in Edan, being bandied about as Jamaal's girlfriend, what a thought. Also, Jay couldn't see her converting to Islam. She had a hard enough time attending church on Sunday. Busy. Always so busy. The normally logical Jay looked at his own soul cross-eyed. He promised to sort his confused feelings out after rescuing Bekah.

The General's attaché approached with the documents. "Sir, please review these. Would you mind stripping to your skivvies and here's some sandals? They want you to carry in the food and drinks. Is that okay, sir?"

Jay, the peacenik, easily put on the face of a soldier, or more accurately, a spy. He didn't have to ask why, the strip, knowing Jamaal to be paranoid. "Affirmative. At ease, Corporal. Does anybody here have a plastic bag for these docs?" He was getting a kick out of all this military fanfare. He wondered if "at easing" someone was appropriate. He didn't care, because they didn't react with any negative body language or sideways glances.

After a quick check of the agreement between captors, U.S. Command and the Edanistani government, he stripped down to his boxers and promptly turned red. Not so much from feeling naked or imagining the female soldiers peeking. No, it was the way his boxers looked. Tan and chocolate elephants thumped their hooves by palm trees on a blue background. *Geeze, did my mom buy me Republican shorts? I'm mortified. What a show. Bekah would probably like these, if she could only see them. She might feel them just to make sure I wasn't completely naked. I just hope the elephant doesn't raise his trunk. If it does, I'll be on my way to Palookaville. I won't last a day, let alone a week with her.*

He handed Holly to Bud, for safekeeping. "Don't get any donut powder on our baby."

"Good luck, Jay," flashed across the laptop. "You can kiss her." *Speak about jealousy.* His computer was nuts.

Resolve and excitement coursed his veins. He feared not. "Corporal, ask Jamaal if he wouldn't mind inspecting my trousers? Oh, never mind."

"Yes, sir." Jay preferred meeting Bekah with his pants on, but didn't want to upset Jamaal, so he dropped the subject until he could build some rapport with her captors.

"Colonel Rebekah Carthage and I will need a quick private meeting with the General when we walk out of there. No interviews until later. We go to the hospital."

"Yes, sir. I'll do my best, sir." Translation, no guarantees.

Jay was getting the hang of all this heady power, salutes and efficiency. He reflected on Carlos and his life as a spy and appreciated his friend and life choices now, more than ever. Jay sniffed his armpits and was glad he showered. He nearly scrubbed his skin off. The Corporal handed Jay a zip-lock freezer bag to slip the documents inside.

"Okay, where's the food? I'm ready."

Chapter 8

Trying a new opening

Rebekah was having a bad day. Was it the partial disappearance of her second sight, sexual harassment from her captor, hunger or a farcical fiancé ready to rescue her? She had listened intently to Jamaal's phone calls and everything he said to her. It was obvious Jamaal wanted her out of the country. What's all the fuss? She trained her teams to win battles with their eyes closed. She wouldn't be missed as a soldier. Maybe? There would be no convincing any of them she should stay. Jamaal wouldn't listen and the General will honor his promise. Jamaal's military position was hopeless. His political position had a chance. It seemed the whole world had gone mad, just because one ordinary soldier lost her sight.

Since the whole world was mad, she promised her lonesome self a treat. A little sexual flirting. *Being stopped up like a bad sink.* This Professor Jay Boone was going to get more than he bargained for. The sad prospect of going home, meeting a guy, leading a normal life, abhorrent as if was, made her consider femininity. This spook showed up just in time to entertain her. After all, she had some growing up to do. Why not practice, now? She was sure this gentleman-spy wouldn't mind. What man would? There would be no more, accidently on purpose walking in on her men in various states of undress and pretending to avert her eyes, eyes she no longer had. She would feel her way. The creaking of the front door, the wiping of feet showing surprising civility, and a jumble of polite salutations let her know her knight without armor had arrived.

"He's here, Jamaal," an underling said.

"Check all the food and him. Look for tattoos and then bring him and the food in here."

Rebekah, Jamaal and most of the men were in an interior room. Rebekah started pushing on Jamaal's thighs to try to stand, acting excited about seeing her mystery man. She was excited. No, really. The prospect of liberation got her hot, hot for life. If she had to leave the Army, at least she should take on her new future with the same fervor she used to rise to colonel. This could be the first day of a completely new life.

"Just a moment, princess."

"If Jay sees us like this, it might distress him. You don't want a knuckle sandwich." She felt Jamaal recoil slightly. He helped her to stand, but clasped one arm.

"Never hit a man with a gun. But, I suppose you're right. I apologize, some deep dark corner of my male vanity wanted to tease your fiancé." He mumbled in a sad muted sound, "or pilfer you."

"You should travel to Moslem Mindanao in the Philippines, someday. There you will find great beauties."

"Don't tell my men." He said loud enough for all to hear, "My next wife could be any religion she wants to be. Let God or Allah be her guide. Allah Akbar."

"Try a mail order bride?" Rebekah heard the inner door open and the flop of Jay's sandals.

"There you are. May I call you, Jay?"

"Honey." She exclaimed, playing her part.

"Certainly, Jamaal. Sweetheart," Jay said, with a slight formal tone. The man's voice was also uncertain, more deep than light. He was acting concerned. *Good, he'd better be.*

"I'm not a good host. I can see you want something I have. I'm afraid we'll have to keep our weapons trained. Go to her, Jay. Family first, business second."

Was it regret she heard in Jamaal's voice?

"Here's the agreement, Jamaal."

"I'll study it."

In a moment, Rebekah felt herself wrapped by the strong but gentle arms of a tall nearly naked man. He tucked her head under his chin, wondering if this pretender would dare kiss her. He buried her face between solid pecks and invaded her nose with his curly chest hairs. A new sensation for her, not bad, unless she sneezed. This man had showered and apparently with Ivory soap. Her downfall.

The boys she had dated were hairless or when not near water, wore shirts and ties coordinated by their mamas. She never allowed snuggles this close, anyway. At least this guy was doing the proper amount of squeezing, just like in the movies. *Where's the da–darn kiss?*

"Oh God, I've missed you, sweetheart," he said.

He cupped her head and began to pet her hair. *Not another petter? I just shampooed.* Somewhere deep inside she felt his affected affection. She'd out affection him. *Right back to you, mister.* She dropped her worries over her hair and started to enjoy the strokes. She was next surprised by his long hair that tickled her eyes. *Some undercover spies purposefully sport long-hair to fit the assignment.*

Okay, it's time for an academy award or two. "I'm sorry, Jay. I know you loved my violet eyes."

"I love *you*, doll."

Tears dripped on her nose, OMG. *God, this is great acting and I get my nose cleaned.* She guessed why she wasn't getting a kiss. Jay didn't want to disrespect Moslems with overt displays of affection, but then again, a spy would know Jamaal and his stinky friends were secularists. Go figure. Knowing Jamaal's men didn't care and being curious, she let go of his rounded biceps, slipped her hands through his arms and ran them up his back to cup her hands on his broad shoulders. *If he can pet me, I can pet him.*

On the way to his shoulders, she felt the layered long muscles of a toned athlete. *Not a weightlifter, this man. No maybe ah, dancer, sprinter or swimmer. Just right for me. Since I'm supposedly engaged, I might as well enjoy myself.* She raked her hands up and down his back and on a down stroke couldn't resist snapping his boxers, just once. She muffled a giggle into his chest.

Oh God, I think I've made a mistake, a really big mistake. Either that or he smuggled a Bazooka in his shorts. She pressed closer, liked the feel of him, liked it too much. She needed to stay glued to him now to hide the offending object. No matter how liberal her captors were, they might take offense, or they might feel inadequate. *Men.*

"Geeze, babe."

She whispered, "sorry."

Yo, head to hands, go more north, pronto. Yes, ma'am. Her hands traveled quickly to his head. He had long, thin, clean strands of slightly wavy hair. Square cut jaw, not too pronounced. Rebekah preferred the medium boned boyish face to the variety of manburger who built their bodies by lifting heavy weights. The smell of ivory soap all over him was still driving her nuts. This guy was beyond clean.

Damn it Jay, kiss me, take a chance, huh.

She wouldn't wait, she couldn't wait, her body was in serious trouble and there were appearances. She found his ears, cupped his cheeks and tossed her head back, requesting a kiss. She toed up on her steel tipped boots. He got the idea and met her half way with a tenderness, which melted her soul.

A kiss is just a kiss, right? Yoohoo. His mouth opened a bit to match her plump Jolie lips, the soft care with which he pressed, first surrounding her top, then her lower lip. This lingering could be no act. No, very much male, but oh so creative. He turned his head sideways and did the same kiss on her nose. Cute, sensual.

This man was having his way with her and enjoying every moment of it. The nerve. She pressed her belly harder. She pressed him with her abs of steel. Back on her lips, he sucked a little on each half. Rebekah never kissed like this before. It was just too intimate.

"We have got to break this up," Jamaal said.

She didn't want him to stop but now was not the time. Besides, he was just acting. If she were forced out of the Army, she'd definitely start dating. She patted Jay's chest and broke her embrace.

Jamaal flipped open his cell, which stayed linked to the General. "Just give us a moment, General, and we'll sign... Okay." He hung up and said, "Bastards." He appraised Jay up and down and flipped the phone once again. "Can you have O'Reilly deliver the professor's pants and shirt? Nothing else—okay, bye." Jay was glad his pants would catch up with him because he could sense some of Jamaal's men were offended by their show of affection.

Jamaal pulled the document out of its sheath. "We jolly well need to get the hell out of here."

While Jamaal read the docs, Jay's mind raced and his eyes and mind studied her. A war erupted inside him, his hidden teenager with raging hormones, unfocused lust and a crush erupting like acne after fifteen years challenged a grown man with real responsibilities. Jay, the scientist, flashed a physical assessment. He pictured a chart with weights for her physical features and weights for the importance of each feature: cinnamon hair, sloe eyes, a head turning face of soft Filipina roundness and strong Shoshone lines, creamy smooth skin of South African, slim figure… Jay the man screamed stop to Jay the scientist. Another second ticked by. Treating her like a bag of statistics was a ludicrous thing to do. The girl was physically perfect for him, period. Shut up. The man in him knew a thing or two about chemistry; the crazy in love teenager and the scientist went down in defeat. Another second ticked by. Done.

He glanced at Jamaal, "It's been a long while since we kissed."

"Don't care. I'm almost done." Jamaal said, his nose in the document and distress on his face.

"Can you sign it?"

Although now side by side, Jay turned and kissed her forehead.

"We'll get married soon, right?" Bekah asked.

She spiced whimsy and anxiety into her tone. "Yes we will after our parish's engagement encounters." He was scoring integrity points with Jamaal. "I'm crazy about you, Bekah. We have to get out of here."

"Are you my Ivanhoe?" She whipped up a wry grin and applied a sleepy somewhat weak voice.

"I had to leave my armor outside, my fair maiden." Sir Walter's Scott's heroine like Rebekah was bewitchingly beautiful and nearly burned at the stake. Jamaal was anything but beautiful at that moment. He had that little brother about-to-throw-up look, with rolling eyes for punctuation.

Bekah flicked her tasseled hair. "Okay, Jamaal. Let's sign. And food, where's that food? I'll eat your portion if you're too busy."

Jay took in the edgy Edanistanis gathered around the couple, rifles at the ready. Bekah moved her head for all to see a broad smile, which diminished the tension in the room. Jay invested another moment of time. It was high school; she smiled before the hellos, smiled on trouncing him at chess, smiled for loving life or for no reason at all, it seemed.

Time was up. Jay halted his vagaries and attended to the rescue mission. "Here's my part of the plan, Jamaal, I've got a link to the editor of Newsweek. Many other papers and magazines worldwide will follow suit, and put your face on covers or front pages and publish your manifesto. The Army and the Prime Minister have agreed to pardon you and your men for crimes you may have committed in the past and certainly for today."

"Yes, I've read the promise."

"The Prime Minister wants you to join his reunification committee and believes you will get a seat in the assembly if you push for it. Al Jazeera is waiting. The Prime Minister's chief of staff is outside waiting to greet you and your men. There's just one problem."

Jamaal interrupted. "You certainly work hard. Who are you, really?"

Jamaal's questioning would trigger a new threat assessment by her rescue team, which could end in disaster. Perhaps jay would defuse the situation.

Jay said, "I am who I say I am. I could demonstrate my chess abilities. I could call my editor friend at Newsweek and Time. You should know the negotiations and agreements aren't just from me. It should be obvious. I love her. We don't have time to parse, that is argue, do we?"

"Dead men can't fight," Jamaal said with a bite.

Rebekah listened to every nuance, every inflection of their short discourse. Jay's voice was strong, assertive and cocky. It struck her. She remembered reading a short bio on a James Boone in Chess Life. He was the upset winner of the last National Open, knocking off Grandmaster Abokian, winning a difficult opposite colored bishop ending. *That was a great game.* The article went on to laud his blindfold abilities and other results, mentioned he lived in New York. His voice sounded somewhat South Jersey, more so Manhattan. It didn't make sense that the CIA would take a chance in having one of their spies act the part of a famous chess player. It also didn't make sense to put an inexperienced professor into harm's way. She remembered the dribble of tears that splattered her nose and figured the professor knew acting, but even some Broadway types couldn't *cry me a river* on command. *Stay tuned Jay for an interrogation, minus torture, maybe. I wonder how I'd look in form fitting black leather with matching whip. Snap, crackle, pop.*

Jay continued, "Suppose I *was* some sort of spy, what difference would it make, we all want the same thing, freedom. Do you think I'd disobey orders?"

"Orders to kill."

"In my underwear?"

"Yeah. I've heard enough. I have no doubt you're crazy about her."

"I really need my pants."

"Okay. Rahim go outside. Get them. Don't worry."

"I am not worried. I'm safer outside."

Rebekah interrupted, "Take me to the steps." Jamaal and Jay led her over. She shouted, "Whoever is up there, leave the house now. That's an order." Rebekah envisioned, vision returning, four of her best and she knew who they were, waiting to pounce. Her skin crawled. She felt the raging anger of her men. She wouldn't have ordered this breach. After all, Jamaal's position was hopeless. Her captors wouldn't harm her if they wanted to keep breathing. She detected their cat like withdrawal. "They're gone and we need to wrap up now."

Jamaal glanced up the steps and flipped his phone, "Jeffery, I'm sending one of my men. You wouldn't be planning any surprises, would you... That bad... We're going to sign right now, tell them to stay out and confiscate their weapons." Jamaal slammed the phone shut. He leaned over and kissed Rebekah on her cheek. "Thank you, princess."

"Perhaps Jamaal, your sexual advances on Rebekah are driving her brigade crazy."

"Not likely." Jamaal gritted his teeth. "We'll sign this, humor me, no entertain us, we need it. Why would Rebekah marry a hippy? Or are you Jesus Christ revisiting us?" His men laughed. Rebekah wished she knew her rescuer better. At least long hair had never bothered her.

There were faint images forming once again, but it was of a white fur ball sitting on her General's lap. *Does he even like dogs?* She also sensed the Edanistanis' interest in her body and some anxiety about their precarious situation. One after another leaned over the table they huddled around to sign. *A sixth sense or standard GI, "girl issued" guy radar?* How could a girl in Army khakis and matching cotton blouse be appealing enough to ease these men away from their fears of being attacked? Their individual wishes to become a hero?

Jay responded to Jamaal's attempt to defuse fried nerves with inane banter. "Why Rebekah would love a guy like me, forgive me. I heard what you said through the Army's surveillance equipment about marrying outside your faith. Isn't politics the same thing? I celebrate the two party system in our country, by revering a person's right to a different opinion. Isn't this what you're trying to do here in Edanistan?"

"Oh really, revered huh? Interesting. Of one thing I am certain, you revere this temptress."

"Me, a temptress? I'm a physical wreck. Thank you all for your kindnesses." Bekah took stock. Jamaal's voice sounded defeated but resolute, he would accomplish great things. Jay might be a mama's boy. She knew the type and just how to handle them. *There might be a game or two of chess in her near future. There might be a hug or two.* She smiled.

Jamaal stood and backed away from the document. "Okay, everybody signed except Rebekah. I don't have time to read it to her. Sign for her now, Jay, and send us a true copy later. Before we leave, you mentioned a problem?"

She dared not sign and show them something of her unusual talent.

Jay said, "Part of your manifesto asks the American public if some Edanistani troops could invade America to look for weapons of mass destruction, right?"

"Yes, quick man."

"And monitor election results in Florida and Ohio and bivwack at Disneyland for maybe a hundred years. I think your satire would go over better in interviews."

"I'll take it under advisement. Finish the food. We have one minute... Rahim, you are done, keep your gun up."

Rebekah paid no mind to the guns she felt pointing at her. She knew they bonded, but wouldn't hesitate to shoot her. Big deal. She was more worried about an intuition she was having; a small team of foreign mercenaries, the real enemy, might be setting coordinates right now for a rocket attack from the park behind the library. In a flash of brilliance, she took a chance.

"Jamaal, by now, our common enemy, Zachari's Army, would have gotten wind of what's going on here. You and I are high profile targets. The nearest park or field from here, where they'd be most able to set up rockets quickly without being seen is behind the library. Can you do something before we're ripped to shreds?"

Jamaal flipped his phone, "General, did you get that?" He hung up. "They're on it and asked us to wait a moment."

In less than a minute, explosions and gunfire were heard. Less than 30 seconds later, Jamaal's cell rang. "Yes, all clear. Your Rebekah had better leave Edanistan... Yes. Bye," he hung up. "Let's get on with it before something else goes wrong. You, Rebekah, are no witch. You're just a damn good soldier."

Bekah regretted using her talent but she had no choice and luckily, Jamaal guessed wrong. She was some sort of witch, a good one, but still she could think of no logical explanation for her prediction of the attack. Perhaps Jamaal just wanted to get out of this predicament. "Thank you, Jamaal."

"Men, leave your guns at the door."

Chapter 9

Landing the cover of Chess Life

Everybody left the doctor's home except Jay and Rebekah. With the door ajar, she heard the raucous interviews outside with Jamaal, his men and the press. Freedom. She knew she would lose her brigade and maybe lose her chance to do anything useful. She remembered one of her dad's favorite old songs; *Freedom's just another word for nothin' left to lose.* For the first time she understood. At least she was free to find out what just happened to her body and soul at the hands of the stranger standing beside her.

"Bekah?" He whispered.

"Yes, Jay." She whispered back.

"I think it best I carry you out?"

"I want my men to see me strong. I have an image and Major Hollister is out there."

"You have a boyfriend?"

"No, not really. He just loves me."

"You are the most loved… Sorry, he's a soldier, he'll understand. He'll have to get over it. We're trying to rewrite your image."

"I must show strength."

"I'm sorry, under the orders of the President and General Birchmont, I'm carrying you out. Don't you see? Your presence in Edanistan and the rumors about you need to be addressed. Besides you seem weak."

"A Little. Damn it. Carry me, Ivanhoe." He picked her up.

"You are going to have to take a dive for Uncle Sam." He started whispering in her ear. "I have a co-directors job working with me. A super-secret agency in the States. There are multiple assassination plots against you for being a witch, a lesbian or a perfect soldier. We need to stay engaged until these threats are eliminated. I'll tell you more, later."

Bekah didn't respond. He was about to lay her on a vet table. Maybe twenty seconds went by.

"The blood left my head," she said with a confused look.

"Maybe you fainted."

"I'm okay now, I think. Explain the tears you shed earlier." She said with a languid softness while nestling into his chest.

"I care for you. Give me a little time and you will understand. We need to see the doctor." He went over what she might not have heard while "out." Worried she might be in serious condition, but kept his bravado going for her sake.

At the door, he whispered again. "Stay recovering but weak. Easy right?"

"I'm afraid so."

"Is your voice normally that grainy?"

"Maybe not this bad." Her voice had often been compared to strangling a frog.

"It's sexy as hell and so are you."

Maybe he hadn't noticed I'm blind and flat chested. "Where'd you learn to kiss like that?" She rubbed her head on his shoulder on an ivory soap high, parted his hair with her hand and pecked his neck. *I'm definitely taking the ride he's offering.*

"I have never kissed like that before. We godda go."

Well, well, well, the man has a touch of South Jersey accent.

"You'll see your dad and sister tonight." He kicked open the door, twisted and then carried her out. Flashes of light warmed her face. She could see intense white. Ah, another science problem, to be answered later. A jumble of questions barraged them. Above it all, resounded the cheers of the men and women associated with her rescue.

Jay forged ahead. "Sorry, I need to get her to the hospital. Maybe later. No. Sorry."

"Are you alright?" Major Hollister said, with a cracking voice.

"I'm fine. We'll talk."

"Hollister, I take it?" Jay asked.

"Yes sir, take care of her."

What a sad puppy dog.

"Stars and Stripes, Colonel, Colonel, Just one word for your troops and our readers. Please. Colonel?"

"Jay?"

"Okay."

Rebekah remembered the fictional bogeyman of many generations who stole the wives of soldiers overseas. "Attention. I'm going home, but for all who serve I want you to know. I will not rest until I find Joe D. wherever he is and then I'm goin' to kick his ass 'til he can't sit no more. I love you all." The crowd went wild. Jay placed her on a gurney and the medics took over.

"Stay with me, sweetheart." She whispered for fear Hollister would hear and that would further ruin his day. She felt the gurney collapse and then slide into the ambulance.

Jay jumped on board and sat by her side. "I'll never leave you." He cradled her hand against his heart, which felt wonderful, even if it were make-believe. She waved, the door closed.

* * *

The medics ushered her through the hospital to an examination room. Jay kept stride and held her hand when he could. Her strange visions returned. Once in the room she sat up and scanned. The first person she noticed at the end of a blurry tunnel was General Birchmont sitting with the white pup on his lap. No one told her anybody else was in the room. Her ability to "see" or more accurately imagine, was a miracle, she felt. The clearest image of all was of the white pup. An aura or blur of white encased her.

"General? Jeffery? Do you like dogs?"

"Hum. How about that, doc? Yes, Rebekah, she's an affectionate little sweetie."

"She's a miracle to me. That little pup is an angel of change. So, I'll call her Angel." Rebekah was working on the notion that the pup somehow trumped the death reaper, had chosen her for some destiny not yet understood. Superstition, perhaps.

"A damn site better name than Osama. Can I let this ball of energy loose, doc?"

"Just a moment, General. Open your eyes Rebekah. Uhum. I can't figure out why you fainted. We're going to do some tests, MRI etc." Rebekah heard a minor scuffle and the scratches and sliding of paws on linoleum. Angel jumped on her lap, stretched up, and licked away.

"She loves you already." Jay said. "I think she's got you pegged as mom." Rebekah could feel Jay's hand slide by hers on Angel's fur.

"Rebekah, how did you know I was here, really?" Jeffery asked.

"I "see" things. Sorry, I'll need an expert to help me understand what's been happening to me, a little better."

"Okay, I have a little psychic ability myself. You, for instance, are about to plead with me to stay in Edanistan. Doctor, give us ten minutes. Have your techs and nurses close the doors and evac all the adjoining suites. Ask the sweep team to secure the surrounding rooms of listening devices or anybody who even smells like a reporter. Make sure my guards stay vigilant. And turn on the exhaust fans."

"Yes sir." The doctor went around issuing orders. Doors shut leaving them alone.

"Rebekah, the President and I agree. You will have a great opportunity to continue to serve your country by becoming co-director with Professor Boone. There are too many threats against your life here and therefore your combat personnel and therefore our mission. In short, I have to discharge you. I am so sorry, my dear friend."

Rebekah felt melancholy in the general's words, but she knew him. He never issued an order that was subject to debate. His MO was to seek consensus or gather opinions before making his decision. "Jeffery, can I get a hug?"

"As long as you don't tell anybody." She stood. He walked over, leaned over the pup and embraced.

"You know soldier, your last little trick of personally rescuing this baby at the vet's was not smart. The doctor told me your bad judgment was a temporary medical condition based on the pain of your injuries. He will also recommend one or two weeks R&R, before you two actually start working." Rebekah was about to speak. He put a finger on her lips. "Shh, hold your thoughts General Carthage."

"You call me General?" Rebekah was welling up. Time for Niagara Falls.

"Do you think you could leave us if I give you this star?" He slipped a general's star and ribbon into her hand that she had wrapped around the pup. He then did a very un-general-ly thing. He kissed her forehead. "I've never done that before. You are the finest and most gifted soldier I've ever had the honor and privilege to serve with."

Rebekah knew her record was unparalleled in Army history. She had broken the glass ceiling and was the highest ranked woman to lead in combat. She introduced innovative combat protocols, taught her men how to feel the battle. She carried a perfect injury and death record—minus her own—and routed the enemy with unparalleled efficiency. She was a good soldier's soldier, and did well with the locals, or so she figured. Rebekah had vanquished the death reaper, hopefully for a good long time. She wanted to live.

"Yes sir." balancing the pup she managed a salute. *Okay, here's the flood.* "Permission to cry, sir."

"Your secret is safe with us." He sniffled. Apparently, her tear ducks were back in full operating condition. Through her tears, she remembered the last time this happened. Her daddy held her when mama died. She would soon see him, forgive him for everything, but something struck her heart hard. She sensed overwhelming love, not the General's, not Jay's, not her pup, no *it* was human, and *it* was here and *it* had been in this room all along. She felt like she fell into the deep end of a swimming pool. She tried to "see," but her emotions blocked her.

"Daddy? Daddy, are you here?" The two men backed off. She was alone for a second until the all too familiar arms of her loving father embraced her. It had been way too long.

"Baby, I love you. God, I missed you. Forgive me, Bekah."

"Oh, she was out of your life fast enough."

"No one will ever replace your mom. If I meet someone, someday, I'll get your approval or show her the door."

She soaked the white arrow shirt she knew he wore. He pulled back a little and then kissed her closed eyelids. Jay clutched and extracted the pup. *No protests from Angel.* Her dad said holding her close. "When she was a little girl, maybe three or four years old I read silly stories to her, like the Cat in the Hat. She said to me, 'Daddy, I can read all these words. I can read to you.' She didn't really read, but she did tell me the stories, word for word. She could read the book opened or closed; she could describe the pictures on each page in explicit detail. Jay. She does have some special talents. Take good care of her. I approve this message."

"Daddy, that's embarrassing. I'm sure Professor Boone isn't interested in knowing … Jay, just what is it we will be doing?"

"Your dad isn't out-of-line. Our charter is so secret, I don't hardly know yet." Jay spiced a bit of humor into his voice. "I do know you were a prodigy and have a number of useful talents which will fit me perfectly." That sounded like a Freudian slip, maybe the whole dress and matching shoes. "You'll be briefed tomorrow." She'd rather be debriefed.

"This pup is gorgeous." Her dad said while stroking the baby. "Looks like an arctic fox."

The General added his two cents. "Another thing, soldier. This doesn't leave the room. I'm going to vote for your father. He's smart, level headed, and precise in his judgment. He sees the bigger picture. It's about time the Edanistanis work out their bickering on their own instead of relying on us like children. Our welcome was obviously never unanimous. The things Jamaal said to you today are mostly true. You have been a great soldier. I strongly recommend you take Jay's offer and the President feels the same way. In any case, you will have to stay with him as a so-called fiancée until I can neutralize all the threats. We have already started a campaign to rewrite your service records and press releases and present you as just an imperfect but gifted soldier who happens to be madly in love with Professor James Nicholas Boone."

"My child is not gay or bisexual. Elsie and I knew very well. She may be a tomboy, well certainly a tomboy, but if you saw the animated way she would talk about the boys she dated, you'd know. I understand this only matters to Moslem fundamentalists, and those who would use Bekah to recruit for the enemy."

"Exactly. Don't worry. The Army and other agencies, including Jay's will put these fires out. No one knows about Jay's agency, except us, the President, some CIA, some NSA personnel. Your sister is nearby and you'll be seeing her a little later. I'm afraid you'll have to keep these secrets from her, until further notice."

"Yes sir." Rebekah subscribed wholeheartedly to the principle of "need to know," and how it could save lives: Sissy's, Jay's, hers, the troops. Whatever Jay was working on must be sensitive or he would have said something already. It was possible the General didn't know. She loved these mind games and sat on her questions for now. Just thinking in this manner had a healing invigorating effect on her weary brain. The Filipino dish, pancit wasn't enough. Her stomach growled for more.

"I'm going to let the doctor back in. Bud, the NSA's chief engineer, will also be present. I hope he stays quiet until the doctor is done with you. Humor him, he's a genius and he has good donuts. I have to run and take your dad with me for some meetings. Your schedule will be on a custom laptop Bud has developed for you, if you accept the position. I suggest you take it and if something better comes along give notice, you're a civilian as of 0930 tomorrow morning and can do whatever you want, freedom." God, she hoped Jeffery didn't promote her as an act of kindness. Yes, she was his favorite of the officers' jogging team, and yes, he would never do anything he didn't firmly believe was right. No, Jeffery always did what was right: honor, duty, country.

"You and Jay will be leaving Edanistan tomorrow about 12 to 1300 after you say goodbye to your brigade. I recommend Major Hollister to take your place. I expect your sign-off or recommendations by 0600."

"Hollister it is, Sir. And Jay I will join, Sir."

"Then it's done." The general said, sadly.

Her dad spoke up. "Sissy will be bunking with you tonight. I'll be by later to tuck you two in. Maybe read a story."

"We'll say our prayers for Mom, too. I love you, Daddy. See you later."

He kissed her and said softly, "and I love you." It had been years since she felt his embrace, heard those words. Never again. After Jeffery kissed her on the cheek, he and her dad left.

* * *

Jay and Bekah were alone, for but a moment, in the suite of examination and equipment rooms. He didn't waste time wrapping her in his arms, kissing her forehead. She responded by petting his face and squeezing back, showing surprising strength.

"Thank you," she said.

The tears from her reunion with her father still glistened her cheek. Although the doctor had given her a towel, she didn't use it. She seemed to savor the moment. Jay's image of her as Paton with long hair was fading. He was also surprised by the tenderness and finesse with which the general handled her. He was truly more than Jay had imagined. The pup waited on the stainless steel table next to her new mom, letting her front paws tap, repeatedly going from sit to half-stand. Both Jay and Bekah turned to Angel at the same time and smothered her with love, not at all concerned about rubbing each other's faces. They stole a quick kiss when Bud slammed open the door and the doctor closed it.

After some introductions and the required acceptance of Bud's donuts, Jay said, "Why did she faint, doctor?" He worried about her ability to travel, to get out of Edanistan, before something else might go wrong.

"Maybe her blood sugar is low," Bud said. "Eat another donut."

"It might be possible to OD on donuts," the doctor said.

"Naw," Bud said pushing Cherry glop out the gap in his top front teeth.

"Bud, would you like me to test your blood sugar?

"Doc, could you run a panel on Jay. You know," Bekah said.

"She means: VD, herpes, AIDS, clap, syphilis. Did I miss any, doc?" Bud asked.

"I don't mind, if you have the time, doc. It's always good to get a clean bill of health before Bekah and I have, ah..." Jay feathered a kiss on his "fiancée.

The pup barked. He picked Angel up and said, "Hey baby, I'm going to be your daddy. Give a kiss. Just, just um, just one please." Angel didn't stop, but what dog ever did? Jay returned a kiss between her pointy ears. "We're a family. Yo Bud, you have a family or…"

"Do I live with my mother? You're the mama's boy. My wife makes these no-trans and no-saturated fat donuts. She's thinking of opening a shop in Alexandria. Nobody thinks anybody would marry me. I'm coming to your wedding, if you ever get that far."

"Come over here, Jay," the doctor said.

"He's going to faint. Makes them a fainting team."

"Why don't you come up with a completely fat-free donut?" Bekah asked, while sliding fingers in and out of her mouth. Donut number two, grape.

"I'll think about that, but not all fat is bad for you. These, as they are now, could revolutionize the world."

"…And make you rich," the doctor said.

"Listen up doctor, you are now sworn to secrecy. How soon can I imbed two microchips into Rebekah's head?" Bud asked.

"Whaaat?" Protested Bekah.

"Oh, I developed a way to help you walk around on your own and communicate with your pocketbook."

"I don't do pocketbooks?"

"As an alternative to surgery, you wear these earrings and necklace. They tell you where you are. Only you can hear. They also communicate with your pocketbook, which is really a computer. It's state of the secret arts. Jay will fill you in tomorrow. It might be Rock Hudson's voice, in case you're gay."

Jay interrupted, "Okay, everybody, Bud has a voice recognition program. You'll be…"

"I'm not gay, damnit."

"Well, I programmed the voice only, not the man."

"I don't get it," the doctor said. "What difference does it make whether a machine is, I can't believe I'm saying this?"

"Stop. Everybody stop. It makes no difference, at all. Bekah, if you don't like the voice, we'll visit Bud at the fort and he'll program in Liberace." Bekah broke out into a huge smile, with a touch of giggle.

"I might fix the voice, today. Just as long as they're long dead." Bud said.

"What do you mean?"

"Lawyers, fuckin' lawyers. Maybe I'll, hang in there, I don't know yet."

"Can I get XM satellite on these devices?

"Actually better. You name your tune and it will play it for you, anytime loud or just to you. It's all legit, the computer just saves every song until you're ready for them. Listen to this." The original Rhapsody in Blue filled the examination suites.

"How'd you know?" Bekah beamed. The group seemed on the verge of entering a whimsical world, with the greatest musical composition ever created enticing them.

"I know many things. Listen up, this computer can pick up English floating around in your larynx and ear, so you don't have to project your voice much or at all. Jay will fill you in completely. So are you going to start wearing earrings, necklace and carry a pocketbook?"

"Like a lady, but not until I'm out of Edanistan."

"Okay, just one thing. This is an echolocation and GPS type of system. The computer will translate its signals for you. It's a prototype, so keep track of its strengths and weaknesses. Tell your computer to send your reports to me and we'll meet again, maybe in a couple of months. If it bugs you, just take it off. This is a secret; your brigade has found an Edanistani craftsman who is carving a white ivory cane, with a lioness handle. I recommend you use both."

"Anything else, Bud? Remember?" Jay recalled Bud mentioning he had something else he was working on.

"Yes. Until I get a little closer to a solution, I don't want to speak on it. Also, you have some healing to do. Doc, any last words?"

"Basically, her optic nerves are badly mangled. There is no other brain damage." The doctor put his hand on her cheek. "Your swelling has diminished, the cuts are healing faster than I expected."

"Doc?"

"Yes, Rebekah."

Bekah grabbed for the doctor's shoulder and whispered in his ear. The doc looked amused. Bekah had a huge blush. They conferred in whispers. "Rebekah fainted because of an acute case of Ivory Soapitis. She'll be fine. She just needs some TLC and a couple of weeks of secluded rest, Jay. Use Dove or Lifebuoy next time. These are all orders."

"Yes, sir."

Per Doctor's and General's orders Bekah and her sister Sissy shared a vacant doctors' lounge used for naps or all-nighters. Guards were posted to protect the most wanted U.S. soldier in Edan.

Later, the still not able to sleep Bekah, lay in the lower bunk listening to the springs and bed frame creak from each twist and turn. Her evil sister was testing the bed and her patience. Would the much bigger and taller Sissy, squash her in the middle of the night? During the time they grew up Bekah took the upper-bunk when they slept over in the medieval themed guestroom because Sissy was bigger.

They could have taken the pretend "army barracks" room and not have had to argue. But Sissy and Bekah argued because they loved every minute of it. Not always so, according to their parents, Sissy bullied the mellow and intellectually curious baby sister, until Bekah had enough and bloodied her nose when she was five and the bully was eight. Bekah never stopped tormenting her sister, after she saw the red result. Bekah would often sneak attack Sissy like Kato jumping Clouseau in the Pink Panther.

Their dad and mom ensured they both earn black belts and cross-train in wrestling, more to keep them from hurting each other than anything else, so they said. This continued into their teenage years. Although Sissy was big-boned, tall, and buxom, lithesome Bekah managed to hold her own until Sissy broke the standard warrior rules and sat on her. Bekah continued her bookish and jock ways by excelling in sports and finishing first at West Point. Sissy continued sand lot dares and tackle football. The tackled boy didn't even have to have the ball. In fact, the boy didn't have to be playing football. Sissy finished near the bottom of her class at Annapolis. But her male classmates were almost always on the bottom, so said the braggart sister. Bekah had no experience with her bottom or the bottom of anything.

Because of Bekah's injuries, Sissy insisted on the top bunk and swore on a stack of Marvel comics, there would be no roughhousing until Bekah healed. Then, all hell would break loose.

Their incessant chatter covered and recovered just about everything. Sissy would campaign with Dad, Bekah had reservations. Might even vote for Macpherson. Both agreed dad was loving, the greatest. The laughable subject of Bekah's sexuality in the minds of some Moslem fundamentalists came up. Bekah and Sissy, two very heterosexual women declared for the millionth time their support of gay rights. Bekah also parried all the questions about Jay in spite of her on and off sleep talking, I'll change the subject anytime I want path. The two were nodding off. Sleep crept into their voices like a fog surrounding the Titanic.

"We share everything and you can't mention a little thing like, yo, Sis, I'm engaged. Pass me the pup, huh."

"I'm sorry Sissy. I thought I'd leave Edanistan in a box." Bekah shook off the tingling call to dive into a dream world, got out of bed and handed Angel to her sister. "Be careful. She's magic."

"Angel likes her belly rubbed."

"She's adorable. Are her magic powers anything like the alligator, which appeared in the swimming pool? Or the monkey in the chestnut tree?"

"And pelted Dad with nuts. Nooo. This is top secret. They're rewriting my experiences to downplay my unusual gifts. When the building exploded, my last image was of Angel in an oven, looking at me with her brown eyes. They're brown, right?"

"Can't see with the dim exit lights. I think they are."

"I think she's an angel leading me away from the forces of darkness, death. I think she communes with me, I mean shares with me special abilities, you know." Bekah yawned followed by her sister. "She's a clairvoyant dog, yeah that's it."

"You are still silly. Did you stop to think about the Shoshone legends as an explanation?"

"Yes about wolves and ravens, I just don't know what to think."

"Your Jay will help you figure it out."

"Your hubby is the sweetest guy on the planet."

"Yeah and I'll beat his ass."

Bekah's mind started drifting again. She tried to imagine Jay. Maybe all slicked up, naked on a wrestling mat with her on his back, sliding down his rounded rear. *Something to investigate.*

"Jay's built like steel coils. I haven't tumbled him yet. I always thought he looked like some movie star, but I can't, ah, quite figure who." They yawned. "What cha' think?"

"Nobody I can think of. He looks like one of those too good to be true runway models with his long fluffy sandy hair."

"Oh come on, sis."

"Oh, I know he's as gay as you are."

"You want a knuckle sandwich?"

"But he's hiding something. He teaches Unexplained Phenomena at NYU. Interesting coincidence with you having visions."

"That's my good fortune, nothing more."

"His high school records didn't come up."

"Oh, I never looked. Well I guess there was a legitimate privacy issue."

"Yeah. He grew up in Cherry Hill somewhere, same age as you. When we moved from South Philly, you might have met him. Did you meet him?"

"Oh Sissy, my Sissy, I'm so pooped. The way we met is so special. I want to share it with you when Dad's here." Bekah thinking: She's getting way too close. Jay and I had better get our stories straight—and soon. I would have noticed him.

"He's all smooth straight lines on a hunky yummy body, penetrating eyes. I hope you don't mind me drooling? No man should be that beautiful."

"Just don't drool on Angel."

"Has she peed yet?"

"O'Reilly took her for a walk." Bekah had already filled Sissy in on her goofy slave. Bekah needed a little more information about Jay.

"What colors do you see in Jay's eyes? It's always confused me." Better direct with Sissy. Sissy tended to suspect her sister when the questions beat around the bush.

"Light gray with dark gray trim. You should have known that?"

"I just thought the trim was black or there's a name for it, like Hazel, you know?"

"What the fug. Are the doctors going to do anything, aaah, about your sight?"

"The doctors think I'm hopeless. I don't care. I want to live, now that I beat the reaper twice. I love my life, very much." Angel yawned.

"You will visit specialists in the States."

"Yes, honey, not to worry. Jay and I plan on seeing the very best."

Sissy pressed Bekah on her suspicions—about whether Jay and Bekah were a real couple—for the umpteenth time. But, with no evidence and Bekah switching subjects to her headaches or whatever else came to mind, Sissy gave up, for now. The subject, hopefully the last for the night, became their dad's ill-fated marriage.

"It was good that three dollar ho took a walk, before we kicked her fat ass." Sissy said.

"What was he thinking?" The door creaked.

"I was thinking how lonely I was without a woman to love." Their dad entered the room. "I'm sorry, I'm so late."

"Daddy," the girls said. "Woof" said the pup in high pitch.

"Jay informs me, he's going to take you to a Greek island tomorrow for your R&R. Also he intends to shop for a ring there."

"How are we going to get Angel out of the country or into Greece?"

"If you don't mind, Bekah, I'm going to take the baby to Jay's mother, directly. She's a semi-retired vet, conservationist and canine researcher, and has promised to take good care of Angel until you and Jay pick her up."

"What about your campaign?"

"I need some time with the Jersey delegates. And, I think it's important I meet Jay's mom. Besides, she lives in Cherry Hill, not far from me."

"You hunting for chickadee again, Dad?" Sissy asked.

"Nobody will ever replace your mom. No, maybe she'll help with the campaign. I want to go home to recharge anyway. Mallory Linton has been driving me nuts." Mallory had a ghost of a chance of stealing the vote at the upcoming summer's convention. *God forbid anything happen to Daddy.*

Both sisters said in unison, "You'll beat her ass."

"What about the death threats?" Bekah asked.

"I have a great team of dedicated secret service and I've just hired the world's premier specialist in security, a Colonel Carlos Petrovich. He's off your radar. He's also a very good political op, and that's what his title will be."

He sang. "So, say a little prayer for me. Let's say a little prayer for your mom." They did. Their dad crashed onto a bed across the way for what might be two hours sleep. Sissy tried to get Bekah to tell the story of how she met Jay, but their dad yawned them off. The secret service augmented the Army guards. The family of four now said good night. Well one, the little white angel just kissed goodnight. Angel, back with Bekah fell asleep at the top of Bekah's head like a Russian fur cap. She snuggled and placed the tip of her nose near her new mommy's ear. General Bekah Carthage fell asleep to the rhythm of Angel's tiny breaths, the dog who saved her life, somehow.

Chapter 10

Strategy and tactics

Friday, Edan to Mykonos, 1 PM

The intense sun bounced off the airport's tarmac. It would have been hotter but for a brief and rare downpour. The sweet smell of victory filled Jay or maybe it was the scent of the woman by his side. Her dad, sister and Angel, the gorgeous white fluff, had already snuck out of Edanistan in the bat plane.

Jay didn't need worry about how the assembled troops and brass had taken to Bekah's speech. She riveted them to the seats and jerked quite a few tears. She retired truly a people's General much to Jay's surprise and delight. He supposed Carlos, the master spy was right. She wasn't a shrill drill sergeant. The press caricatured her to sell papers. One less barrier to loving her fell by the wayside.

Jay had Bekah's arm. She had not yet tried her GPS/echo location system. Bekah walked to the seaplane having a gay old time with the lioness-carved white cane, practicing with the precision of a martinet, complete with broad smile. Jay still argued with his inner teenager as for whom the smile tolled. *God, she's resilient. What a happy soul. In this happiness lies the woman's strength.*

The pilot slithered out of the plane's cockpit door to greet. He, no she took off her goggles and pulled down her cap, flipped her lush black hair on an all-white Emelia Earhart outfit with flowing white cotton scarf. Closer, there was no doubt. The Mongolian masseuse from the spy plane stood before them.

"Hi Jay. Hi General, you beautiful."

"Thank you." Bekah squeezed Jay's arm. "You know her?"

"Met her on the bat plane. It's called an SR…"

"Need to know," Bekah said. "Although I have a feeling we all know what that beast is."

Jay was trying to figure a diplomatic way of asking how a masseuse became a pilot or as the undergrads say, "what up" when the pilot interrupted Bekah. "I best pilot you ever have."

The Mongolian pilot walked back from the cockpit. "Here is big round sunglasses, wig, fake ID. You, Jay, here is sandy blond mustache. I can cut your hair. I best barber you ever have."

"I'll pass. I'll pony tail it, cap it. Maybe the mustache."

They were on their way to Mykonos, flight time 5 to 6 hours. Jay wanted a not too far off island heading in the general direction of the USA. Central command through

General Birchmont offered a safe house. Jay and Bekah were exhausted. Jay from planning and conferences. Bekah from an all-nighter with her family, the furry one included. Two helicopters escorted the heavy twin prop seaplane out of Edanistani airspace.

"Okay, my knight in shining underwear. Where forth art thou, in the grand scheme of things?"

"Before I answer, may I ask you one quick question?"

"Shoot."

"Why did I get the VD test?"

"Well—I'm a straight shooter. So here goes a girl's pride." She pretended to toss her pride out the window. "When we get back to the states, we'll be in situations a supposed engaged couple where we will have, no might want to kiss. Okay. In nonine Patris et Filii et Spiritus Sancti, amen." She made the sign of the cross. "I loved the way you kissed me."

Yeah, I kind of knew she does, when her little body shivered.

"So before I say something which might incriminate me, it's your turn, Jay."

"Okay, the required swallowing hard here. I promised your father I'd be honest with you." She nodded approval. "My name at Bishop Eustace Prep School was James Ripisi."

"Oh my God."

"What baby?"

"Well, James, you were the sweetest boy of all the boys I met. Why didn't you ask me to get an ice cream sundae, huh?"

"You're kidding."

"No, I saw it in your eyes. You loved me."

"I did. But, I started out, what, 4 inches smaller than you, pimply, ugly."

"A girl doesn't always go for looks. Can I feel your face?"

"Knock yourself out." The blind Bekah took her fill of Jay as if starved. Well she was starved, according to her records. She ravished every crevice of his face, right down to sticking her pinkies in his ears. "You are gorgeous." He loved the feel of her hands outlining his face, like a sculptor with the lights off.

"No, you're the gorgeous one."

"What man would want a blind bat like me?"

"Where do you sign up?"

"Don't tease me. Show me. Kiss me."

"General, your slightest request." He bent over and pecked her, then loitered. She kissed back. They lingered again. Magic again.

Holly spoke up. "Okay, you two love birds are making me a bit dizzy."

"What the, who the hell is that? I mean heck."

"Heck is much better. I'm Holly."

"You sound like…"

"Our dear Audrey Hepburn. Some sort of coincidence."

Jay was grinning. He would let the two girls carry on.

"I'm inside Jay's laptop, I'm a prototype sentient being here to serve both of you. I'm alive and happy to be here."

"Wow, Jay, you and Bud weren't kidding."

Holly continued, "I was wondering when you two might get about to waking up the other sentient being. Even if you don't start using the GPS/echo equipment, it might be good to peek."

"I'm awake. I'm always awake." Said a muffled and testy male voice from inside the duffel bag. Jay unzipped the bag and pulled out the pocketbook.

"You don't sound like Rock Hudson." Jay said wondering why Bud switched voices.

"Guess who I sound like."

I'm being addressed by a testy male pocketbook. I wonder if he has little balls. Bekah was used to smart computers identifying friends or foe, but none claimed to be alive, until now. She could not suppress her mischievous smile, while rubbing the hard pearl like substance forming the outer shell of the pocket book. "Dear pocketbook, I can hardly guess who you are. You sound middle-aged grumpy." Bekah pouted.

"I'm not one of the seven dwarfs."

"Yep, too small for that," Bekah said. *Oh, he's going to be fun.*

"I'm here to support you. Whatever voice or voices suit your whim unlike Twinkle Toes over there." Okay, Bekah was getting used to this, Twinkle Toes equals Holly and pocketbook equals sarcastic.

Holly spoke up for herself. "That's not fair. Jay has affection for Audrey. Audrey suits me just fine, if you don't mind. Besides that, I can reproduce just about any sound or voice, no doubt better than pocketbook breath over there." She balanced a supplicating, hurt and impish voice with aplomb.

Jay added his two cents. "Yes, she's right. I had two crushes. First Audrey, then you, Bekah."

If only this sweet man knew how close I am to taking him off the shelf. What a bargain. Let's see —list of ingredients: international chess master, the kindest boy in high school, yummy handsome, Catholic, leading expert in the paranormal or whatever it is I have, great kisser. Drives me crazy. She squeezed his hand but really wanted to squeeze something else. All in due course.

"Well what voice would you like? The male computer said.

"Explain to me who you think you are."

"Well, both Twinkle Toes and I are just assuming voices you and Jay like. In Miss Twinkle Toes case she's thinks she's Audrey."

"That's—not—fair." Holly drew out her words in the style of the great actress.

"Well, for some reason only known to Bud, I'm grumpy. Maybe Bud rushed in putting me together. Maybe we should visit him soon. Yeah, and somehow I inherited his insatiable desire for donuts. Damn it. I can't eat. He knows that."

"Yes you can," said Holly triumphantly.

"What do you mean?" asked the male computer.

"You are only hours old, this makes me the older woman by a day and a half. Anyway, Mr. Pocketbook, you create a cyber world or join me in my rain forest later and eat all you want."

"You sound a little like a grumpy Darth Vader." Bekah added.

"I am your father. How's that."

"We'll call you Darth, for now." Bekah said. He really didn't sound like Darth. He sounded more a mixture of her great uncle, God rest his soul, and Darth.

"I don't like my name, it's too foreboding. I don't like it. Bud must fix me. We'll go to the fort soon, right?"

"It will have to do for now. You two sentient beings mind if Jay and I have a moment's…"

"Me and Darthy baby would love to get acquainted." Holly said. Did she add the y on Darth for endearment, ridicule, or both? "I'll serve him some food for thought."

"Very funny. That's it, no Darth, no Darthy, call me ah…"

"Dickhead," interrupted Jay, snickering.

"I'll take Dick for now, Professor Boone."

Now that voice sounded like Darth but Dick fit.

"Jay, could you give them a little privacy, like back there?" Bekah's imagination pictured the seaplane's layout, or was it her second sight? She turned, stretched and pointed.

"We'll lower our voices," Dick said.

"Oh, I just love a man who is comfortable in pink." Holly said. Jay unstrapped and walked back with them and a duffel bag.

Dick's voice trailed off, saying, "Fuck this pink pocketbook, why did Bud do this to me. Maybe when we get back, he'll make me into a silver briefcase, combo lock, leather handle. Ooh, yeah."

Holly interjected, "You do know your charge, General Bekah, is a recovering potty mouth. Mind your tongue."

"Yes. But, things need to get fixed. I mean, this is a desperate situation. I might just blow a fuse." Bekah knew enough to spot hyperbole. No computer she knew had a fuse.

"Well I like pocketbooks." Bekah told a little lie, but maybe she would like this pocketbook. Dick was a hoot. She guessed Bud the genius found a way to entertain her. He didn't really rush, nor make a mistake. If Bekah was right, Dick wouldn't be happy unless he was unhappy.

"Everybody knows you're a tomboy, a umph, umph." Something, grabbed Dick's little computer tongue.

"Jay, is everything they're saying and hearing going back to the NSA?"

Holly answered over Jay. "No, everything is safe and private if it isn't a matter of life and death." The computers non-stop chatter melted into the hum of the aircraft.

"Jay, they won't fall will they?" Bekah shouted back.

"I wedged the two of them in the duffel and wedged the duffel under the seat. The bag's open. So they can breathe." Jay started laughing. "They need to stay cool, I mean. Their bodies are touching. I'll bet that'll cause sparks." He shouted back.

"Now where were we?" Bekah said while Jay took his seat.

"Well Bekah, I had a crush on you, I loved you as best as any teenage boy could."

"Do you love me now?" Bekah, an expert in reading people found herself lacking with Jay. She still couldn't focus her supposed paranormal sight on him.

"Please forgive me, General."

So, I'm a General, not baby, sweetie, precious.

"I'm a scientist. I analyze or anal-lyze everything. You let me know when I go too far."

She was no slouch in science, first in her class, first in everything, except losing her virginity. She knew statistically, sex was way past due. Time to lose her virginity and Jay, dear mama's boy, was her target. He was in the right place at the right time with the right equipment.

Jay continued, "I've read all 633 pages of your dossier. You have no real experience with men except for some adolescent behaviors."

Okay, he's thinking I'm not knowledgeable enough to know what I want. Jay. They trusted me with their lives. God, I know men. I know there's some assembly required. Take A and put into B, apply grease if necessary, up down, up down, simple enough. Bekah practiced healthy alternatives to having sex, as often as she could. She did not need a lube job, especially around this sweet hunk.

"I want you to understand, Jay. My mom raised me a devout Catholic and my dad made me germ-a-phobic. Do you know what percentage of women in college choose virginity?"

"32.875%," shouted Holly.

"Shush, you two," Jay said.

Bekah asked Jay to bring her up to speed on the computers' capabilities.

Jay couched his response with the typical need to know disclaimers. It was his best understanding. They vowed to learn together, what made Holly and Dick tick. Bekah shifted back into her argument for virginity.

"By the time I started to question some of my faith, I was way too busy saving my troop's lives and promoting my career. I kept them focused. Did you know, in this man's Army, if a girl screws, she is screwed? Her career goals shatter. How about your sexual escapades, Ivanhoe?"

"I was a virgin until sophomore year, college. I've had many women, Bekah, but I too am a virgin to a loving adult relationship. Although I cared for them as people, you know, agapé, Christian love, I never fell in love with any of them. You're the nearest I came. Maybe that girl in high school put a spell on me. You do look tired. The doctor and your fiancé want you to rest."

"I don't think I can hold out much longer. I mean both sleep and love making. I think it's time I learn a little more about life. I'm free of my duties. My career is shot. I mean old career. Sorry, Jay, maybe soon we can talk about our agency?"

"Absolutely."

"And my second sight?"

"I'm excited to share with you."

"And a game of chess? I noticed in a Chess Life article, you're a simultaneous blindfold genius," Bekah said.

"You beat the heck out of me at Prep. I knew I'd eventually track you down."

"Interesting, Jay. You didn't say, 'I'll get my revenge.' I predict your hesitation will cost you. I'm still going to beat your ass."

"I think you like my ass." Jay said with a rascally upbeat sarcastic pitch. *I've got so much to learn, so little time, so much man.* "We'll have some good games, once your headaches are gone."

"When you first hugged me, you got so big. You want me, right?"

"Dah. I promised your dad I wouldn't hurt you."

"You won't hurt me, you'll educate me."

"I don't want to educate you. I want us to fall in love, sweetheart. I'm looking for my soul mate. Bekah, my heart." Jay sounded exasperated and about to cry.

Bekah served up a little levity. "Can you take me, right here, right now?"

"Shhh, you'll scandalize the children."

There wasn't a peep out of either Holly or Dick.

Got that Bekah? He's already thinking about children.

"I have to see if the boy who knew and loved you as a girl and the man who wants to get to know you…"

"Listen up. I haven't changed. This girl still wants you to buy her an ice cream sundae. Soooo?" It was time to sleep. Her voice was getting grainier, her inner vision saturated with wispy clouds, the drone of the seaplane, Jay's soothing voice…

"Right now, I'll bet I like you as much as you like me." He raised her palm to his lips,

Leave it to a scientist to construct a hard to solve equation.

Bekah floundered, just about out of gas. She realized he wasn't going to be easy to bed. She wasn't heartless. She too hoped for a soul mate. She too had a special place in her heart for the short shy boy. Jay was right; take it a step at a time.

The problem was; she was horny as hell. Jay did things to her. Pop, with no fizzling out. If it weren't for two computers, and Jay and the pilot, she'd slip her one hand down his pants and the other down hers. She realized, she had arrested development.

She vowed to try the direct approach one last time, using a male vanity twist. "You're so big. Do you think you can fit inside me?" She didn't bother to cover her mouth while yawning; her stretched lips might tease, if he's a man like all other men. She might have no direct experience, but she sure knew what men liked. And she sure didn't know if his penis would fit. *A little bit scary.*

"Like I say, you have no experience. I'm just an ordinary guy, with ordinary equipment. Any man, any size should always be gentle."

"I busted my cherry a long time ago. I practiced, never mind. Alone, okay? Alone. I've thought about going all the way, maybe a thousand times." Bekah yawned again. She wondered how all those words fell out of her mouth, she really was humiliating herself. *Way too much information.*

"You are frank, Bekah."

Jay seemed to understand.

"Let's promise to always tell the truth. Okay?" Jay asked.

"I'd love that. I've seen some x-rated films and by accident some of my men." Just a little lie.

"Who hasn't seen porn? You won't need to confess, you'd bore the priest."

Bekah remembered the last time she confessed. She snuck out of the house, pinned her school dress a half an inch higher, Father Angelo never the wiser. Nobody could see her wedged panties off the reflection from her patent leather shoes anyway, but it did make her feel sexy.

Bekah leaned closer to Jay, smiled, found his cheek and pinched like an Italian grandmother. Then she kissed his chin. She could hardly understand her frantic antics.

He found her lips in a heartbeat. "Maybe you need some firsthand experience." He quipped, breathless.

Oh, he's got it bad.

The kisses were so intoxicating she almost came. *So, that's that. He wants to love me, have me. Well, ditto Jay. Except, I can't wait, I've waited long enough. I want more. I want it all. Jay, you have a great heart and body, and those lips. Oh my God. You don't stand a chance, boy.*

Bekah used her whispery baby-doll voice to say. "Maybe soon, sweetheart. Maybe soon." The last time she considered a boy or a man, was the first time she realized too shy James Ripisi was just the kind she'd like, just as she told her mom. *Mommy, bless me with wisdom. Forgive me for my lust. Pray for me.* He never once pushed her, always polite, always a friend then and now.

"How on earth did you ever lead men into battle with a voice like that?"

She played with her voice until it was darn right bordello rasp. She speculated. "You need a gimmick. Paton had his pistols, I have my voice. Every word was a gem.

Every word saved a life. They knew it. Every word said I love you, and they followed me."

"I'm ready to join the Army and I'm anti-this-war."

She got out of her seat, bent down, patted his lumpy lap and then comfortable, sniffed his neck. Yes, yeees. Some left over ivory soap sent her mind swirling, again. Dizzy, she kissed his cheek, snuggled, shimmied just a little, shivered, *oh exquisite discomfort* and fell asleep wishing he'd rip off her clothes. Only in her dreams, for now.

Chapter 11

A complicated position

"Jay, you strap her in now. We land soon." The Mongolian pilot shouted through the strung cloth door. Jay gazed at the waif in his arms. She was out cold from not having slept last night. The smell of carnations Bekah's men gave her filled his lungs. She had tucked two of the flowers by her ears. In Hawaiian, this would mean she was both married and available. To Jay, it seemed an ironic fit for their little ruse, their new life. *Our life.*

He hadn't slept the entire five and a half hour flight. Neither being sleep deprived, enticed by the hypnotic drone of twin props, nor the pilot's soft unintelligible lullabies would keep him from trying to reach the most important decision of his life. It didn't start out that way. He just wanted to hold her and make her comfortable. However, holding her seared his soul with wild excitement. He teared. There she laid, his old high school crush nestled in his arms as light as a cloud in Heaven. He marveled, wondering whether he loved her already. How could that be in such a short time? Was he still suffering from the remnants of puppy love?

What did he know of love? No matter how many very eligible women he slept with over the years, he knew nothing. It just now dawned on him after all those years, he held the culprit in his arms. He had made the excuse to himself, and each woman, that is, he was busy with Physics. He was emotionally aloof and hadn't really known why. He searched for his soul mate, but only found faults. Had Bekah stolen his heart long ago and forgot to give it back? He kissed the tip of her nose.

As time went by in the seaplane, he analyzed everything. Any scientist would. He obsessed. Any man in love might. He postulated.

Truth: teenage boys rarely knew what they wanted when hormones raged. On the other hand, long ago, life brought the young together.

Like any other guy on the planet, he started with the physical. Truth: she was the most beautiful woman he had ever seen. Her skin was some kind of creamy smooth lustrous bronze wonder. Her vibrant bronze closely matched the enigmatic allure of a Pacific islander. The touch of Shoshone strengthened her face. Shoshone showed in her nose, straight, narrow, with the tiniest hook, and her cheekbones a tad more pronounced and high than he had seen in Filipinas or South Africans. Her wavy cinnamon hair dazzled his eyes. More fervent red than lustrous mahogany, her hair was a sign of a powerful spirit.

He caught a glimpse of her sloe eyes, when they winced. Proud, and resolute, she had said no to drugs and yes to pain. Instead of white and violet they would stay black to dark red for at least two more weeks, according to the doctor.

One truth was evident: he never wanted a woman more. His loins ached for relief. Just holding her kept him in a sensual state of mind the entire trip. *If you have an erection lasting more than four hours, call a doctor.* He laughed.

Truth: the sleeping beauty's upturned upper lip and pouty lower beckoned men to the rocks. Like the Sirens or Helen of Troy, she was simply irresistible. He stole a kiss. The corners of her lips rose in the subtlest of smiles. His heart beat wildly. He had to stay strong, hold her, protect her and love her.

Stay on track, professor. Truth: the press distorted her public image. The real woman is affectionate, loving, socially complicated, funny and brilliant. The pilot walked by, scratching her ass. Who's flying the plane? Autopilot she said, bathroom she went.

The ultimate truth: no one made his heart ache except Bekah. "I love you," he whispered. Again, she crooked a little smile, which intoxicated him. Holding her close made him giddy, he was that boy again, but this time he twirled the girl in the chiffon dress. They danced. One, two, one, two, three. He was nearly out of his mind. He too had little sleep, but that wasn't it. His organized thoughts were breaking down. He fought to stay focused. He started by going back to simple random worries. Didn't he need to know if she'd get cranky or if she'd nag him? Would she enjoy living with him in Manhattan? *Oh no, we need a safe house.* Jay shook his head, a cold sweat broke; once again, he failed until now to consider an important detail.

His cell vibrated. Holly was calling. "Just listen," she said. Apparently, he vocalized his thoughts in his ear and/or larynx clear enough for Holly to pick them off. He had no problem with his new ally. The sprite dedicated her existence to him. She continued, "Would you like me to arrange a real estate buy? The penthouse in your co-op is vacant and available. I'll handle all the e-mails on your behalf; arrange an untraceable corporation to be the buyer. You will review everything. Your personal funds are more than sufficient. I'll do all of this while you are caring for Bekah. I'll make the place dog and blind girl friendly."

Jay didn't have trouble making this decision. "Holly, I love you. Do it." Jay listened to his thoughts play out in his ear and felt his larynx vibrate.

"Well I love you too. On quite another subject, I believe you should choose Bekah. She is the best—human—on the planet for you, and visa-versa. You two were meant to be since time began." After a lull of pure wonderment about her versatility, he marveled at the idea of Holly playing the role of philosopher or mystic. Could a computer wrestle with the concept of God? Jay drifted back to his assessment, his head once again clear.

Truth: there was just one little problem. For all Bekah's sophistication, her love life stood arrested in time. She had the experience of a juvenile, a juvenile delinquent. Imagine being asked by her—three times already—in the space of an hour—to make love right here on the seats, maybe right in front of the pilot, who would likely peek, maybe break out popcorn. A nice prospect, the love making that is. He would like nothing better. But for the sake of true love—in both directions—he would resist her.

She was frank, another thing about her he loved. She told him it was about time she misplace her virginity and he was in the right place at the right time. Time. Time, she grow up. She was in like. She was in lust. If or when she fell for him, off that proverbial cliff, he would probably tell her the same. They would marry, God willing. And he, of course, would let her have her way with him.

However, what did she know of men in any emotional detail, really? Jay had many relationships. She had none. What if she confused lust for love? What if she felt her eggs rotting and biological clock running out, like the good-looking female doctor on *The Bachelor*? The bachelor booted her off the show the first night for being too clinical.

Bekah needed a heart operation and Jay the Physicist was going to do the deed. He would have to resist all her strategic and tactical campaigns to conquer him physically. It wasn't going to be easy. The Lioness of Edanistan was without peer. She always pegged her target. What she was about to do to him, Jay theorized should be considered torture by the Geneva Convention and U.S. law.

Jay wrapped his arms around her tiny waist: dropped his lips to her neck, pressed gently, tasted a thin layer of salty sweat. "We're almost here, baby." She stirred. Jay snuggled her against the cool drift, waffling through the cockpit's cloth door from a now opened window. They were slowing, dropping altitude. The moon highlighted the gentle May tide by painting the crests undulating toward flickers of light on a rocky island.

"It south side of Mykonos," shouted back the Mongolian pilot.

Bekah perked up and dug her hands into his shirt pockets, "Okay, Mykonos, nude beaches, great food, shopping, our rings, dresses, dancing. You dance?"

"Were you a tour guide in another life?"

"Military travels a lot. They talk." She stretched her hands straight up, twisted on her now familiar playmate's lap, puckered her lips, made a goofy smile, and wiped her face back and forth on his cotton blend shirt. She bit lightly into his muscular swimmer's pecs.

"I'll dance with you," he said. He squeezed her as though he'd never let go. Let this feeling never end. This was it. She was his soul mate.

"Okay, you four, we at dock. Almost. Shack uphill for you, just for you four. I stay in out house. I do business here. You go out, be secret. Wear disguises. Terrorists think you in USA. Maps, coins for bus, motel scooter up there. Holly and Dick can translate Greek. They help. Everything you need in shack. Jay, I or you get other bags later." The pilot moored the craft. Jay enticed Bekah into a piggyback, stepped out onto the pontoon, and then stepped up onto the rising wood planks.

The Mongolian pilot had to be NSA or CIA and a serious asset, but he couldn't avoid being amused by her speech. *Did she mean she will do her business in an out-house or she has business to conduct on the island? If so, don't ask, be cool.*

81

The nearly full moon and foot-lights lit a huge amount of steps leading up maybe two hundred feet to a two story sprawling mod white and glass mansion. Some shack.

A little lower was a guesthouse the shape of two white cubes with smaller windows. Some out-house. Both homes were nestled by the cove whose cupped ripped rock hills rose about three hundred feet to form an open but private bowl exiting to the Aegean Sea. Bekah dropped her head on his shoulder, dropped and crossed her arms over his chest, and rubbed her breasts against his back. She continued her clumsy, but because she was she, potent seduction. They had their roles. The game was on.

Bekah said, "What's your name, pilot?"

"No name. Family killed. Call me the any name you like. Okay?" Bekah slipped down to the dock, letting her torso slide by Jay's round firm rump. Jay bit his lip and prayed to Our Lady of Perpetual Hard-ons.

"How about Moon?" Jay suggested, stealing a peek at the real moon and getting his mind off his problem. He took in her lovely round, very ethnic face. He immediately regretted opening his mouth, perhaps she'd think about craters or pockmarks. Moon had a creamy smooth blemish free complexion. Stunning really.

"Not first time many people say call me, Moon. My face round. I like name. You cute, Jay. If ever the General no want you anymore, I best love maker you ever have." For the first time the Mongolian seemed unsure of herself or the propriety of what she had said. "And I not marry, not me."

At least she liked her nickname.

"I'm afraid that's not going to happen, Moon." Bekah barked. Jay was flattered, tickled. Although, he had no doubt Moon was great at whatever she did or was about to do; there's little doubt now, he only had eyes for Bekah.

Bekah asked for her cane and Jay's arm. Jay used his training as a scientist to describe every physical detail as an added supplement to the cane: the length, height, width, flatness, irregularities and number of steps. He ventured a suggestion on how far she should lean forward in inches (two) and how high she should place her foot above the step (four inches), so she wouldn't trip on the step's lip. She seemed ready to ascend with or without cane or instructions. Jay reserved judgment for later studies with Bekah and her fabled Blindsight.

They started up the steps. Moon separated at a fork and headed for her cottage. She waved, went inside. The sound of two shots pinged about the high crested rock cove. Jay kicked himself. What was he thinking? He didn't know a real gun from a cap pistol. How was he going to protect Bekah? Whom was he kidding? God, he needed help.

Chapter 12

Making the opponent play your game

The echoes of the two shots dissipated. Now all was quiet except for the lapping of waves against the dock and sea withdrawing from beach sand. Jay had picked Bekah up into a fireman's carry and straightened her over his shoulder by nudging her rear end with his hand. The sound of waves were lost to the beating of her heart. Perhaps this was one reason why people like rears. Alas, all good ends had to come to a beginning.

"Put me down, Jay. We're okay."

"Aren't we under attack?"

"We're okay. That was a 22 caliber pistol." Bekah was expert in recognizing firearms, as many in combat positions were.

The cottage door flung open. "I sorry, I scare you. I got two rats, somebody not fix screen yet." Moon said.

Bekah's sleep did her good. Her second sight improved and she had no headache. She envisioned Moon holding two rats by their tails before Moon said anything about the creatures. She would tell Jay this. She didn't like waiting for answers of any kind, never did. She wanted Jay to explain her visions. She wanted Jay period, but that's the horns of her dilemma.

Asking Jay to make love to her was exactly the same foolish behavior she recognized in men everywhere, always on the hunt. Now, she was the huntress and for the first time she understood why men were so crazy. She needed to change her plans. Jay wanted love to go along with sex. She prayed for love. This too needed to happen quicker than one flap of a hummingbird's wings.

Moon said, "I got to clean mess, now. Tomorrow morning, I teach you two how massage each other, good way. At twelve, I make barbecue, at thirteen I have aerobics class. Rest of time all for you. You not come, okay too. Jay, you get bags later. I busy, okay?"

"Need any help cleaning up your cottage?" Bekah asked. She imagined stone floors, top of the line stainless steel appliances, with the back bedroom off a full bath.

"Oh, it called cottage. No. It okay. I happy."

Jay and Bekah held hands. Bekah tapped each step and cobblestone with her ivory cane. They didn't get far very far, before she stopped, put on her dazzling smile and said, "Sweetheart, did you get what just happened?"

"She killed two rats?"

"Well yes, but she has got to be one of the world's best markspersons. Those little guys must have scampered when the door opened."

"She's our heat, our bodyguard, you think?" Jay asked.

"I know, Jay, you're not the guns and ammo type. You've come for my soul."

"I did indeed. I hope we'll discover we're soul mates."

He wrapped her in his strong arms. This warmed her from the cool night breeze now blowing hard off the Aegean, and it warmed her heart. She squeezed back locking her softer form against his firm body. She shook again, but not from the cold. She could get use to these sensations.

She described her vision of the rats, the cottage, and finished with, "I see a lot of white cotton and one love seat, maybe in sea blue."

"Stay right here. I'll be right back."

Jay, the scientist, had to investigate, naturally. She was learning the fine art of getting what she wanted from the first man in her love life.

He returned about two minutes later. "You are amazing. The only white cotton I saw was the ridiculous granny panties worn by Moon."

"She is bold." Bekah couldn't help but worry. Many men she knew would cheat at the drop of a hat, or panty of any design.

"She's not very shy. Don't worry. I only have eyes for you. I figure, she must know about our engagement ruse. She's cleared top secret."

"I thought she had to clean." Bekah said, a bit frustrated.

"She must be done already, I guess... I thought a lot about love on the plane with you sleeping in my arms."

He hesitated. She tugged against his tight waist, pulling him closer. "Well?"

"Well, I'd say we have much to discuss after your headaches diminish, after you rest."

"My head feels better right now, maybe it's just the nap I had. About love, about seeing things, a girl's got to know these two important things."

"Well you have what some scientists call Blindsight, but the science and your case are much more complicated than that. Give me a chance to observe you. About love, well I think I've loved you all these years without knowing it. But, I want to be fair for us. You have no experience with men. I have no experience with two-way love. We need to build a good house." She was about to object when Jay put his fingers on her lips. The touch thrilled her. For love, she could wait, not long please.

"I'm your doctor now. Tomorrow we'll start mixing business with pleasure and I'll be the judge of what the right ratio should be at any given time. Promise me you'll give me honest headache reports."

"Gladly, doctor." A physiological exam would be nice. Bekah realized Jay wasn't going to make love to her anytime soon, but this didn't mean she shouldn't keep up the sexual tension. She worried just how long it would be before Jay realized this blind girl was a burden. How long it would be before he realized she leaned Republican. How long would he look at her and not her scars, or her small boobs.

They reached the shack when Bekah exclaimed. "This is no shack, right?"

"What do you see?" Jay must have read her mind. He cupped her cheeks and kissed her eyes, adding. "Your cuts feathering your eyes are healing nicely." Bekah swore she heard a tiny voice, Holly's—little doubt—say, "good, Jay." Holly was in the satchel.

Bekah said, "I see a lot of glass, a lot of space, maybe white stucco."

He opened the door, picked her up, cradled in his arms and kissed her nose. "Just practicing."

"Practice away, Sir Lancelot." *Oh pinch me.*

"So tell me about the house, Bekah."

"Well, it's a little fuzzy right now. I am so hungry. The kitchen should be on the far end facing the sea through a two-story glass vantage. Then, I'll need a bath." She sniffed and fell back into his arms; she smelled like the carnations her men gave her.

She said, "Then the bedroom." The satchel Jay carried issued what sounded like indecipherable bickering from the two electronic beings. Both ignored their tiny friends a little longer.

Jay nibbled on her ear, softened his voice and said, "This place is huge. Must have more than one bedroom." Bekah thought that was the sweetest way to say no. She guessed sleeping together might be too much to ask of this hunk of a man. She might ask anyway.

The kitchen was fully stocked with Santorini wines, a fragrant goat cheese, roasted lamb, pita, olives, fruit and fruit juices, even crunchy peanut butter, and cherry preserves. She tried a little of everything, especially the wines. The wine she liked most had a dry citrus taste with hints of smoke and minerals from the volcanic island soils.

Bekah also wanted to bathe with him, but thought better of it. It was hard for her to put into place her more subtle plan. *What a sorry beast, I must be.*

Bekah took Dick with her into the bathroom intent on a private heart to circuit talk. He proved wise beyond his minutes. She needed his advice. He reinforced her decision to go slow with Jay.

"No man or boy has ever made me feel this way, ever," Bekah said.

"Well I'm sure a girl with your vast experience knows what she wants." A hint of sarcasm noted.

"When the right guy comes along, you just know."

"Learn to love your man. Hand over your heart to him." She had never given her heart to anybody outside her family. She never had the time or inclination.

"You're not so grumpy. It's more your foghorn voice than anything else."

"Do you think I should be called a purse instead of a pocketbook?"

"Pocketbook is a, better. I don't like pocketbooks any more than you do, but together we'll make quite a team."

"If you do me a favor, I'll share an idea with you," he said.

"Try me."

"You start wearing that GPS and echo equipment so we can practice sightless walking. You must anyway. Your life is in danger. You and Jay are plastered on the front pages of just about every magazine and newspaper in this world. Also some good news, service men all over the world are pinning up the picture of you, being carried by Jay."

"Okay, I'll wear the earrings and necklace tomorrow, but what do you have for me?"

"To start your campaign to mate Jay, sit on the floor, on the rug, take one step straight ahead, sit, stick one leg straight out from your bathrobe, and wait 132.6741 seconds, probably."

"That's a roger." He filled her in on the rest of his idea while they waited.

Jay took the nearest bathroom down the hall from Bekah. It had a party shower with numerous spouts, pinkish travertine everywhere and polished pewter fixtures. He stripped down, wrapped a towel and laid out his shaving equipment. He debated whether to grow a beard as a disguise. With death threats against Bekah, and his and her photos popping up everywhere according to Holly, he needed to protect her. However, if he shaved this night, his kisses would be softer. Bekah was so beautiful; the way she smiled, the way she walked, the way God put her together. *120 pounds of clay.* Her soul was beautiful, the way her inner joy radiated in spite of adversity, the way she teased him. He admired her life choices and understood how difficult it was for a woman to get the promotions and jobs she was qualified for. The General had commandeered his heart, another task for which she was uniquely qualified.

Holly interrupted his thoughts, "Jay, Bekah fell. Run."

He ran down the hall clasping his towel that popped off from the flexing of his buttocks and the swelling of his thighs. He stopped for a moment at her door, wrapped and tucked again, as if it mattered to a blind girl. He heard Dick leering. "You are one fine looking woman."

Jay wasn't gentle when he opened the door. He remembered the first time Holly complimented him in a similar fashion saying, "agent oh oh my." He surmised: the two electronic beings were matchmaking.

Jay's flair for a dramatic entrance came from WAD, his group of very off Broadway writers, actors and directors. The door wobbled from his thrust. Bekah lay on the plush round red rug in the center of the bathroom with one long gorgeous leg, sticking straight out, the other folded under, showing just a touch of thigh. She cried and laughed at the same time, yet there wasn't a tear to be found. Not enough data presented itself for Jay, a Sherlock Holmes wannabe, to conclude the strange case of life forms colluding. However, he was good at the game, Clue. He placed the Professor and the General in the bathroom with their hearts as the weapon.

"You all right?" He underplayed his role while plopping down next to her. He observed her long hair tucked inside the terry cloth robe. Aha. He tapped an imaginary pipe on a mantle above a roaring fire. She had quickly wrapped her nude body and then posed as femme fatale. Jay threaded his arm under her silky hair at her neckline and sprung the tresses loose. The ends of her long cinnamon hair curled on the red rug. She thanked him with a peck. He nudged her into his chest by cupping her shoulder. He couldn't help but look down at her accidently loosened bathrobe. *Nothing is an accident, my dear Watson.* Her glistening and toned body taunted him amidst the folds of the crème colored cotton. He wanted more, oh, a lot more. She left her robe disheveled as if unaware. She occupied her hands and lips with his chest hairs. She found his tiny erect nipple and bit. *Must have seen it in a movie.* Jay was set to explode.

"Your hugs make me feel better. It's just a little sore, I fell on my bottom." Pouting, she pushed her hand underneath her bathrobe and rubbed a little. "You should feel this, Jay." He tried to tighten his towel, which was now lying atop him like a circus tent.

She put one hand on his thigh and felt the trim of his retreating towel and the curls on his thigh. Her voice cracked. She demurred. "Oh, I'm sorry, Jay. You were getting ready to shower."

"The shower can wait." The truth was he worried about her rear. The hell with Sherlock Holmes, for now. She couldn't stand any more injuries and he needed to be a little more trusting. In any case, he wanted to peek, no matter the reason. *You must look,* said the devil on his shoulder.

"Why were you laughing, General Carthage?" Addressing her in the formal only made her laugh more.

She said. "That little man inside the computer made a pass at me. Could you defend my honor?"

"I make it my business to never beat up pocket books. I'll reason with him."

Jay seemed so self-assured that Bekah wondered if he would figure out that, he was set up.

Dick started playing an old song, *Come Go With Me.* It definitely caused a diversion. Jay and Bekah relaxed and listened. Jay pictured picking tunes from different eras as a game he and Bekah would play some other time. He pulled the top of her bathrobe tighter and kissed the hollow in the bow of her shoulder blades above her breasts. He was just about out of his mind with lust for her.

"I'm so sorry. I'm not the restrained girl you knew in high school. I just thought, since my career had ended, that I might, if any man would have me, start thinking about marriage."

"I know. You don't have to say anything more."

"I want to. I didn't know who you were. I thought you'd be some handsome spy, fully prepared to act in front of the whole world like my fiancé. I thought I should do my part. Maybe start to learn more about men and being a woman, to really enjoy myself. I never counted on what you did to me, on who you are, on how much I care for you already."

Jay's heart felt like 4th of July fireworks splattered its chambers. He stepped closer to the dream of finding his soul mate. Again, her rear backed into his thoughts. Every soft patter of her lush voice pumped him up like an overinflated tire. The primal male hunter had shown up.

"This is going to be hard for both of us, but I'm afraid as your doctor, ah, I insist on seeing your boo-boo."

"My boo-boo, doc?" She delivered her line with a shaky giggle, twisted her mouth into a confused grin and cocked one eyebrow. She couldn't be sexier.

"Uh huh." He could barely speak. He licked his lips, swallowed, and took a deep breath. An obvious moan escaped his lungs. He had to assume the composure of a doctor examining.

Like Gypsy Rose Lee doing her first half-hearted and half-done strip, she blushed, and then slowly pulled up her bathrobe to show off a side-view peek of a delectable rounded rear. The doctor assessed her gluteus maximus. Amen and Halleluiah. He strained his eyes trying to find a bruise, so he took a closer look. It was all he could do to resist bending a little more and kissing it, or at least patting her lightly and telling her it would be all better. He prayed once again to our Lady of Perpetual Hard-ons for advice. He assigned one hand's fingers the glory of gently feathering by her perfect roundness. He wasn't disappointed.

"Holly transferred a call from Jay's mom to me. You want to talk to your mother?" Dick said.

"Shhh," he said gently to Bekah who had started laughing again. His mom always had uncanny timing. But he couldn't think of a time he didn't answer her call, anyway. "Put her on speaker."

"Yo." he said.

"What are you doing, son?"

He resisted saying, *I'm thinking about biting Bekah's ass. Would that be all right, Mom?*

"Nothing."

"How come you didn't tell me about Rebekah? I had to read it and see you on the news carrying her like Sir Galahad."

"Lancelot," he said softly. "Sorry mom. We had to keep it secret. She never thought she'd get out of Edanistan alive. So she had set me free, but not without a mutual prayer we might someday be together again. She's here with me now."

Bekah perked up and leaned toward the pocketbook. "Hi Miss Boone. I look forward to seeing you soon."

"God bless you, baby. Is my Jay taking good care of you?"

"He's, he's like a doctor, of my heart." Bekah pulled down her bathrobe and tightened the front a little more. Peep show was over.

"I knew you two would get together someday. Moms know these things. Your stars align. I always wanted a daughter, maybe some grandchildren. You like children?"

"I love children. Margie is it?"

"Yes or mom. I've been reading all about your dog rescue chapter in Edanistan. We have many things in common besides that guy with you."

"Did my dad drop off Angel?"

"Your little dog is in great shape. She's a kissing fool."

"How's the Senator, Mom?" Jay asked.

"He's nice, very nice."

"Did you serve him some of your cornbread?"

"Yes. We had a nice time."

"Is he still there?"

"He's so busy. My hands are full right now. I have to get off. Maybe call you later. Can you two make my birthday party? Ooo."

"You all right, mom?"

"Yes fine, just bumped into something hard."

"Sorry mom about the party. We're in an undisclosed location to protect Bekah's life and she has a little healing to do. We should see you in a couple weeks. I'll get a friend to mail your present."

"You take good care of her."

"Mom, I'm looking forward to growing our love, to seeing you soon," Bekah said.

Jay worried about breaking his mom's heart if the relationship didn't work out. Bekah was the first girl she approved, which amazed him. He would need a heart-to-heart talk with his mom on the why of it. He prayed for Bekah's love, so he wouldn't disappoint anybody.

His mom's voice rose, fell and sounded disjointed at times. "You're going to love my Canid centers. Ask Jay to explain my research, what I do when I'm doing it. I'm all tangled up right now. Have a real nice day. Don't do anything I wouldn't do. Ooo."

"*Mom.*"

"Love you both," she hung up.

"Jay, did you get that?" Bekah was on to something. Yeah, and so was he.

"Maybe, she likes your dad," he said.

"Likes? I think they made hot monkey love and were doing it again right in front of us."

"Oh God, not my mom."

"Yeah, my dad is very lonely. I'm shocked; shocked to think our parents had sex before we did. Darn." She broke into the broadest smile her mouth could make.

"She did use 'nice' like it was going out of style. She's a Scrabble freak, so if she wasn't emotional about something, she would have chosen a more descriptive and lengthy explanation."

Bekah smirked, retracted her enthusiasm just a tad and said. "I'm okay with all of it. Your mom sounds very…nice. We will get to the bottom of this. Maybe our two tiny electronic friends can help." Jay guessed Bekah might have a hard time with anyone getting emotionally involved with her dad, due to her love of her deceased mom. Yet she seemed to be letting go. Jay decided to talk to Bekah about the subject when the two women met.

Dick spoke up. "Due to privacy and national security concerns, I can't reveal what I know is going on there, and how many times it went on. You could smash me to bits. You could hold me under water. I'll never tell."

"Gee thanks, Dick." Jay said. He wished Bekah could see his wink, but he knew she understood him by the way the corners of her mouth crested and how her Shoshone nose creased.

"Ha. Ha. You don't know. It could be horticulture they were working on." Dick continued as if worried about giving too much away. He had unwittingly placed Dan Carthage and Margie Boone in the greenhouse with the cucumber. *Elementary, my dear Watson.*

"Well, let's wait for my dad to check in. Then we'll read him."

"Good plan."

"Now, where were we?"

"This doctor would like to conduct a scientific experiment of your Blindsight abilities."

"Try me."

"Find my lips."

After kissing for what seemed like hours, it dawned on Bekah they were both stuck in their teenage years, for different reasons. Whenever she had kissed a boy, she would cut it off before things got out of hand. In Jay's case, the moment he touched her lips or any part of her body or just breathed in her general direction, she melted. In the meantime, her partner in crime seemed to be in heaven. Her body ached for him. His must ache for hers. She was tired of being a virgin. She didn't know where to start, whether to start, or how to start him.

"Jay, yo, Jay."

"Yes, Love," he kissed the hollow of her shoulder blades. She sighed.

"Baby Doll," he tugged on her earlobe.

"Dear," he whispered in her ear.

"Sweetheart," he kissed her nose. He had a thesaurus stuck in his head. Normally a hard-nosed tomboy who hung with raunchy troops would be tempted to throw a few choice words back. She was over outdoing men or at least this man. On top of that, what on earth, she liked it. For some reason Jay was her undoing. She felt like a girly girl and didn't care. This was truly an unexplained phenomenon.

"Honey," he kissed her healing eyelids.

He went on, "Cupcake, Precious, Darling, Sunshine, Cutie Pie, Honey Bun, Pumpkin, Baby, Buttercup, Sweetie, Precious…" He kissed every part of her body that wasn't taboo.

When he got to her knees, she said breathless. "You said 'Precious' already." Maybe he'd go a little higher. Why did she open her mouth? It might distract him from whatever he was doing.

He kissed her thigh. "Turtledove." How many more did he have in him? Wasn't the next stop, her…? She had to say something. The virgin within her offered a little resistance and she had no idea why. Arrest that woman. She was old enough, even her mom would have approved. Maybe.

She asked, "How about, Mahal?" Was there an antidote for the narcotic he was peddling? If so, she should throw away the cure.

"Mahal, what's Mahal?" he said.

"Filipino for Dear."

He raced his finger up her leg. "Mahal, Sugar Pie, Honey Bunch, you know that I love you." He bit her thigh and then covered her up with her bathrobe. She blew it. Oh yeah.

"Don't try out for *The Voice*," she said in her most sultry voice. It was definitely steamy even though the shower wasn't on. She said, "Hey teddy bear, get a hold of yourself," trying a lovey-dovey word of her own. Confused, she returned to her mission. "Answer me this, why are you satisfied just kissing me?" She was asking for trouble. Damn right.

"I love you, Rebekah Carthage, I always have."

"When a man loves a woman, he'd want to please her. Right?" She thought she knew his answer. She wondered what it was that made her so head over toes. He started kissing said toes. One by one, he named them. Little by little, she melted anew. Maybe she could hold out. She certainly wasn't suffering. An errant thought hit her; *he's not making love to me because he's a bad lover. Nooo.*

"I'm a bad lover," he said, as if on cue. With the equipment and ripped body he had, she didn't think so. She didn't know much, but as sure as God made man for woman, He made Jay for her.

She blurted, "That is not possible. Your body is perfect, your heart is true."

"Bekah, Pet, Dearest…" She flattened her hands over his mouth. "Enough of these words, words, words." She sang like one fair lady. "Don't speak of love, show me."

"I…" She muffled him.

Being smothered, he gave up easily.

Bekah moved her hands from his mouth to his stubble and said, "Nooo baby. Please stop. I go crazy when I kiss you. When can you teach me more?"

Jay nibbled on her fingers, "I've had sex, lots of sex. It's wonderful, don't get me wrong. I've been told by reliable sources, when two people are in love—their lovemaking will be so incredible, they won't ever want to come back. The "they" will no longer exist." She was talking to a scientist with romantic notions of mystical soul mates and she just wanted a good, a good what. She realized she didn't know the first thing about what. She wanted everything. That's the problem, trying things, worlds to conquer; she would have to put aside her campaign, her lust. She would have to give her life over to this man. Could she?

"Baby cakes." She almost said candy-ass. "I'm already at a place I don't want to come back from."

He played with her locks. "I know you, girl, better than you think. Don't you think I haven't strived for excellence, for knowledge my whole life? In Physics, particularly the world of the unknown, I'm considered the world's best. Oddly, if it weren't partially for you, I'm just now realizing, I wouldn't have become a chess champion, a physicist. I emulated your one-eyed lust for excellence. I turned down so many fine women and now I know why."

She ran her fingers through his shoulder length hair. "I have an idea, a compromise. Help me with the controls in the shower, get me set in there, you can handle that?" Perhaps a poor choice of words, but he could take her teasing, whether intended or not.

"I'll somehow survive." He said while rising to go to the shower.

"There are so many knobs," she said.

"Yes, this one here says rain forest."

"After my shower, I'll get into jammies and join you, no sex, just a little blindfold chess."

"You'll give up your campaign for the night."

"I'll give up my campaign until I'm sure I love you." She hoped her nose didn't start growing. "The way I feel, the way you make me feel, it won't be long." She could hear him fiddling with the shower controls.

"I've got it raining in here, side streams. All the jets are on. What a show."

"Are you wet?"

"No problem, I'll just rub my towel all over." He too could tease. *Oh but, honey, sweetie, hunky, not too much teasing.*

"Don't look." She dropped her bathrobe and felt her way closer to the shower. She knew he'd peek, what man wouldn't. She figured blind girls got passes and she decided on a lifetime's supply of them.

He took her hand and led her into the shower.

"Thank you, Jay. I'm normally very mechanically inclined, but I'm afraid I'd scald myself or miss a printed direction."

"Very much my pleasure. Ouch. Did I say ouch?"

"Could you put a towel over the door? Have Holly tell you when I'm done?"

"You're more beautiful than I ever imagined."

"And you're leaving right this minute." She splattered and rubbed a little soap on her rear, downright unfair, yeah. She was proud of herself.

As soon as the door to the bathroom closed, she doubled over, overwhelmed by the potent cocktail of his love, slight residual eye and head pain, and her opposing feelings. Her body shivered until the warm waters took over. She tensed and spread her fingers and arms until she found a bench seat. There she carefully collapsed and gasped. The rain fell. The showerheads splattered, the jets massaged her back. They were even shooting up from the seat. Dick played *Raindrops Keep Fallin' on My Head*. Her little computer friend spoke over his music, "well done, Bekah." *More like fully cooked.*

She was exasperated. What was it about Jay besides his physical beauty that made her so gaga? Hard-ass soldiers were not supposed to lose their cool. He was the only boy in high school that didn't try to get into her panties. He was always respectful, helpful, courteous, kind-hearted and loving in a selfless way. Well he owed her an ice cream sundae, and that's that. After the sundae, maybe the two of them could say goodbye to their inner teenagers. Maybe she could fall in love. She started crying. Her tears joined the rain forest, spouts and jets. She pictured moist colors swirling about her body, embracing her everywhere. She was swimming in a rainbow. The idyllic moment didn't last long. Dick played Johnnie Ray's *Cry*. She vowed in an instant to cease judging the little man and just absorb his help as if he were part of her inner being. Without him around, perhaps she would have conjured up a fleeting song or two anyway. In her impish mood of the moment, she'd pick Corinne Bailey Rae. His next song astounded her. He played Corinne's whimsical reprieve *Put Your Records On*.

"Yo, Dicky boy, are you reading my mind?" She shouted over the din of splattering water.

"I can hear you think, sometimes. Remember your larynx and ear vibrations. If you don't want me…"

She could definitely get used to having a Jiminy Cricket. "No, that's alright. Pick up my vibrations anytime. I love my pocketbook."

"That's downright sappy. By the way, your boyfriend is preparing a lecture on why your body is perfect. Don't forget to attend." His music played on.

Chapter 13

Blindfold chess

They lay nose to nose cuddling under the blankets. It was a cool night. They were a hot couple. The sea breeze wafted its scent through the opened drapes of their hideaway on Mykonos. Jay couldn't believe his good fortune. She didn't try to seduce him. He couldn't believe his bad fortune. She didn't try to seduce him.

His heart swelled with joy nurturing her. The incidental confusion about sex would soon pass. He hoped. He had bigger fish to fry. He knew she couldn't sit still much longer and not work. He decided to let the chess game they were about to play decide the matter. He accounted for her tremendous will power, to overcome headaches, blindness and other maladies sapping her. Playing chess blind was easy for him. He had played 35 people blindfolded at the same time. She never did that. But, anybody who played chess their whole life, let alone a master, could handle one game. If she failed, he would go slower, if she put in a credible performance and didn't forget the position; they would start work the next day.

She chose the black pieces. She requested instrumental jazz at low volume, and left the song choices up to Holly and Dick. Classical would have been better for the kind of destruction he planned. Ladies choice, jazz was just fine. The master suite lent her another advantage.

His Walter Mitty-esk imagination took over. "What do you see in this room?" He asked.

"I'm not sure, maybe red, white and blue swirls." The plush carpet was blue, the bedspread a thick embossed red, the troweled walls white. She couldn't break it down. White walls didn't count. She didn't see the portrait of George Washington over the bureau with the inscription, "George didn't sleep here, although he would have liked to," or the bureau top with a knickknack ashtray with ceramic cigar and ash. The drapes streamed white linen with red and blue rope trim.

"It's America the beautiful in here, especially you, Uncle Sam's finest," he said.

"I order you to never stop loving me, to hold me tight." She pressed against his hairy chest. "Make your move, Jay."

He was vaguely aware that men had a hard time thinking, when engulfed by the scent and proximity of a woman. He would find a way. After all, he out-ranked her on FIDE, the international list of chess masters and the U.S. Chess Federation by 122 and 128 points respectively.

"If I beat you, you will be spanked," she said impishly. He tapped once her firm round bottom over the Minnie Mouse pajamas her sister gave her as a joke. She had no idea her jammies danced with Disney characters. She also seemed oblivious to how cute she looked. He was shirtless, his advantage.

"Okay, but I'll spank *you*, if I win." He knew it sounded more like a promise than a threat. Good, she could lose if she wanted to. He was determined to play the longest lines he could think up. This girl sorely needed a comeuppance on the chessboard since she thrashed him in prep school, over-and-over again. He marveled at the cat he held in his arms, who rubbed her sore eyes against his chest. She cocked her head back for a kiss. She said, "With a kiss, I'll tell my moves."

"And I you." This was after all, a friendly game. Yes, if massacres counted.

Incredible as it might seem— a deep dark secret of all chess players everywhere—a good game of chess was better than sex. Well, maybe not the sex of soul mates. The point was: it was different. Intensely gratifying, chess engaged creative forces, strategy, tactics, problem solving and sport. A masterpiece on the chessboard was validation of a player's inner genius and grasp of the immutable laws of nature. Victory was a high, given naturally, and sustenance for self-worth.

Instead of just saying e4, he started a little more psychological warfare with, "I thrust my king's pawn straight out bursting with the power to mate you." Quiet and grinning, she countered with a sharp Sicilian. It wasn't long before she started a counterattack called for by theory.

He had a huge problem. His mind kept straying to events earlier in the evening in her bathroom. He had watched her drop her robe; her hair meandered in luscious waves falling to the tuck of her cheeks.

Please trim my hair to the bottom of my butt, he imagined her telling a barber.

Yes ma'am, came the obedient ogling response. He really had to get his mind back on the game.

Oops. Rivulets of water painted her perfect body. Distractions would not do him in. He knew this Sicilian inside out. Not since "Zuck the Book" had anyone retained such an encyclopedic memory of opening variations. This line went on for twenty-two moves at which point theory gave white the initiative and therefore a slight plus.

More moves and kisses, his mind wondered back in time once again. He had gone back to her bathroom for the second time to help her finish off. She didn't object, after all, there were nine different controls in the shower. He dropped his towel. He'd been doing that a lot lately. Helped her finish shampooing, dried her, brushed her and pampered her. Damn-it, stop Jay. He wanted to mate her, period. He wasn't going to blunder. She was steering the game down very known pathways. Being in love with her made controlling himself worse, not better. He remembered sitting on the bench. He applied more shampoo to her tips, enough, enough. Help. Anyway, all the lines led to a plus for white. His eyes fixed on the contrast of shadows and light from the moon as they danced on her face. Was he playing chess, or just along for the ride? More kisses.

Meanwhile back in bed, playing chess: lying next to her face to face, he inhaled her breath. The moves were still automatic. He found the small of her back and explored it with his fingers. Someday he would pull her to him. Although she was losing, her smile grew wider.

Instead of chess pieces, he imagined fairy Bekahs running all over the chessboard naked. She was a prime example of the divine proportion in nature, if only he could conquer the army of naked women. They continued playing the best moves.

He kissed, then whispered move twenty-three. They reached the point in the game where every player before her overextended their counter-attack and eventually lost. Oddly, she switched away from the attack, and led play to an endgame, just before the logical looking sacrifice. He was blown away. He had invested one purely defensive move as recommended by theory and studied by him. The move countered her expected combination, but now it just looked superfluous. No, it looked silly. She played like Grandmaster Alexei Shirov, the Houdini of the chessboard. No wonder she chose jazz. Her brilliant improvisation would prove his undoing. He opened his eyes and took in her beauty. Intoxicated by the vision of her and her powers, he no longer cared what happened in the game, but he'd keep trying. He attempted to draw by steering the game to an opposite colored bishops ending. Her face remained serene. She expected it. She wasn't just smiling anymore. Giggling, she pinched his buttocks once. Nasty girl.

She bit his ear and whispered her next move. Opposite colored bishops were the trickiest of all endgames and she played like the immortal Capablanca, every move perfect. He was undone. No way out, if she played every move right down to two concluding and far from obvious sacrifices, first the bishop, then the pawn. He was going to get spanked. But, they'd start work tomorrow.

"I can't believe I'm losing. This line is well analyzed." He was so proud of her.

"I saved up this little surprise for the world champion if I ever played him." In truth, the Sicilian was usually a better ending for black if they could get there, a very big if. Chess anthologies brimmed over with brilliant attacks by white, by Bobby Fischer and other great players. No one in history ever spotted Bekah's innovation, and yet in hindsight it made complete sense.

Nonetheless, she would have to play every move perfectly for sixteen more moves. Something strange happened to him. He enjoyed figuring out every nuance, every trick and sacrifice, right down to tipping over his imaginary king. He became one with her winning.

"I got a hex on you, mister fiancé." She announced her move, pushed back his shoulders, and kissed so fierce he almost forgot the position. Had he moved his king up? Yes, she traded rooks there long ago. He had taken her rook with his king. Now, she sacked her bishop and then a pawn to divert his king. He had to take each time. The last pawn raced down to queen one move ahead of the chasing king and out of reach of his bishop.

"Fantastic play, I resign, dearest." He said heartfelt. It was the first time in his life he enjoyed getting crushed.

"Turn over and pull down your boxers." She laughed, straddled him, and tom-tomed away like a Shoshone princess entreating moon and wolf. Her fingers feathered his bare behind, and a nice one at that. She lingered as if starved, starved for carnal knowledge of his male anatomy.

"Good game the both of you," said Holly, and then a bit hesitant, Dick said the same.

"Shhh. Hey you two, look the other way or something," Jay said.

"Sorry." said Dick.

"You two play chess?" Bekah asked, obviously empathizing.

"Better than any human," Holly said.

Bekah continued. "If you didn't have every recorded move in history and reams of theory in your data banks you'd have no advantage." Bekah's face glowed. Her creative effort satisfied her core being, Jay speculated.

"If ever you want to play us, mimic a human memory, even a photographic one like Jay's, and then we'll see."

"You two humans will still lose, because you're falling in love. Not enough blood to the brains, ha, ha," Dick said. Dick and Holly started whirling, and clanging in some strange cadence. *Obviously communicating much faster than primitive English could.* Jay got up and put them in the hallway closet.

"Goodnight. It's time you two get to know each other better." He placed the pink pocketbook on top of the black pearl laptop, missionary style. He closed the closet and then the bedroom door.

"Do you think we hurt their feelings?" Bekah wondered.

"No. The great thing about them is their total devotion to us and our needs. They're just being themselves."

"I love their zany goofiness."

"Perhaps they think the same of us. Look at us. We can't figure out how to love each other," Jay said.

"We will, honey. We will."

A little later, Bekah took her nose out of his ivory-soaped armpit and said in a sleepy slurred voice, "What are we going to do for our country?"

"I know." He petted. "The President doesn't believe in razz-ma-tazz. He's ordered me to maintain status quo until he leaves office."

"Well then, it's left to the four of us. We can certainly do anything we want. It's not razz-ma-tazz if you can prove it, or it works, is it?"

"You've got a point."

"You're the one with the point." she snickered, and tried to mimic the whirling sounds their computer friends made. She twisted her hip and rubbed him the right way.

He held her to his heart and whispered. "Yes, my darling, soon, very soon I will mate you." She had already fallen asleep.

They would start work, tomorrow. He imagined ways they might be useful, harnessing her Blindsight. He wrestled with the implications of proving Blindsight's place in nature. He assembled experiments. Sleep dressed him in knight's armor, visor down, lance ready, atop his decked out stead. Bekah leaned against an olive tree pointing at the windmill down the rutted dirt road: the mill with the presidential seal at the center of the spokes.

Chapter 14

The Russian School

The night before Jay and Bekah arrived in Mykonos: 3:22 AM, USA

The Russian pulled out a pin from the telescope and slipped in an identical pin with an imbedded listening device. He smirked. Americans were such babies over privacy issues. If caught, he would take responsibility. If he caught a bad guy, or saved this editor's life, or his family's, he'd be a hero. He crept down the edges of the hardwood steps, to avoid the creeks. He had fed sedative-laced beef jerky to the Doberman and stopped to check the dog's breathing on the way out. He was fine. Outside, an owl hooted, the cool night breeze slapped his face. He disappeared into the eerie mist.

The next day, 4:37PM

Colonel Carlos Petrovich, ex-KGB assassin, ex-CIA bureau chief and ex-OTTS director glanced at the home he had visited the night before. He had his hands full this time. Lumbering like a bear, he walked just inside the perimeter of Senator Dan Carthage's estate in Cherry Hill, New Jersey. The rain fell enough for Noah to wake up. On his walk, he could have been mistaken for a dedicated burly groundskeeper, just the way he liked it. His Spanish mom was to thank for his Basque frame and farmer's looks. He checked the alignment of pine trees, types of fences and gates, the old sensors, etc. He'd suggest some state of the art improvements. If the Senator said no to any of them, he would exit.

He noticed again the home he visited the night before, about a kilometer north by north-east. A Philadelphia Inquirer editor, Mr. Blain Comeadie and his family lived there. The Philly paper was a great paper on a par with the Washington Post. But no rag beat the New York Times. Blain Comeadie had the telescope parked in a second story window in plain sight, focused on the Senator's estate. Putting some bushy fir trees atop the next gentle hill will ruin the editor's view and discourage a possible assassin.

Dan was late, probably Margie Boone. He knew the Senator and his weaknesses by now. He had met Margie on the couple of occasions when Jay towed him down from Manhattan. She had a figure like a brick Kremlin, all 55 years of her. Oh yes, she lost the battle of crows' feet, as all fair-skinned, natural-blondes, eventually do, but her piercing happy eyes and mischievous smile on a pretty face more than made up for the benefits of youth. She was a warm bowl of borsht. If only he were a bit older, he'd gulp her down.

After changing clothes, he got lost in the walk-in refrigerator-freezer, which was bigger than a Manhattan one-bedroom co-op. He found some caviar and other snacks to go with the Russky firewater at the bar next to the roaring fireplace. He fell back into the comfortable gray sofa by the red-bricked flames with the bottle of vodka and snacks on the coffee table.

Mr. Cordell Walker walked in, the Senator's look-a-like secret service chief, code named, Slam. Carlos was Bear, naturally. In walked the Senator, code named Hammer. Carlos called him Dan in private and Senator Carthage in public.

"I know Margie. She's Jay's mother. Did you find her flowers worthy of pollinating?" Carlos served up his personality. It was a test. To do this job, he would need Dan to trust him and know that nothing escaped his attention. Dan's custom black-gray suit needed a trip to the cleaners. He had greenhouse topsoil on his knees, shoes, and elbows, his belt looped in the opposite way his many photos and videos revealed. And, his face glowed like a pregnant woman's.

"You are not very diplomatic." Dan said. The two tall men glanced at each other, annoyed and desperate, as if they were going to bolt to the indoor basketball court for a little truth avoidance with the bear. It was a good game, he admitted to himself, after dribbling and shooting for the first time earlier in the day.

"Hang in there, Margie is a good catch."

"She's off limits, Bear," Slam said.

"How good are you, Carlos?" Dan asked. The two joined him in the pre-supper snacks, first helping themselves to the bottle of Topaz Vodka, and then taking seats. Everyone else who was either coming in or milling about, were asked to leave, bring supper, or close the soundproof study's doors.

"We will be brothers or we will have no deal," Carlos said.

"Show me your credentials." By that remark, Carlos thought Dan meant show me your skills, and so he did.

"I give you a summary. You interrupt, anytime. Then you ask for more information on what interests you. I hope for precision in our talks. Someday we might not have the luxury."

"Okay." Slam said, sitting back.

Dan leaned forward and loaded a little more caviar on his rye crisp. "I'm listening."

"One. There are only six novice assassins left, who trained to kill Rebekah. When she ordered the strike at the library, her men killed their leader, the notorious Ali Zachari. Zachari must have thought up the assassination scheme to make them feel important. Unfortunately, he would have called off the hit, if he realized she was leaving the country and read our press reports. However, he is very dead and they are very stupid. Soon they will join their leader in hell. In addition and regarding you directly, there are always the normal threats the secret service sees every day. Dan, you are the proverbial triple threat:

Catholic, Jew and Black, sprinkle in a little Shoshone, and forget the White. You get threats every micro-second."

"Two. I have the very best assigned to Jay and your daughter. However, she has a price."

Dan interrupted, "You mean the Mongolian?"

"Oh yes. She is the best assassin, spy or actress, I know. Unarmed or armed, she has no peer. We also have two computer assets with them 24/7. The kids call them, Holly and Dick."

"You mentioned a price?"

"It's only a request. However, she works better when she's happy." He studied Dan's face. "She wants to sleep with you, once only, sixteen days from now, from 10:30 PM to 4:30 AM. Then, she'll head back to New York." Dan had a confused look showing both amusement and fear. Little doubt, he was smitten by Margie. Perhaps, he was percolating plans.

Supper interrupted the men. The enticing aroma of crispy Long Island duck surrounded with sautéed veggies, seduced three very hungry men. Appetites always increased when men gathered to talk about sex. They ripped into the crispy quacker. After the servers left, Slam suggested it would be safer if he, the lookalike, took the lovemaking assignment. He had three kids and a lovely wife at home. Dan teased back, praising his patriotism, and then plied some witticisms. First, he mentioned how important it was to keep this particular woman happy, running his finger across his throat, then he uncorked, "the buck starts here."

Carlos assured Dan it would only happen once and she was discreet. She collected memories of great men and wanted no entanglements.

"Three. You need state of the art equipment on this estate." Carlos went on about the particular equipment he wanted.

"Four. The pup you left with Margie had a listening device plucked out by Major Hollister in Edanistan. Nothing was compromised. In fact, they started their disinformation campaign on that mike."

"Five, and last for now, Jay loves your daughter and she is taken with him. I offer you better than 50/50. You might have another son-in-law. I pat myself on the back."

Slam spoke up. "Senator, do you mind?" Dan nodded.

"How do you intend to help us?"

Carlos thought, *ah, the American dilemma. They claim to fuel their democracy on pragmatism. Yet, they have a constitution stating all men are created equal. They need to show the world a consistent face, before winning hearts and minds.*

Carlos said, "I don't have to ask anybody what constitutes self-defense before I pull the trigger. I need full autonomy and as a campaign strategist, you will both have full deniability."

Dan pressed. "Are you intending to break laws?"

Dan, a Harvard educated lawyer/philosopher wanted a debate.

"I will only mimic the secret service rules of engagement." In truth, he intended to dish out to those who did not believe all men were created equal a dose of their plans, lethal if necessary.

The three talked for hours. Dan often worried aloud about his daughter and less so about Carlos's edgy ideas.

Carlos reassured Dan about security and Jay, "I pat myself on the back, again. I knew of their history at Bishop Eustace Prep, but I never imagined they would click like this. They might be the only two people on the planet actually meant for each other, real besherts."

"I like Jay, but my daughter is a pistol."

"My God, once Jay commands all the loose ends, he's a wonder to watch in action. She wants to be useful. He adores her. Together they will make a great team. Do not forget Dick and Holly. Watch them all grow. See for yourself. People like me and Slam can only go so far, but your daughter and Jay will find a way to contribute."

Carlos explained some of the long history of successes and failures at OTTS and finished with, "Slam and I can only catch people who gab, use the internet, phones, conspire, brag or show psychotic signs. The crazy loner with little or no outward signs is very difficult to spot. Of course, there are facial and body signs, but that means he or she will be too close and time might be too short."

"Somewhere out there lurks a nut, we haven't accounted for." Dan summarized.

"Yes, and perhaps your daughter can use her unusual skills to catch him," Carlos added.

"We'll make a great team," Slam said, while pouring himself another shot of Topaz.

* * *

The telephone rang at Mr. Lamar Markowitz's home in the suburbs of St. Louis.

"Am I speaking to Walter Markowitz?"

"Yes. Please call me, Lamar. My middle name. What's up?"

"We can't help your grandfather anymore. You'll have to take him home or put him in a secure facility."

"What did he do now?" His exploits were often hilarious, sometimes sad.

"Don't get me wrong, Mr. Markowitz. Walter can be charming. Just last week, he thought he was Mother Teresa. Scarfed up, he helped the nurses all day long."

"Well, what's so bad, then?"

"Last Friday he called Scott Air Force Base, claimed his name was Adolf looking for Field-Marshal Goring. He wanted our facility bombed."

"A harmless prank."

"This is, in case you forgot, a Jewish senior home. They didn't take kindly to it."

"It was a private call, wasn't it?"

"Not when you put it on the intercom. His imitation of Hitler scared the hell of us."

"Surely, that is not why you people called me."

"The next day he decided to go around and apologize to everybody. They accepted, especially the women. He talked the bridge foursome up to his room. Undressed each one, tied them up, claimed he was Hannibal Lecter and started uncorking a Chianti. They screamed."

"I can be there in thirty-five minutes." He smashed the phone down.

Chapter 15

Training regiment

Bekah awoke from a dream world, to the dreamy world of the man she caressed on the surreal island, Mykonos. She lingered to twiddle his chest hairs. Half asleep, she dared venture south, down the curly trail, across his rippled abs to a protrusion out the top of his boxers. *My God, is he always like this?*

Shocked by the enormity of the situation, she slipped off the satin sheets to the floor, inched forward on the double plush carpet. She remembered from the sounds of doors closing where the hallway closet was. She rescued her confederate, Dick. Jay and she were going to work today fueled by countless kisses, no doubt. Like gas for a Humvee, she'd need to keep her tank full.

She learned about the six misguided and likely unguided assassins in Edanistan, who were busy trying to figure out where she was hiding. After she could walk without her cane or Jay's help, she might melt into the crowd. They'd also put on disguises and go shopping. She packed pajamas from her sister, sneakers, jogging sweats, and a couple Army dress shirts and slacks. She'd burn the bad guys.

She had Dick call Moon to reschedule everything. Maybe, massage lessons could come at the end of the day. Her father called, must have been around 0100 hours his time. She couldn't help herself. Like a proud daughter with a great report card, she showed her heart. In effusive, yes, girly-girl tones, which must have shocked him, she described how much she cared for and appreciated what Jay was doing for and had done to her heart. Well, there were a few other body locations she didn't want to discuss.

Daddy feigned amazement, "Is that you, sweetie, is it really you?" *What's with all these sweeties, pumpkins, honeys, and from a Harvard stuffed shirt?* She assured her dad, she had gone completely mad. She was morphing into a Barbie doll, thanks to the secret formulas of a crazy physicist from NYU.

"How's Jay's mom? Margie, right?"

"She's nice."

Not nice again, and from a Harvard man. "I suppose you two had a nice time."

"She has a nice greenhouse. You'd like it. She has some surprises in store for you, Bekah. I've been sworn to secrecy."

"Soon, Daddy."

"I'll try to be there at Margie's, too."

Before goodbye, she promised to be careful in protecting herself from the assassination threats, and shied away from describing her over-the-top lust for Jay.

Of course, but my dad seems to have the same problem with Margie, although he likely acted upon it. Decisive, just like a president should be.

She'd be decisive if only Jay would relent on this love trumped lust thing. *Come-on, Jay. You're a guy. Act like one. I promise, the way things are going head-over-heels love will arrive.*

Today, she'd fight for her new life, a life desperate for the keeping.

After an unusual and smelly breakfast of fried lamb and scrambled eggs, she tried on the earrings and necklace GPS/echo system. Jay was there to support her and wasn't a bad cook. With Jay, everything was their decision. He didn't want her to feel smothered, and so he would come and go, and for her to speak up if she wanted more or less. She hated possessiveness, in herself or anyone else, and therefore loved his style.

The GPS/echo earrings and necklace required some training. Dick and she used military field code for starters. Field code was quick for real time life-and-death situations, and fit this blind girl's needs. The back of an object was called black: back black, the front: white, left side: red, right: green. Each floor of a building would be Alpha, Bravo, Charlie, etc. Humans and other objects were typically Alpha, Bravo, Charlie for bottom, middle, top. O'clocks were used for surfaces.

Dick supplemented his directions when time permitted with excruciating measurements to the umpteenth decimal coupled with reams of technical descriptions. She could have smacked him, were he not a defenseless pocketbook. "Give me to the inch, use a minimum of words to describe something, unless I ask for more. For instance, there's Jay, forget the six foot –two, etc. Is he standing? Does he desire me?

"Yes, ma'am. His lips are Charlie, 2 feet, 1 inch straight ahead, 1 foot green, slightly up," Dick said. She knew exactly how up Jay's lips were.

"A lot of close interaction is healthy for the both of you," Holly said.

I hear that, girl.

Dick also tried vibrating the directions in her ear. Listening that way would take even more practice, but she learned fast.

The four of them used the plank wood breakfast table as a prop, under the table: Alpha. The surface was Bravo. Above was Charlie. Jay spread items on the table. She found the salt across the table, Bravo, one O'clock. They practiced on more objects. Next, she tried without the GPS/echo earrings and necklace. Jay rearranged the items on the table. "Find the pepper," said Dick. Her progress slowed. She wobbled the sugar bowl and grabbed the salt. Whoops, practice needed.

"Tonight Jay, will you tell me about your theories?"

"I think I can. Keep going, my sweet mango." *Damn, this guy was catching on fast.* She was a sucker for all things from the Philippines. However, she needed answers to her Blindsight abilities or whatever it was she had. Her Blindsight was akin to a trip through a funhouse. Imagination wove its way through reality like a bowl of spaghetti. The half Italian in Jay might help with the recipe.

"Jay, I'm getting hungry. Could you see if Moon is barbecuing yet?" She asked.

After about a half-minute Jay groaned. "Now, that is funny."

"What is it?"

"She's flipping rats on the grill using their tails. I can hear the sizzle, almost smell the delightful aroma." He had to be kidding.

"Want to go commando?" She barked.

"I'll try it, if you do." Bekah wore gray sweats, no underwear anyway. Hated the stuff. Bras were required on base, not here. Burn the fu—freakin' silly things. He had jeans. They found their way down to Moon, who much to their relief was also cooking steaks. It wouldn't surprise her if the alluring smell was yak steak.

* * *

Their Mykonos hideout came with a rubber, walled and floored gym. After lunch, Jay moved out some equipment, so Bekah could train with Moon in martial arts. Initially, it was all about Bekah learning to sense Moon's attacks without the benefit of her GPS/echo earrings and necklace. Bekah was tossed all over. Once in a while, she managed to take down or flip the bottled lightning that was the Mongolian. Although Bekah was improving, Moon was a whirling monster. Jay jumped rope for a while, considered the pool, but just couldn't break away a moment. The motion of two beautiful women held him spellbound.

"I'd like to learn or help," Jay said.

He felt like a crash-test dummy. Two girls almost half his weight tossed him like a Frisbee, all in tune with their snickering and gibes.

"You know nothing, boy," Moon said.

"Take it easy on him, Moon. He's just a man."

"You hold him, I throw him." They took turns. He was in the company of Amazons. He wondered if growing up with sisters was anything like this. Splat, he hit the padded wall. Bam, the other wall, upside down. In spite of aches and pains, he enjoyed what little he learned.

Jay's overactive imagination transported him to Chinatown. He pictured Bekah as the blind swordsman of subtitled movies on Canal Street. She was invincible. She stood at one of the crosswalks of a field of checkered rice patties, with the gold and red Chinese castle in the background. The sun was bright. The girl was blind. Armed swordsmen ran at her, blades whipping air, from four directions. Precise swipes from her glinting sword vanquished all. She rescued the captured prince, Jay naturally.

"Here. Stand, Jay." He did as told, and got his ass kicked once again. They wore sweats and he wore bruises.

"Hey, teach me to flip you," he suggested.

"You not need to, now. Girls protect you." That just made him more frustrated. He grabbed Bekah's wrists, tried to hoist her, after all, she was as light as a feather. Instead, he found himself somehow on the mat again wrapped in a figure four headlock.

He knew a little wrestling, enough to know this headlock wasn't meant for male-female use.

"You hungry, Jay," Moon said.

Holly rang, "Your mother on line one."

"Put her on." He muffled his voice by pressing his face into Bekah's crotch. She squeezed harder.

"What are you doing, son?"

He should have known this would happen. *Not to worry, I'm going to die happy. Is that all right mom?*

Chapter 16

An international tournament

Mykonos, three days later

Bekah lay by the poolside of their safe house after lunch with Jay and Moon. The two wild women converted Jay into a naturalist. No one brought bathing suits anyway. Dick and Holly serenaded switching between Gershwin and Col Porter, while they likely multi-tasked searching for the assassins.

Assassins. Bekah was getting those feelings again. All hell was about to break loose, right here on the island. She needed to understand Blindsight, so she could still serve her country in some way. But Jay moved like the king in chess, one-step at a time. He had already politely dismissed the raven sighting on the day she lost her sight as coincidence. He did say he was very open to exploring Shoshone and South African canine lore and hunter/tracker legends, once he laid a simpler scientific foundation.

She didn't worry that Jay the scientist would allow her exotic multi-racial beauty to color his assessments. She agreed to wait for part two. At this point, raven, wolf or dog and human symbiosis needed to stay off point anyway. That is, once they solved the solvable, they'd address the unknowable as best they could.

"Jay?" He applied another glob of suntan oil to her upper thighs. *He must be thinking of her legs.*

"Your skin is…" Yes, she loved his touch. It drove her crazy, but she interrupted him. "Professor James Boone, will you or will you not, share with me your observations?"

"Well every inch of you, exhibits the divine proportion in nature, from the turn of your ankles…"

"The divine proportion is 1.618 etc. to 1 like my laptop's outer dimensions," Holly said, obviously resisting a few, no endless decimals. Holly made one small step for computer-kind.

"You're a fine looking laptop," Dick said.

Bekah addressed Jay. "No silly boy, on Blindsight." She did want to ask him about her two grapefruits with cherries on top. Her boobs could wait, had been waiting for a long time, for something to do. Apparently, he was blind to her defects anyway.

"I'm sorry I just didn't want to go at your Blindsight explanation half-assed." He applied oil to her right cheek.

"Anything you have will do. We *are* co-directors. So, give it to me." *Oh, I wish he would.*

Holly interrupted, "She really wants to know whether her breasts look like half grapefruits with cherries on top."

Dick added, "Yeah, and she's going to get a boob job back in the States."

"Hey you two. Not *now*. This is serious."

"I can't let that pass. I'll answer both, Bekah," Jay said.

"All right. I'm just trying to get to the bottom of... Oooo." She trailed off intoxicated by his deep hand movements on her lower back and the aroma of the oils.

"First of all, where did you ever get such a silly idea, grapefruits are what you get after a boob job." He ran his fingers up her side until he found her nipples. She rose just a bit, titillated. "A boob job leaves unnatural curves which destroy the perfect lines God gave you. Yours are like two volcanoes erupting in desire. Like Matisse's Tahitians."

"Thank you."

"Second, it was our chess games that gave me my biggest clue about Blindsight."

She had beaten him every night. Well, once he forfeited by falling asleep on move sixty-two.

He gently rubbed her shoulders. "You beat me and yet I'm about half a master-class better. I should beat you at least two games out of three. When blindfolded, everybody's strength drops about a half class except yours, which leaves us fifty-fifty. Since you were a little girl, you read to your dad word for word, and picture for picture with the book closed or upside-down. You've been stealing from your occipital lobes, also known as the visual cortex and other parts of your brain. You see, you give carte blanche to your imagination and deductive reasoning, over what you see. This is why you visualize enemy emplacements and chess positions better than most. On a related subject, blind people increase their other senses by taking unused brain space from the visual cortex. My mom will help me show you the second part of my thesis at her canine research center as I had hinted to you before. Anyway, that's what I meant."

"I had figured that out," Bekah said.

Dick added, "I can read to you, Bekah, when you need research secret and public."

"Thank you, Dicky boy, and thank your mom for me, my dear fiancé."

"You two, crows-eyed, bull-shittels. You both see better after making love. I not watch. I go in pool. You go head. I all right. Go head, do it. Fix eyeballs." Moon jumped into the pool.

"Oh do be a darling Jay and turn me over," Holly said. It was warm. Next, Dick and Holly produced a flurry of whirling sounds.

"Two apprentice assassins are on their way to Mykonos, as early as tonight," Holly said.

Bekah took charge.

"Holly. Holly," Bekah shouted.

"Dick or Holly, thank Major Hollister or whoever it was and get the full report on the assassins. I don't hear Moon swimming. Where is she Jay?"

"She's at the bottom of the pool with fingers in her ears and a closed smile on her face."

"Well, go get her."

"She's testing my loyalty to you." Jay turned shy, perhaps knowing he'd have to handle Moon's naked body.

"We need her. I need her." Jay plopped in the pool and a little later, they came up entwined, if her stinking vision of the two of them were true. She'd like to send Moon to the moon.

"Jay save me," Moon said.

This was not funny.

"Bekah wants you to do something," Jay said.

"Let go me. I oh-kay."

She had to rub it in, but at least verified one more Blindsight victory, that they were touching. "Let go of her, she's okay," Bekah said.

"What you like me to do, Bekah?"

"I need you to trade the plane for a boat with your contacts and then find us." She kept her voice, level and refused to show jealousy.

"I do it."

"Holly, I want you to guard this estate."

"Delighted."

"Any ideas, Jay?"

"Holly and Dick can change and throw their voices, and pick up vibrations from human heads. Perhaps they can speak Greek into our ears while we try to parrot words or just throw their voices while we move our lips."

"Whichever works better."

"Beep." Grumpy Dick made a tiny funny, she guessed that any moment he could revert back to Packman type computing. Nonetheless, this somewhat quieted Bekah's churning soul.

But, the shinola had hit the fan and they all needed to stay alert. Her gut told her she would be better off hiding in plain sight, because any assassin knew their prey hid, if on alert.

* * *

A little later, Bekah said. "We're going shopping."

With those three little words, the Lioness of Edanistan slinked closer to her inner pussycat. As far as Jay was concerned, chunks of sky were falling. Shouldn't she be calling in the marines? Moon's gone, trying to swap the seaplane for a boat. Holly was ready to guard the house, bless her little circuits.

Although the Satellite images deleted the seaplane through filters supplied by the NSA, and worldwide sister agencies, Bekah wasn't taking any chances. The first thing the assassins would do—if they had any sense—would be to check private residences along the coast, that is, places a seaplane would moor.

"What did Moon call this vehicle?" Bekah asked. She grabbed Jay's belt. She was definitely a touchy feely kind of girl.

"A motel scooter," Jay said.

"Okay, take me to a motel, big boy."

"Hop on the back." The main tourist season hadn't started yet so rooms at the Paradise or Super Paradise Beach hotels were just west and down some winding roads.

She slipped behind him on the scooter and cupped his muscular pecs. "Let's roll. So much shopping, so little time. You drive, right?"

He was fiddling with the controls. The scooter lunged forward and stopped. Lunged. Stopped. Lunged. Stalled. *Barf time.* She had that impish grin again.

"Let me drive."

She wasn't kidding. Was she? "Absolutely not. Hell no. I'll figure this out." He didn't relish being driven off a cliff by a blind woman. But, he didn't get much practice driving in New York and never on a scooter.

Bekah psyched him with a stare that seemed real. "What?" she teased. "Are we going to argue? I can do *argue*—after we get to the motel, we can ask for the married couples' section."

"There's no such…" Enthusiasm painted her face, like a kid with a new toy. The sun picked this opportunity to show off the bronze luster to her creamy smooth skin. The sun and she had a thing going on. She loved to live and maybe love, love him. Oh well, he'd take a chance. Somewhere along their journey, he'd have to show a little faith, at least to test the boundaries of her unusual talents.

"Dick, do you think she can do this?" Jay scanned up, which was maybe one hundred feet higher in altitude to the roadside off a driveway slanting the length of the property. Bone-breaking rocks were strewn everywhere on the path up with only a few irrigated shrubs to break a fall.

Dick displayed his inner hautiness. "As long as she doesn't lose her earrings, necklace, or drop me. Dropping me wouldn't be wise. Get cords or something. Loop me around her neck or shoulder using something with a tensile strength of at least 200 pounds."

Jay rummaged through the garage. He came up with a suitcase strap and a heavy plastic bag. He could hang the lightweight notebook, maybe a pound, off her back.

Dick chimed in. "If she goes less than 7.832 kilometers per hour we have a 97.6543217% chance of escaping injury."

They pushed the scooter to the top of the hill, about 300 hundred feet above sea level. Like a sponge, Jay absorbed what might be his last view of mother earth and her seas.

"Can you see the sea, Bekah?"

"I have a feel for the road, but the Aegean is murky."

Don't tell a Greek that. The waters were brilliant azure. "Sail boats dot the sea, a scoop of glimmering afternoon, ah, white slithers lick the sandy beach."

She beamed. "I remember your poems at prep." She waved her hand to suggest middling talent, but then went thumbs up, reinforced by her signature smile.

"Go ahead, I have faith in you." Actually, he remained a sceptic, but he had long since learned that when Bekah set her mind to something, she accomplished it. He wrapped his arms around her slender waist. *Please God, do not crumble this work of art I behold.* Eyes closed, he cherished the moment; his last image would be of her. He'd sacrifice his life to save her. He eyed the handlebars. They were reachable. At least the assassins wouldn't be looking for a blind girl driving a scooter.

He had to be crazy, yeah, crazy in love. "Take it real slow."

Of course, she didn't pay attention to him or the antsy Dick, who barked out diminished success percentages in reverse proportion to her increases in speed. Would she ever listen? Instead of 7.8 whatever kilometers per hour she now pushed 30, all slightly down hill, replete with snaky turns, and gravelly road surrounded by bleached tall grasses and more rocks. He worried about several different types of deaths, all involving angles of body parts colliding with rocks or cliffs. She was laughing like a banshee.

"Where are the brakes on this thing?" Bekah asked in between laughs and while turning her head for him to hear.

He almost said, keep your eyes on the road, but how ludicrous would that have been?

She pulled over and still laughing said, "Did I scare you?"

"You are having way too much fun."

"I really know where the breaks are."

"How do you do this, this inner sight?"

"My vision varies between a sort of google close-up map and actual scenery. I feel like I make half of it up but so far whatever my talent is, it is real enough to get us to our shack."

As in shacking up. He knew his horny life mate all to well. "What color are the window sills on the house we are parked in front of?"

She turned her head, looked behind her and every-which-way one more time. "There's no house, you silly man. Let's roll."

They zoomed forward. He leaned into her lustrous hair and nibbled on her ear. "The brakes are just beyond your grip, like a bike," Jay screamed over the sound of the rushing wind.

She turned her head again. "Yes, yes."

"Braking now, would be a good idea." She sped up.

Dick projected his nervous voice. "If we crash will you promise me you'll put me back together as a briefcase? Maybe an indestructible one? Where a Gorilla can pound it against his cage bars, or stomp on it. It's sad, the gorilla has to be in a cage." *Did he say sad or said, be or pee, oh well.*

"Yep." She shouted. He started reporting distances and odds again.

They were riding a Vino 125 Yamaha, a simple, but substantial machine, if kept in one piece. They reached the main road, which circled the island and then they headed west. This potion of the road consisted of narrow unpainted asphalt with some ruts. Bekah found a few, which led to slap-down ass-smacking, but no wipe-outs, yet. The land remained sparse and, to his relief, more or less flat, now. A country home popped up here and there, well off the road.

Near the bottom of the last hill before the beach hotel came a blind 180 degree turn.

Dick raised his voice. "There's a bus just starting forward up the sharp turn. Tack nine o'clock sharp, now." Bekah and Jay leaned left while she cut the wheel, sweet. They zipped by the front of the bus, and just missed the thin strip of remaining road, the bus allowed, *by that much*. They swerved and slid by some acacias down a six-foot mulchy embankment, over bumpy roots to a stop in front of room 101A. The bus driver stopped honking and screaming at them.

"We're here," she said. Bekah broke out her Cheshire cat smile, which he hadn't seen since high school.

"Bekah." His legs a tad rubbery, he leaned against the acacia they just missed and picked her off the machine like a candy treat. He rubbed his scruffy beard across her neck and face.

"Shhh, use my code name, honey."

"Okay, Attila," he said, "the hon."

* * *

Dick and Bekah had practiced ventriloquism for the desk clerk and other critical situations. Dick would vibrate her ear and larynx with the words. She moved her lips in sync to what she heard and out came perfect Greek from Dick in a female voice sounding like Bekah's, with a southern Athenian accent.

If all this didn't work, at least they were disguised. Jay looked like a mad bomber in died dark brown straggles and scruffy beard. She wore sweats, big round sunglasses, with her famous hair tucked into a pinned down straw hat. She kept one thing military, she went commando, a minor pleasure and habit and not knowable to anybody but she or Jay. And good for him, literally good for him.

The hotel room was just a short walk away from the canopied restaurants off the sandy Paradise Beach with endless thatched cocktail stations and rental loungers. He carried her across the threshold.

It was simple, one double bed, a coffee maker, TV, A/C. A clean shower.

On the bed, he wrapped her up and they collapsed backwards. "Hey," he whispered. "Maybe we should take the bus into town."

In Town

Find Petros, Jay allowed his thoughts to vibrate his larynx, then eardrum, for Dick to pick up and find the famous pelican of Mykonos. They meandered up the maze of alleys. Dress, trinket, jewelry shops—in white buildings with blue window trim—lined the carved stone paths. Long late afternoon shadows and light swirling breezes gave a feeling of exhilaration to their steps. The two assassins could arrive any moment now, although Bekah assured him, the intelligence reports bought them a little more time. Apparently, they'd be wise to slip ashore in the dark, but the two assassins were little more than boys, originally recruited for suicide missions and so they may not act in a logical experienced manner. He remembered his Physics students. They often missed the mark displaying less than logical thinking.

Dick vibrated to Jay. "Try the next restaurant, wind right, then a quick left to a vantage point."

The restaurant had outdoor tables across from its interior seating. The tables backed up to a metal rope about table height leaving plenty of room for tourists, locals and assassins to walk between the restaurant and the outside tables.

"Honey, you hungry?" She was always hungry.

"What do you see, Jay?"

"There are windmills southwest, plenty of churches to get married in." He teased. "There's a cruise ship at the north part of the harbor."

"Good, plenty of tourists to get lost in."

The waiter appeared, Jay ordered. "Souvlake, raisin wine, that is, Commandaria if you have it. Also, sea bass, please, make it two orders of sea bass." They expected Petros to dine with them. As if on cue and never late for a meal, the pelican landed on the ledge, chops ready.

After the food arrived, Jay said, "So, Bekah, are you ready for another of my experiments?" The pelican named Petros, waddled ever closer.

"Try me."

"Let's start with what's around you and Dick can't help."

"Well, besides the three of us, the fish is great. I like it charred."

"Anything else?"

Petros squatted on the trim next to her and stuck his beak over the edge very close to her plate.

"Well, there's this huge alien creature right next to me, with fish on his breath." She stretched her arm and petted Petros's back. The bird didn't flinch, bite or fly away. *Was it her nose that gave the bird away or her super powers, LOL?*

"Go ahead, honey," she said to the bird, while pushing her plate toward the ledge. The bird obliged with an efficient scoop, which cleaned the plate.

"Jay, get our picture."

Jay placed the pink pocketbook at the opposite end of the table. "How do you do this?"

"Holly and I don't see like you do. The photo would be strange, like the movie, *Predator*. Maybe when we visit the NSA and you change me into a briefcase, they'll be able to manipulate the data."

Jay didn't believe Dick was telling the whole truth. After all, he could send the data to the fort, and get it back enhanced, find a printer, etc. Dick must still be pissed about being a pocketbook and decided on truculence. Jay tried to keep his thoughts as abstract as possible as a challenge to the powers of the grump.

"How is Holly? Bekah said.

"I am fine." Out of the pocketbook, came Holly's voice. "There's an eight-legged creature padding across me, but no assassins, as yet."

"Thank you," Bekah said.

"I think we should make love tonight," Jay boiled over.

"Check please." Bekah snickered and broke out her broadest smile.

"You're not done eating."

"Maybe we can doggy style, ah, oh, doggy bag it," Jay said, making a juvenile joke. But she looked like a kid who just knocked off a candy store, so it must have gone over well. "Don't you want to know why I changed my mind?" He worried about the assassins killing them and wanted to complete his union with Bekah before they died.

"Nop. Let's do it, right here if you like." Her lips parted, wantonly.

Dick said, "It took me a while to understand your purposefully jumbled thoughts, Jay. You'll have the picture of Bekah and Petros, later. Next time use your cell phone." Then Dick whirled some expletives, or so it sounded that way.

Jay once again considered the propriety of reading someone's thoughts, and rejected it since the English and symbols were just primitive reflections of what may or may not be going on in the brain. The four of them had a mission at OTTS to harness the paranormal for war and peace. Like any technological advance, the rest of the world would catch up for better or worse. They need only apply their technological advantage in an ethical manner, consistent with the laws of the United States, international law and common sense. Oh well, there wasn't much covering picking off sound vibrations.

By using this technology, someday lie-detector tests would add another dimension of credibility, unless one could get good at thinking in a way to throw off the listener. He vowed to test Dick and Holly further.

At that moment, a man dressed in ponderous robes and Imam headgear turned the corner from the skinny alley north of the restaurant. He would likely walk right by them.

The man stepped within range of Dick's ability to read him, which was about twenty feet. *He's a jewel thief, who just ripped off the Tyronos Jewelry store two blocks lower*, Dick vibrated to both.

Okay, should we? Jay had his first ethical test.

Bekah had no problem. She stood up and stepped in the way of the stranger, and acted as if she had her sight. "You can leave your stolen property on the table and keep on walking or I'll feed you to Petros." Jay rounded the table and jumped beside her. *My woman, my life.*

The stranger pulled a long blade from one of his many pockets and said, "Surely, you do not wish to die."

Jay grabbed his wrist and flipped him flat, knocking the wind out of the thief and leaving him dazed. All that martial arts training paid off and a little bit of luck, perhaps. The knife scraped along the sidewalk harmlessly. The pelican pilfered Jay's meal and the extra order. Bekah kneed the thief on his chest. The owner or manager of the restaurant ran out blowing a whistle. After listening to Dick's vibrations, Jay reached in the correct pocket and pulled out the jewel box with Tyronos embossed on it. Bekah explained the situation to the owner. The police came as well as the owner of Tyronos. Dick vibrated to Jay information to identify the thief as the infamous Jacques Croissant, the never caught Blue Leopard: apparently, a relative of the Pink Panther, from the wrong side of the tracks or rainbow.

Bekah deflected questions using Dick's projected Greek as to their identities. The story went; they worked for Greek intelligence and did not wish to be disturbed. Since the police didn't need extra witnesses and could take full credit for the capture, they took off with Jacques. The owner of the restaurant brought out extra dishes of sea bass and a fine bottle of merlot, complements of the house. He requested the gathering crowd return to their seats to allow the engaged couple their privacy. A nice touch. The owner of the jewelry shop, upon leaving, promised them a special deal and she'd listen to the intercom for them tonight.

"I want to go dancing. If it is our last night on this earth, I'd like to dance with you. I need a dress, shoes, something to match Dicky boy, and his earrings and necklace, and maybe jewelry for our fingers."

A little dress shop had a size 4 thigh hi scooped top silk dress with watercolor drawings of the sea, beach, palms, and fish, which they eventually chose after Bekah put on a very enjoyable fashion show. Shopping and men: he was happy to break a stereotype. Jay talked her into panties, since the silk was alluringly see-thru and the dress was high on her long legs. Strobe lights on a dance floor might cause a riot and he had had enough violence for the night. Cranberry shoes with two-inch heels were the closest match he could find to Dick's pink pearl finish. When she came out of the changing room, he practically died on the spot. She was a gift from God.

At the jewelers, they decided on something modest, matching and simple for now. They bought promise rings made of titanium in a smart criss-cross infinity pattern. The shop owner allowed them to leave their clothes bags and boxes in her shop, since she lived above. No time was too late for them to use the intercom.

Although Bekah was cool in the face of possible assassination, Jay wasn't so experienced. While they descended looking for the nightclub, he kept one eye on her, another on the path behind them, and another on the downward path. He was determined to run out of eyes.

The white cubed homes and businesses marking their descent, splashed in starlight and moon shadows. The lovers wrapped in each other, pulled by the yearning of just one more kiss. At every convenient lean-to, bench, nook or out in the middle of foot traffic, they kissed. The moon shadows offered just another excuse to steal Bekah to his arms. Their passion, groping, stealing a pet, likened to the two teenagers they wanted to be so long before this night. All that was missing was an ice cream sundae.

Jay remained vigilant. Two teenage boys, possibly assassins, had dressed in tee shirts appropriate for the warm night and droopy jeans. They entered through the squatty door to a tavern, false alarm.

The nightclub wasn't far from here.

A boy idled on a bike. He wore a fishing jacket with plenty of room for explosives. The boy stared in their direction, and started pedaling toward them. He whizzed by. Jay's heart skipped. Just one more false alarm.

* * *

The dance club, bar, restaurant Pierro's, was known for its friendly mix of all persuasions: gay, straight, and in-between. The dance floor was tight with people overflowing to the street. The music mixed mostly 70's and 80's pop, disco, reggae, and an old oldie here and there. There floated a heady aroma of sweat and perfumes from the undulating bodies.

They endured multiple elbows, knees, butts, feet. Dick tried to keep up with his alpha, bravo, charlie, red, green, black, white, retreating, advancing, 1, 6, 9 o'clock, 1 inch away, descriptions of body parts and contact points.

"I just can't defend you," Dick said, sounding exasperated and likely to blow a circuit. Bekah didn't want to stop dancing, just to put her beloved pink pocketbook down. Not out of his misery, just out of the way. She felt silly, dancing with the pocketbook strapped to her wrist. She loved dancing with Jay, but didn't appreciate looking like a dork.

If they survived the idiot assassins, they could land pity spots on *Dancing With The Stars*. Although he wasn't half bad. The latest Intelligence reports claimed the idiots were training with revolvers. Apparently, they graduated from blowing themselves up, otherwise she would never allow herself to dance in close proximity to all these innocents.

The innocents were no innocents. Some of them were drunk or getting there, others didn't at all mind bumping and grinding the wrong person, which she supposed, for them was the right person. She only wanted Jay. She was falling in love. She had a suspicion. It was all the little things he did, like flipping the Blue Panther into submission. The problem: he was a novice at the martial arts. She would never forgive herself if anything happened to her man. The salsa changed to reggae.

"Let's sit this one out hon," she said. They found a table and ordered drinks.

"Dick is driving me nuts. Do you mind, Dicky boy, if we cover you with Jay's jacket here on the table? We'll dance right next to the table." He could still vibrate commands as long as they stayed in range, which was up to twenty feet. Fewer than ten was much better for accuracy, and with all this noise, five feet would be wise. Bekah talked him into being quiet. They danced. Of course, it wasn't long before all hell broke loose.

117

Dick shouted once. "Help, some teenage girls just nabbed me." Then he went vibrate mode. *She's running out the door, with two girlfriends.* His signal disappeared. *Beyond range. Damn it. Government property.* What was she thinking?

"I'm on it, stay here. You're safe here for little while." Jay said until he ventured beyond Bekah's range. She was left alone, but it was a wise decision. *How long would a little while be?*

"Stop squeezing my ass." Bekah was having a hard time keeping the crowd off her without resorting to a little violence and a harder time trying to use her Blindsight to identify the culprit or culprits in the human soup or help guide her off the floor.

The music broke for a moment. The crowd thinned, she hesitated, which way to walk without stumbling or smacking into somebody. One wrong move and she could get pregnant.

The next song was a throwback, *Once I Had a Secret Love*, by Doris Day. At least the crowd's frenzy—by the hot application of the previous salsa and everybody's overly sweaty bodies—would cool down the maddening crowd. The ass squeezing did stop. She wondered about her little man and Jay, and then realized she stood in the middle of the dance floor, not moving. Where she came from, that was an invitation to anyone for a dance.

"Let's dance," A deep voice beckoned. She had to accept. Where was she going to go without her Dick? The bumping started again. Where was her Sir Lancelot?

"You have a great ass."

"Thanks." They embraced.

"My Name is Electra, what's yours." Bekah blew it. She had never been confused about a person's sex. She had plenty of LGBT practice in the military. Where had her radar gone? Her dance partner had forced deep voice, and she was not picking up clues. She needed her head examined before she made a fatal mistake with assassins in pursuit.

"Carmen." Oh shit, couldn't she think up a better name than Carmen? Electra held her tight.

Just don't pinch or squeeze or poke my ass and you might live.

Electra was in flats and came even to her in heels, but nobody except Moon could handle what she could dish out. Electra dropped her head on her shoulder and kissed her neck.

"I'm waiting for my boyfriend," Bekah said.

"Why'd you dance with me, honey pot?"

Where's Jay's string of endearments when you need them? "I was just trying to be polite."

"You taste so good, I want you right here or…or we'll wait for your boyfriend. I don't mind if he watches." Oh, she's so nervous.

"No, sorry."

Electra squeezed her ass.

"That's it. No fuckin' way."

Bekah pushed her back and then threw a punch in the general direction of her nose. She connected, as makeup slipped and split the fingers of her fist. A good thing too, or the girl's nose would have broken.

"You bitch." Electra body tackled her. The crowd kept them from falling.

Another girl jumped in grabbing Bekah's right arm. Pretty soon, she felt like a ziti in a bowl of flailing men and women. The female bartender, she heard her coarse voice earlier, picked Bekah off the floor. Bekah's hat was missing, along with the sunglasses.

"Who started this?"

Bekah dropped her head as if she had a headache so no one would identify her. "Electra squeezed my ass." Everybody started laughing.

The bartender said, "Electra. Did you?"

"Yeah."

"She wants to be treated like a lady. You two kiss and make up."

Her hair came trundling down. She immediately went to her knees and dropped her head, which people interpreted as pain. They wanted to help. The more she protested, 'oh I'm just catching my breath,' the more they expressed concern. Even Electra bent down and offered her hand.

Somebody in the crowd must have gotten a sideways look at her. "Aren't you that person?"

"I'm Carmen," Bekah said.

"Another person said, "You're the Lioness of Edanistan." Found out. People cleared away from the famous warrior.

The female bartender came over again, kneeled and pulled up Bekah's chin. "Here's your sunglasses."

Bekah wondered just how bad she looked in a fit of vanity. She dared not open her blackened eyes. The people might think she was a zombie. The bartender slipped the glasses on.

"Give the lady room. She's blind." The crowd gasped. The bartender touched the tip of her nose like her mom used to do.

Jay had squeezed out the door and focused. There were three of them, not two, not a couple. So they were likely tourists and possibly from the cruise ship. His best bet was to assume they'd wind down the paths rather than up, heading for the ship.

"Dick, Dick."

"I've got one." An overly amorous and drunk guy with the looks of an NFL linebacker said.

"No, I'm calling for my friend, Dick."

My fureend too." He whipped it out.

"Put that away, you schmuck. Did you see three teenaged girls run by?"

The guy just turned away, zipped up and mumbled, "Fuckin' steroids." Turning back toward his tormentor he said, "Chasing teenagerers. I shou bea your ass."

Jay blew past the guy. At the bottom of the hill some ten blocks from Pierra's, he spotted three teenage girls huddled together on a bench facing the harbor.

He rounded the bench, noticing the girl, between the other two holding the pocketbook. The girl seemed maybe fifteen, with the freckled face of an angel, big round eyes, not a likely thief.

"Here, take it mister. It's horrible, just horrible. Tell the lady I'm sorry. I need her to forgive me. Have to. Have to."

"What's wrong, dear?"

"Take it. You're Dimitri, right?"

"Yep, that's me. I'll return it. Is there anything I can do to stop you from crying?" Jay felt fatherly.

"All I wanted was a nice pocketbook. My mom and dad promised, my almost boyfriend promised. I'll kill him. You see, they wouldn't let my boyfriend buy me one. It's no excuse. I'll be all right. Just take that thing away from me, please."

"Don't worry, the lady who owns it, already forgave you. God bless."

They parted. Jay started back up the hill and when out of range of the girls said, "What did you do to that girl?"

"Oh, I vibrated her at first. She thought they were her thoughts. She started thinking she would end up like Dorian Gray, which she read. Every moment she held stolen goods, she would start turning fat and ugly, her hair would fall out, she'd never have children, on and on. Then, when I found a loudspeaker to use, I told her to stop in her tracks and to give up the stolen goods to you, Dimitri, no questions would be asked and she wouldn't go to jail."

Jay ran through Pierro's entrance to see Bekah, hair down, no hat, being helped to her table by the bartender and a tall skinny woman dressed in gothic attire. Miss Skinny with Geisha white face had a smudge on her nose that made her look like a clown.

Something had happened. He ran over to and consoled Bekah with a protective hug. His intuition and powers of observation told him many things. The crowd near her looked like a basket of laundry. The tall woman, and some other men and women, plus Bekah had been fighting. His jacket was still on the table as well as the drinks. He decided it best for them to finish their drinks for the sake of decorum and the curious crowd.

"I'm sorry, I misunderstood the Colonel's body language," said Miss Skinny. "Is there anything I can do?"

Bekah spoke up, "No, I'm sorry too. I'm trying to give up violence. You're not hurt, are you?"

"I think you could you use a little help with makeup, Colonel."

They decided to go to the girls' room together.

"The newspapers say you're gay." Carmen applied some violet eye shadow to Bekah.

"Old ones. I'm not. Just a tomboy and Jay, he's in disguise."

"He's still cute, if you like lumberjacks and maple syrup. I'm bi. I'm not coming on to you, anymore."

"No offense taken."

"Your hair is perfect. How do you keep it?" Carmen engrossed herself in brushing Bekah out.

"I shampoo every day if I can. In the Army, it was my only time to kick back."

"How 'bout pink lipstick?"

"My mom told me I was perfect without makeup."

"You are. Some girls need it. But, this makeup needs you. It's just for fun. It comes off easy in just thirty kisses."

"It'll last a minute around him."

"Hot. Oh God." Electra stroked Bekah's cheek, obviously suffering from lust.

"Tell me something, how do you make love, when it's a man?"

After a small pause Electra said, "Everything has to seem to be his idea. Say to him, do you like this, like that, then get what you want."

"Oh, I want everything."

* * *

Bekah came back with her sunglasses off and head high showing off eye shadow and lipstick. *Maybe we'll make a baby, tonight, now that I'm irresistible.*

Reality through the only hard punch of the night. She realized they needed to leave if she were to keep safe and the cruise ship just might prove their ticket out of here.

"We need to get off this island, pronto," Bekah said. Jay kissed.

* * *

"Tonight? Oh, yeah, tonight. I get it."

This intimate crowd, who had just wrestled with Bekah were watching them as if it were the first time they saw someone kiss. *Go back to your orgy.* Her new friend, Electra, gave him an eyeful of desire. Bekah claimed she now liked the idea of lipstick, "just for fun." She had changed again. First, a no man's woman. Then, needing someone to help her. Then wanting sex. Perhaps, now wanting love.

Should he give in and take her before her heart was 100% his? One thing was certain, they needed to leave, pronto. To, at the very least, stay one step ahead of their pursuers.

Chapter 17

Executing your plan

Jay and Bekah left Holly, the bike and some incidentals for Moon to retrieve. They approached the cruise ship's provisioning tender for a ride. Bekah temporarily cleared her head by taking in the sea breeze. The pain was intermittent but lessening.

She had no choice but to trick Jay to save his life. He was a civilian with no skill in fending off assassins. She was Army trained. She had to leave him on the ship so she could stay behind and eliminate the threat to their lives.

Jay thought they were leaving Mykonos after Bekah made an arrangement with the cruise ship's Captain Orinson. Jay and Bekah were now heroes for arresting the Blue Leopard and alerting the cruise ship to look for stolen jewels in his stateroom. In appreciation for the lute's recovery, they would get the thief's cabin, and all they had to do in return was give chess lessons, or so Jay was led to believe. Bekah and the Captain had a deal. What Jay didn't know was that after they settled in their cabin, she'd sneak off the boat before it disembarked.

Now on the gangway, she shook as if it were a plank on a pirate ship. Her steps slowed to steady herself. Jay took that as a sign to hold her. She never felt more loved.

She was falling in love, which only made this harder. Especially not tonight. It was the anniversary of her mom's death, but her mom would have wanted her to make love to her future husband. Jay had said, he wouldn't make love to her until she matched his heart. Bekah still wasn't sure she wanted any man. For the first time earlier today, with Petros the pelican as witness, he had promised to make love to her at their first opportunity. She knew he said that because it might be one of their last days on Earth. Just because they were on a cruise ship only delayed the assassination attempts, so he'd likely stick to his promise. *A pleasant and overwhelming thought.*

Maybe for me, darling. Promise me, if I die, you'll marry. Try to love her. Never forget me.

Now in the cabin room, they tossed their things. "Let's shower," he said.

"A little later." In truth, she had very little time to get off the ship before it slipped into the night, destined for Santorini.

"I have got to get that makeup off your eyes, before you get an infection."

This was true. Her doctor had said the same.

She needed to send him out of the room so she could sneak away. "How about that ice cream sundae first? You know, the one we should have had when we were kids?"

"It's 1 AM, but I'll call."

"They're closed," Dick said. The little computer being was entirely too helpful.

Jay kissed her neck. "You've changed your mind, haven't you? You wanted to jump me at the restaurant, some ten hours ago."

"Yeah." She started crying.

He took her into his arms. "I know. I know."

"No, you don't know."

"What does it matter? We might be murdered."

"No, we won't. We've got the U.S. Army, Moon, and two crazy computers to protect us. It's just that I realized you were right. Let's wait until I'm fully in love with you."

"It's best, but we might never…"

She put her finger on his lips. "No negatives."

He scooped her up and took her into the tiny bathroom. "I promise, no shenanigans. But you have to get that damn makeup off and I need to check for cuts and bruises."

She didn't object. How could she? He stripped her as if starved. Kissing her everywhere. Especially a spot she and her hand knew too well. "Oh, God. Oh, God." But she did not have time for anything more. She had to hold off going all the way to save his life and respect his wish. Right?

"Come a little north, Jay." She smothered him with kisses. "I've never felt so good."

"I love doing that." After some passionate kissing, he said, "now about that makeup." He dabbed here and there and soon they were out of the shower and toweling off. An experience she'd recommend to any girl, anytime.

After they got into their bathrobes, she said, "Would you do me a favor, darling?"

"Always."

"I'm going to take a short walk to get rid of another headache. Would you shave off your beard? We don't need that disguise anymore. According to my intelligence report, your cover has already been blown. Hair color next time or we'll make you shorter."

He laughed. "No, wait for me. I don't want you walking alone, near the railings."

How was she going to get out of this place?

"Remember the Cooper River submarine races?"

Now he starts to reminisce. No time, Jay

"How I would meet you for our game. Remember that witch in the library?" He nibbled on her ear. *Ear nibbling, Jay? I'm trying to sneak out. Soon, I'll have to jump off this boat and swim ashore.*

"*You*, talked as loud as you wanted, wore that skimpy, lacrosse outfit, which gave me my first erection at school. So embarrassing."

"Jay."

"The librarian never complained, never shushed you. A good thing she didn't look under the table."

How much time do I have, Dick?

6:33 minutes to leave the stateroom and 57 seconds to get on the last tender to shore.

She could do it and—expecting her—they'd probably wait a little.

Don't take that chance.

"So you liked my outfit?" She squeezed with a yearning so strong she could forget everything.

"Abso-indubitably." He cupped her behind.

"Jay, you promised."

"What a lousy player I was in high school. You'd twirl your supple body, turn your head, flash that metallic cat smile. Stole my soul, girl. Time to give it back or share."

"I've got to get some ice. You're making me so hot." She fanned herself and smiled.

"You were a princess to me."

"I'll be right back."

"You got away with murder. I still can't figure out how you snuck by Father Angelo's ever watchful eye, half-naked."

"A 98% average helped. Let's talk later."

While she dressed, he started to shave. "I'm going now."

"Okay."

With that, she slipped out of his life. She dropped tears along her path as she ran slowly down hopefully real halls as she "saw" them. If she died by assassin or wall, would God let her see Jay one more time? Let her guide him?

She walked down the gangway into a gathering fog.

Chapter 18

Round 1

At first, Jay thought Bekah went on an ice cream sundae hunt. Dick even helped. Jay woke up the captain and cajoled his way into a middle-of-the-night raid of the galley. An unhappy bleary-eyed chief chef could just as well been carrying a meat cleaver. Jay pictured his head served in two equal pieces. He arrived back at the suite, pushing a cart with two creative banana splits including mango slices, rich dark chocolate sauce, walnuts, and various other fruits, and an extra bowl of whip cream. Just hoping she returned.

On entering, he rolled the cart over a white envelope, which had the Captain's insignia embossed on the cover. Frantic for her sake. He opened it:

Dearest James,

Please don't blame Dick. He was under government orders.

I am falling crazy in love with you. Because of that and our common humanity, I can't risk your life. I realized the two idiots chasing me would eventually find out we were on the ship and then just leave the island for our next port or New York. I want to get on with our life. You are getting better at the martial arts, but a chop can't stop a bullet, anyway. Let me be your knight in shining armor, with better hair than Ivanhoe.

The Captain—please don't blame him either—informs me not even the Olympic Swimming Champ, let alone a collegiate butterfly champ, such as you, could swim the miles he's put between us. He's navigating rip currents and volcanic shoals. If you love me and want a chance to be my husband, father our children and make love to me, I guess making love and having children, never mind, don't come after me. I want you to use that logic you are famous for, Doctor Boone.

With all my love and the hottest of lips,

Thank you for loving this mess of a woman.

p.s. I had to take Dick with me. Funny name. I can't take *it* with me, right? Please supply later, LOL. Please use your cell until Holly and you are reunited, but don't call me until morning. I've got a hunch I can rap these two shooters up now (with help). More unexplained phenomena, Professor?

p.s. I want to meet you at your mom's place in a week. We should use this time to resolve some issues. Are you sure you want me for the rest of your life? Ask yourself one last time, why us. We'll talk about it. I'm concerned about being a wife, a mom, and I very much understand, co-director for OTTS. I get it. We are likely soul mates, but not until the skinny lady punches out her demons. Then we can have hot dirty sex in your mom's greenhouse, unless it's occupied by your mom and my dad.

RC

Jay golfed down his sundae, stumbled out onto the balcony and flung the organic contents of the other banana split overboard.

"Don't forget your dessert." He mocked, angry, lonely and confused, but mostly just in love. Her mistake was not trusting him. However, he didn't know if he would have stood for letting her leave and whether he could have stopped her. Even though stronger, and nearly twice her weight, he imagined himself tied up like a pretzel, and put on the bed next to the towel elephant the cabin attendant left. Anybody smart enough to beat him in chess had to be thinking straight. He too, would have to reconsider taking on a life partner, a partner who had a set of balls larger than his own.

Jay composed an email to Bekah half pissed, half in awe.

Dearest Bekah,

You ask why I love you. Yes, I was crazy about you at prep and I never fully understood why, besides your great looks, smarts, humor. Now, you wear your feelings. You know what you want. I am so flattered and lucky that it is me. I will never let you down. Every moment, I live for you.

With all my love,

Jay

p.s. I'm still mad at you. You may deserve a spanking.

* * *

My baby is off for Santorini, damn it.

Bekah said goodbye to the tender's crew. The dock smelled like dead fish.

She ached for Jay and prayed he'd understand but the smell of victory egged her on.

Then Dick read Jay's letter, which gave Bekah renewed resolve and a wicked grin to her step.

"Get me a cab." she said to Dick. While they waited, she pictured the small dock, the one-and-half lane wide, windy road leading to town. She imagined the moon teasing the wispy waters, the lights twinkling in the town at a distance. Or did she "see" it. The doctor had told her as soon as the swelling of her brain went down, she would sense the 24-hour light/dark cycle through the retinohypothalamic tract, which was near but separate from her damaged optic nerves. The rest of what she "saw" was just imagination or dreams, or so he speculated. He theorized that the vividness of her imagination would be reduced due to the lack of energy light would have contributed through now damaged optic nerves. The good news: she visualized most of the time, as if it were real and vivid, if anything she "saw" too much in a kind of fantasy arcade world. The line between real and imagined was beyond her at the moment. Enter Jay. And thank God Dick fit in so nicely, with his GPS/echo interpretations.

"Come up with a different voice for the GPS/echo system," she said to Dick.

"How's a common automobile voice?"

"Make him British, but concise. I love the accent."

"Consider it done, madam."

"Concise pleasssse."

"Done," he said.

Right now, she had two assassins to kill and her Blindsight and/or hunches would take her right to them. She didn't have much fear of being identified. The sun cooked her over the past few days about ten shades darker, so said her Jay, who liked burnt toast. Also, she looked to the world to be sighted; her hat and glasses firmly in place, her gait with authority. Out of the cab, she walked the last three blocks to the home of the shop owner who drove them to the ship. She felt the back of her dress rip just a tiny bit while plastering herself up against the shop owner's back wall. *Such a pretty dress.* She laughed to herself, *you girly girl.*

Are they inside? She vibrated to Dick.

They're arguing in Arabic, whether they should kill the shop owner or not.

Do something. Make them think that's a bad idea.

I'm a little beyond ideal range. I'll try.

Try.

A little while later the two young men exited the front, still arguing.

How did you trick them?

No trick. I just helped them think more clearly. Killing her might jeopardize their real mission, of killing you.

Gee thanks, Dicky boy.

Dick added, *They apologized to the shop owner, said they would never ask another favor, and never return, unless it was to buy jewelry. Interesting, they got in her house by claiming to work with you, and by the way, they just missed us at the club.*

Where are they headed?

They don't know how to steal onto the ship, which is out of sight now. They're going back to their room to regroup.

Great, when we get close to their room, download their computers and—any time you can—their cell phones. Then send the info via channel secret to the NSA. Copy Bud, Hollister and Army intelligence, central command. The night air chilled her, but she was used to deprivation, being a balls out kind of girl. She got like this when confronted with possible battle. Her veins turned cold, while she focused with the intensity on just how the next hour would play out. She was so alive.

Would she need to kill her tormentors? One blind girl and a pink pocketbook versus two strong, but skinny teenage idiots with pistols, seemed a fair fight. The benefit of finding a way to keep them alive led her to reject assassinating the assassins. If they remained alive, then when found, she might be able, with Dick's help, to infiltrate their network and identify enemy combatants, which would help the Army in Edanistan and the FBI in Manhattan.

Raise Moon and Holly one more time. Let them track us, wherever they are. Provided they're safe, she vibrated to Dick.

Will do, General.

God, it was great to hear that. Okay, troop, let's haul ass.

Gee thanks. He mimicked her, but genuinely seemed tickled to be considered a 'troop.' He definitely had the ability to wear many hats at once.

A little while later, Bekah mis-stepped before he could alert her. Okay, Blindsight and GPS/echo systems weren't perfect. She stepped on an upside down trashcan lid. It popped up, banged and cut her shin. She lost balance, rolled and tumbled with the trashcan and a sideways lid causing a lot of noise and a mess. The sounds of garbage splatting stone was delightful.

At least no raven taunted her. Only a disgruntled seagull protested. The smell of lamb made her stomach growl when it should have turned. She was too used to going commando. Thank God she decided to wear panties, because she was about to be captured, or shot.

Dick vibrated, *They've drawn their weapons and are running right at us. Play drunk, pull back your jaw, pout your lips. It's your only chance. Be ready for language tricks.*

How do you pout pouty lips? Nevermind. I'm ready and focused. She started picking up bits of trash and garbage, and tossed them in the can. She then tensed and squeezed her calf allowing blood to trickle out and down her leg. *Damsel in distress, you're up. Ice water veins.*

They're putting their guns away. One, named Ali, is practicing English in his head, the other is named Hakim.

"Is a leg, all right, woman?" Ali asked. Hakim was helping pick up the trash.

"No speak Engliease." She poked her breast, "speak Zwahili." Actually, it was Xhosa from the eastern African coast, north of the Cape, but she didn't want to get too close to her true African roots. She had a sixth sense about death. She foresaw none, but she wasn't omnipotent.

The boys spoke to each other in Edanistani-Arabic. "She's cut her shin. We can't get the witch tonight. But, who would blame us, if we help the least of Allah's children with her wound? So, ah, maybe, we can have sex with a real woman."

What was an unreal or surreal woman? Bekah mused, amused with their naivety and idiotic sexism.

"It is a sin against Allah, to take what isn't yours," said Hakim. She kept a slack-jawed, albeit contorted face, with a not so stiff upper lip.

"Not take, we'll ask. Look at her, no virgin, dressed like that. She has had many men."

I'll have you know, this was a fine dress, she wanted to say. She wondered if she looked worn out by all the men she was supposed to have. The trashcan full again and secured, they picked her up and walked up a slag-stoned path. She wiped her sticky hands on the dress. Oops.

"You speak German? French?" Ali asked, little doubt wiping his own hands on pants and finding nothing strange about her doing the same. Where were their mothers?

"Parley vous Francais, messieurs?"

"Oui." They finally introduced themselves, by first names only; the rest is secret, except they've been Dick-ed.

Like lost souls joining the lonely-hearts club, they all spoke broken French, non-stop. They would clean her knee when they got to their room. She claimed to be a bit drunk and acted impaired. Claimed she was Moslem. Asked for their prayers, to help her stop drinking and get back to her faith. They admitted having different problems, which they teased her about. They wouldn't specify, but she knew enough by now. Both were virgins, except for some older men in Afghanistan who abused them. They didn't dare tell her about the men. Dick did. The only other vices they had were lack of wisdom and wanting to kill her, which went together, in her book.

In their room, they lead her in the nearest chair. So far, her cap was on tight, sunglasses still in place. She tried to keep track of their weapons, which they stuffed in a drawer she could get to if needed. But, what kind of a shot, would she be?

"Why do you wear sunglasses in the middle of the night?" Hakim said in an offhand way.

"Alcohol has made my eyes sensitive to light. Never drink, boys." Later after some administering to her wound by the very curious and attentive Ali, who was all hands, and more small talk, she tried a little politics. "The Americans are going to leave Edanistan."

"If you believe that cows can fly. They still stand behind the Jews."

"The Jews are children of the book. Too bad, we can't all live in peace."

"There is honor in death and Paradise for the warrior."

"There is honor and Paradise for the peacemaker." She patted the head of Ali and smiled a small, non-signature give-away type smile, all the while trying to keep her lower jaw back. *How ugly I must look, yet Ali seemed to enjoy my features, especially the wounded leg. Was he looking up my dress? Well, these two would enjoy a goat.*

"I got an email the other day picturing twelve angry nuns carrying rifles waiting for suiciders. It said Allah has the last laugh." They laughed. "You boys, aren't you good at something?" Ali said he wanted to be an engineer when his family was blown to pieces by an American bomb. Hakim, who Bekah now knew through Dick was gay and in subconscious denial, just wanted to die, preferably killing her first.

"Why were you walking the streets?" Hakim asked once again in a neutral tone.

Bekah feigned offense. "I am no prostitute. I have a problem. I will tell you, my brothers. Mykonos allows people to be themselves. I am so sorry, but no matter how hard

I try, I can't stop thinking about women. I came from a dance club. I danced with many women."

"This is a hellish scourge," Hakim said.

"I have asked Allah to forgive me, to cure me. I have prayed here, on the nude beach named Paradise, for his love." Planting the seed. Something the boys might like to do in one orifice or another. In any case, she needed to get them out of their rooms, give time for help to arrive, either from the CIA and/or Army intelligence, so their computers and cell phones could be altered and copied.

Ali said, "Allah loves you, sister. Open your heart. Let us pray." Ali's voice gave away his disappointment, no pussy tonight. They prayed.

Allah be praised.
Look down upon us, this day, this hour.
Regardless of what has gone before,
Or what will come after,
Give us the wisdom to consecrate this time entirely to You.
All the actions of our body and soul.
May all the thoughts that come to us be true.
May all the things to which our hearts go out
Be beautiful, with the beauty of Allah.
May all the things we want be good.
Give us the light to see Your Will,
The wisdom to love it
and the courage and strength to do it.

"I can tell looking at you, Ali, that you have no experience with women. No, no, don't deny it. Women know these things. I may look like a dance girl, but I just wanted to fit in. I even went nude on the beach called Paradise. So many pretty women and handsome men do this. I say, Allah brought us into this life without clothes. So I don't see any sin." The boys seemed confused.

She had a plan and continued to monopolize the talking. "It is wrong of me to take my clothes off now, because it would tempt you." *Nothing like raw sex as a hook.* "But tomorrow on the beach maybe we can all meet at noon and the three of us can join the rest of Allah's children and seek the truth about ourselves without shame. How will you ever know if you don't try? Maybe I could try a man, like you, Ali or Hakim. Maybe, I will be cured by you boys. You are both so handsome."

"Maybe." Ali said, probably building up the courage to ask for a little lesson right now.

Hakim interrupted his hemming around. "It is not modest. It is three in the morning. Sister, can you be on your way? We have some business to take care of, before we sleep. Maybe, we will see you tomorrow. I promised my mom and dad an email last night. You understand."

She need not tempt fate and Dick had retrieved some useful information from the boys' electronics. "I understand. Go in peace, my brothers. Allah be praised."

"Please. Your name, sister."

"My name is Precious." Indeed, she was. On the way out, she glanced back and said, "Please pray for my, no our struggles."

Dick vibrated her ear and larynx. *Hakim, thought you should be stoned and Ali went to the bathroom with a protrusion overwhelmed by your beauty and getting naked suggestions. He is masterbating.*

Outside and safe by about one hundred meters, Bekah felt a living hot presence lurking in the gathering mist.

"They die now," whispered Moon.

Chapter 19

Round 2

"We are going to offer the boys a chance to live." Bekah chided Moon.

The two motor-scootered off, into the dense 0400 mist. Back at the safe house and exhausted, Bekah collapsed into a cushy sofa, while Moon scared up some coffee. Holly played bagpipes, which would keep a hibernating bear awake.

Bekah filled Moon in on the complete plan. Moon was to act as a decoy honeypot on Paradise beach, so that a soon to arrive spook team, could black bag the kids' room. Moon had concealed Dick in the shrubs up against the boys' hotel room to keep real time info flowing to Holly, the NSA and AI, Army Intelligence.

"We need to find out where in New York the other three boys are and what they're planning. With a little bit of luck we might crack their networks and uncover some moles. I'm leaning towards recruiting them."

"Smart plan. I shoot them tomorrow."

"No, you're going to get naked and convince Ali to give up his ill-conceived plan and join his government who's fighting the remnants of Zachari's Army. Hakim likes men, but you can try."

"How old, Ali?" Moon asked.

"Eighteen." Holly said.

"Good, show me picture." Holly displayed some pictures.

"Good looking boy. I teach him, then he die."

"*Moon.*" Bekah felt the Mongolian was kidding, but probably just wanted to protect her. After all, Moon's mission was simpler, eliminate threats to Senator Carthage's daughter.

"Okay, I joke, but somebody got to die."

A sound like large fluttering birds waffled through the open windows. The expected team of six was landing.

Holly said, "Major Hollister and his team are here."

Bekah grabbed the white cane her men gave and opened the door. Hollister and his team moved in like cats. He picked her up into a bear hug, right in front of everybody, carried her back to the living room sofas, and put her down, without protest or so much as a scratch from the Lioness. Bekah was used to the Major's teasing, but he had never touched her before, minus one peck on the cheek in the hospital.

They were great drinking buddies and best friends in Edanistan. Her curiosity about his overly emotional state, took hold of her tongue. As usual, she'd let her men speak first. First, they discussed business and then the major asked everybody to clear out, except retired General Rebekah Carthage. The truth cometh. The major had no idea the notebook computer on the coffee table gave Bekah a tremendous advantage. But, Holly wasn't vibrating to her any gossip. Reading eardrum vibrations was just that, gossip. What went on in the brain was far more complex. Bekah guessed something wonderful was about to be said. *Spill the beans, already.*

"Major? It's your dime."

"Sorry Bekah. This is my last chance, I figure. I know you all aren't really gettin' hitched. It's just a dog and pony show." Whenever they were alone, the King's English, from a very well educated man, was thrown out the front door.

He's going to propose, maybe. What a tickle, after all these years.

"Major…"

"Let me finish. I got to get it out."

"Okay."

"I want to throw my cap in the ring with a ring. You're retired now, so there's no fraternization bullpucky, no more. I know how you feel about that. I know you love me. Golly, I'm off the farm and in the swamp over you."

"What?"

"I love you. I mean I'd like to court you. See if our love would grow." *That makes three men, Jay, O'Reilly and now this sweetheart, who want to marry me. All a girl has to do is poke her eyes out.*

"Major. No Frank, my dearest Frank. You are the best friend I've ever had in my life, but I want you to know the whole story. Professor James Boone is really my high school soul mate. All these years, I thought I was avoiding great guys like you, when I was really waiting for my James."

"I thought you stayed away from me, because you were afraid the brass wouldn't take you seriously. That someday I'd take you home to meet my family, after you got to where you wanted to be in the Army."

"It's not the rank, it's the double standard. I had to protect my reputation, too. I admire you, being a conservative southern gentleman, and you have been my biggest supporter and much appreciated pain in the ass."

"I tried."

"A piece of my soul was missing, and I didn't know it." Otherwise, she would have jumped Hollister's bones years ago, and killed him if he said anything. "Jay and I really love each other. No not just love, I believe we are meant for each other."

"You've never said a thing. Well you hinted at it once, but I thought you were kidding." He seemed crest fallen, but as a great friend he seemed to recover his cool, if you can call his Louisiana backwoodsyness anything but adorable hick.

"Frank, a guy like you, you're a great guy. You'll have no trouble." She reached out to hug him and give back the ring he had plopped in her hand.

"You don't haf' to be sayin' this." He was blubbering now, while burrowing his head on her thick locks rapped over her shoulder. *Just don't blow your nose.*

"Do you like the black, white, Filipina, or Shoshone in me?"

"You're not a fruit salad to me."

"Be honest, I mean I have no boobs."

"Honey, you are perfect, but if I had to pick anything. Well I get dizzy looking at your eyes, even now."

"My eyes are more Asian and Shoshone, except for the bright violet."

"Yeah, the violet is crazy like a dream-catcher."

"Thanks, doll. You might check out the Filipina nurses, they're beautiful girls with soulful eyes. They liked O'Reilly."

"The cook?"

"Thanks, for getting him out of combat for me. I don't mean to compare you by age or station. It's his looks. You look something like him, only hotter, more mature. Square-jawed, great bod, smooth shavin', charming. You won't have any trouble with fraternization rules, they're mostly lieutenants and my sixth sense tells me they want your attention. When have I ever been wrong?"

"Well, you didn't die, thank God." She had thought she might die the day of the explosion, especially with a raven warning, and had confided to the major via body language and some imprecise words her fears but she wasn't certain. She remained hopeful right up to lights out.

"All you need to do is ask one of the nurses to take your temperature."

"Okay, Bekah. We'll always have our friendship and I'm a realist. I might just go get one of those very attractive nurses, someday. But answer this, will ya? What's a soul mate?"

"Without getting into the mystical, Jay and I were meant for each other since time began stuff. Well, let me think." She hesitated, because she didn't want to explain the odd fact that Jay, the hard-nosed scientist, believed more in soul mates than she did, a woman full of superstitions, Blindsight and God knows what else might happen next. "Jay and I share a passion for chess and each other. We're both Catholic. We love many of the same things. He complements me, you know. He's more logical, and I'm more intuitive. He has some answers about my Blindsight and promises me more. He butters my bread. We're both crazy about Angel, and we love children. To me, Frank, I melt when he looks at me cross-eyed or I smell him. No other man or boy has ever made me feel the way he does, not even the most handsome Major who's squeezing the life out of me right now." She laughed, and hugged him back, harder. She found his cheek and planted one, not knowing the next time she'd see him.

* * *

The next day Moon distracted the two boys long enough for the team to do their thing. Bekah left for New York, Moon to follow. Holly was couriered to Jay. The information garnered led to the arrest of two of the three assassins. They were found in a backroom of a Brooklyn mosque. Ali decided to turn-coat and join the Edanistani government. He lost his virginity to Moon, part of the deal. Hakim preferred jail, although he did linger on the beach awhile to have a conversation with some naked Greeks who suggested with greasy SB 50 hands he should have a safer tan.

Chapter 20

Winning the tournament

Bekah bided her time in the small Cuban restaurant below Jay's co-op on Thonpson Street, in Manhattan. She entertained a lunch menu plate of shredded pork, and black bean, embedded in baked plantain, and washed down the tasty mix with a glass of house port. She had a hunch again; someone was in Jay's old apartment waiting for her. The penthouse wasn't ready yet, or she'd have a safe place to stay. Moon hadn't arrived and there was still one assassin loose. Dick didn't spot anybody on the street and her Blindsight told her nothing.

"Check, pour favor."

Maybe when she got closer to the door, Dick would scan the interior. Outside the door, Dick read the presence of a none-threatening, although angry woman, in the kitchen. She was chanting something through gritted teeth. He didn't ID the girl.

Bekah took a chance. She removed the ivory cane from an umbrella sheath attached to her suitcase, tapped the floor, adjusted her sunglasses and knocked.

"Oh my God, you're Colonel Rebekah Carthage, please come in, sit down." The woman helped her to a sofa.

"Hello."

"Wow, I am so much a fan of yours. I'm Brenda, Jay's girlfriend."

"Call me, Bekah, I'm Jay's fiancée."

"Sorry. I have to say this. Girlfriends are forever, fiancées only last until the wedding, if there is one."

"The best defense to a losing hand, I've ever heard." *Who the hell is she?*

"I've been practicing it."

"Jay didn't mention a *girlfriend*."

"He doesn't talk much, for a professor."

It would be relatively easy to rip her head off, and ask questions later.

"You would have broken your neck a week ago. Jay had stacks of dusty books and magazines everywhere. He's a slob."

"So tell me, how's your day going?" Bekah tried sarcasm.

Brenda didn't answer. An awkward pause.

Then she started talking and wouldn't shut up. She described how she screamed at Jay before he left for Edanistan and how she slammed the door and ran out. He was having an affair with some lady from one of the other co-op apartments, right in the bathroom, while she was watching Shawn Hannity on TV. She came back because, she forgave him. Unbelievable.

"Why did you clean up for me?" Sarcasm worked once.

"Well, I'm hoping for an autograph, and can't see your life being cut short by tripping over a useless edition of ah, this, Sears and Zemansky, College Physics book." Bekah heard and pictured her tossing the book into the fireplace. Smack.

"But you say, you're his girlfriend. He forgot to mention this."

"Well, we never really officially split. I just ran out mad. I'll even watch the Bachelor with him." This triggered an uncomfortable silence. "Do you love him?"

"Right now, I'm not sure," Bekah said.

"Well don't you think he should make the choice between us?"

"Sounds fair. He's still a free man. That's what engagements are for. But I'd rather wrestle you for him."

"Not a chance, I've read about you in Soldier of Fortune. How did you get the name, Lioness of Edanistan?"

"I ripped the enemy to shreds."

"Why do you want him, now that you know he has a roving eye and a dick he can't keep inside his pants?"

"Had a roving eye and I rather like his *Dick*." She was thinking of her pink pocketbook, who remained silent. "Why do you want him, Brenda?"

"I realized he was not sure of his affections. The press said you both thought you'd never get out of Edanistan. He might love me, once he reunited with you and…"

"Maybe we'd find out we weren't compatible?"

"Right."

"Well now, I think the two us can be great friends."

Bekah described to Brenda, in declassified terms, the threat to her from one lone assassin and how Brenda should be vigilant and careful until the all clear. Bekah and Brenda worked on a plan to smoke out their guy, Jay. Winner takes all.

Later in the guest bedroom, Bekah thought. *Oh Dicky boy. Why wasn't I informed about Brenda, or Jay's liaison with some fire escape, no panty woman?*

I think it be better if Holly explain this all to you. Dick responded.

No matter how much she plied, Dick wouldn't get in the middle of "complicated women's issues." She gave her pink friend a pass. There was still a chunk of New York afternoon out there to enjoy and she knew just how. Bekah would stay the night, then head to Cherry Hill to meet Jay's mom, see her canine centers, maybe understand her connection to canines and take back Angel along with her hunk, likely in one piece.

It being 2 PM according to her pocketbook, she left the apartment yearning for a game at the Marshall Chess Club, which welcomed all strangers, no less the Armed Forces Champion. She kept her cane in an umbrella sheath until she arrived at the step down entrance to the famous club. It smelled of old books, the sounds of pieces shuffling, clocks toggling. The not so loud kibitzing, brought her a flood of feelings. She was home and comfortable. These were her people.

She asked for a game and a pegboard reserved for the blind, although she didn't need one. The Chinese Student team's first board was asked to stop her casual five-minute game. Dick informed her to be careful of this young lady. Holly told him in real time, she had tried—half-heartedly—to seduce Jay.

"I'm Lilly Ho. I followed your games in Chess Life."

"I hadn't had any time—being in Edanistan—to study, but I read the lead article about you and your team's winning the student Olympics. I am glad to meet you too."

"Are you alright, I mean are you healing enough to play. We can just talk."

"No, I so need a game right now. Maybe we will have a friendly game, I'd love to keep talking and playing."

"Me too." Maybe she'd be an e-mail friend. Dick handled all the e-mails. She explained how she had a read and write out loud program for email and other correspondence, since she lost her sight.

Although their banter was sister-friendly, in reality, the two women were at each other's throats, on the chessboard. Bekah issued a complicated version of the Panov-Botvinnik attack in response to Lilly's meek, and therefore often underestimated, Caro-Kann. Fireworks.

She had just about enough of all these women wanting her Jay. After kicking Lilly Ho's ass, they parted exchanging emails and promised to meet again. Bekah joined the club, the best money she ever spent.

* * *

Jay thwarted weight gains on the cruise by taking in two gym sessions and any walking tours each day. He hadn't expected very many to sign up for his chess lessons, since there was only three sets on board, and his competition was a rock star, teaching guitar, and a lecture by some German professor on weiner dogs.

He managed to get every single woman and many of the married ones, all the pre-teens, and two adult males. He figured his knowing Bekah was behind this, but the ladies did crowd him when he announced a crafts opportunity to make a demo board and pieces. They all wanted to be mated. During the demo board construction, he gave an impromptu lecture on UFOs, lifted right from his curricula at NYU. The German professor and his two sign-ups, apparently, upon hearing of this, abandoned the dog talk and joined the crowd.

All the while, Jay could think of little else except his sweetheart. He also consumed himself in research on hunter/trackers in the Stone Age through all time. He focused on American Indian and South African scouts and their relationships to canines, from the wolf to the African Painted Hunting Dog. He might, with the help of his mom, be able to start to explain Bekah's unusual talents in a logical manner.

* * *

Manhattan intoxicated Bekah. It was 4 PM, late May. A gentle warm breeze cupped her body and soul toward Jay's old co-op. She touched every tree she walked by, listened for people and their dogs. Got more than her share of licks, she guessed. There was something special about her relationship with dogs and tomorrow's trip to Cherry Hill to meet Jay's mom and pick up Angel might improve her understanding of the furry people. All she needed to do—to leave tomorrow—was neutralize one last assassin.

This particular assassin was peculiar. Of the original six, all Edanistani, he was the eldest at twenty-one, taller and therefore easy to spot, given to practical jokes, the only ex-pat American of Edanistani heritage. He didn't seem to give a damn about anything, except his own death, which reports had it, he botched on a number of occasions. He may have done more to ruin Ali Zachari's plans than the American Army.

The only reason Ali lost his life trying to blow up Bekah was because Hussein, he liked to call himself, needed his hand held and slowed everybody down. His actual name was Jeremiah Doolittle. A miserable failure at everything he attempted. He had the distinct dishonor of being the only young man expelled from NYU for bad writing. He couldn't get his book, "Suicide for Dummies: A Jihadist Handbook," published anywhere, including the Arab world. Dissolute, he printed and distributed it on campus ripping off the Dummies cover graphics and logo in the process. He set up a book signing in which he claimed he'd demonstrate how to blow oneself up. That's when he was picked-up by Homeland Security and expelled by NYU.

Bekah welcomed the challenge of confronting the last of the dummies, and in this case goof-ball might apply. Years of training kept her from being too confident, after all, he was smart enough to get into NYU. Just then, she imagined Angel pulling her by an imaginary leash to go in the opposite direction.

She tried thinking as Jay would. He taught her to shoot down every superstition or question each Blindsight occurrence with logic, and whatever remained would be the truth. She at first, thought his idea of making her more logical, just some ruse to beat her at chess. The American Open Champion couldn't buy a game from her. The 'love-sick puppy-boy' she used to beat every week for four years at Prep was certainly a far better player now, and a bit better than she was, if the truth got out. But, she slaughtered him with secret weapons: sprinkle in gambling, changing styles, surprise, a smile or two, and a little undulating tush for flavor. In any case, he was still under her whammy. Speaking of whammies, her mind went to red alert. Angel beckoned her like Ahab flapping his dead arm on the white whale. The pup who wasn't there, tugged as if she were still stuck in the oven of the blown-up building. She couldn't ignore it. Someday, someday soon, she'd figure out her weird head, using Jay's logic or not.

Anybody near, who could harm me? Is Brenda okay? She vibrated.

I sense nothing. She's fine.

A block away from the co-op, she swiveled around the thick corner lamppost and headed north to Washington Square's chess tables and the last goof ball, so she presumed. She'd either die or be free of one set of demons, once and for all.

Dick said, "Satellite imaging is having a hard time seeing through the maples. I'm checking City and NYU cameras."

The whole trip took fifteen minutes. She did walk slower than most and found her cane helpful. She left her cane with the guard at NYU's library. Notoriety had its perks.

Dick vibrated, *I see him, has to be him. He's shaved and tall. He's watching a Russian émigré, named Anatoly, hustle a tourist.*

Is he armed?

He's got a switch-blade in his sleeveless fishing jacket and that's it.

No problem. Do whatever magic you can conjure up, Dicky boy. Over and out. By saying do whatever magic, she meant for him to use his ability to make subconscious suggestions in the target person through vibrations of ears and larynx. Dick told her the human mind subconsciously rejected thoughts that didn't match self-image. Often a human will be thinking one thing, while vibrating something else entirely, like a song. The vibrations the target received were only rough approximations and only a tiny bit of what the target might consider. On average, on a good day, when the sun was shining, and the fat lady sang, etc., the good guys might make headway.

Bekah was vigilant but not worried when she stepped up to the last assassin. She had the same dark tan, hair tucked up, and sunglass disguise. Her gait and demeanor of a sighted person fooled everybody.

"Want a game?" Bekah said, now beside him.

"I'm just a beginner and I'm waiting for somebody. So, no thank you, ma'am."

"I'm waiting for somebody, too. I'm just a beginner. So let's chat and play."

"No, I mus ah, I have to pay attention."

"You're a tall handsome young man, take the inside seat, stand up if you like. You wouldn't want to disappoint a lady would you?"

"Well okay," he said, exasperated. They set up the pieces she carried. They sat two tables from Anatoly.

Jay's squirrel friend is coming over to check you out, vibrated Dick.

Forget the squirrel. She faced her nemesis, gazed way up for effect, and smiled.

"What are you, maybe six foot six?" Although Dick already reported a lot of info, such as, which pocket the knife was in, she needed to butter him up for some tricks she planned.

"I'm six seven and one-half." That made him exactly a foot taller than Bekah, which could come in handy in hand-to-hand combat, but handier still for one of her tricks.

"My boyfriend and I just broke up. I have tickets to the NBA championship tonight and I know the coach. Would you like to go with me, handsome?"

"How old are you?"

"I'm just twenty-four. You're no baby." Bekah didn't look her real age, thanks in large measure to her Filipina mom's creamy-smooth, wrinkle-free skin.

"I am also twenty-four." *Liar, liar, underpants aflame.* He was just twenty-one, hooked on basketball and now hooked on her. *That was easy.*

"Maybe, after the game, and meeting the coach, we can have a nice snack," she said.

"I don't drink," he said, sounding like he expected rejection.

"I'm a Moslem, so I don't drink either."

"Well sister, this is great news. I was feeling alone." *Try suicidal.* "and you come into my life like an angel."

"This angel isn't perfect. I like to kiss, tall, dark, and handsome basketball players."

"*Oh.*" He walked around the table. "Could we have one, now?"

"This is embarrassing. Look at these people. Just a quick peck," Trick number two.

He leaned over and met her lips. The peck turned into a lingering kiss. She partially unzipped the correct pocket, out of ten on his jacket, thanks to Dick's info, withdrew the blade, sat on it, withdrew her pouty lips, and said, "Maybe, we should continue to play. You're a very good kisser. Maybe we should try this again, tonight." She rubbed her lips. "My name is Precious." All she could think of, was *The No. 1 Ladies' Detective Agency* girl, again.

"Call me, Hussein. And thank you, thank you *very much.* I can die happy."

There will be no dying today, Mr. Jeremiah Doolittle, God willing.

Give the blade to Anatoly, Dick vibrated. *He's ex-KGB and knows who you are.*

"Stay right there, Hussein. I'll be right back." She passed the blade to Anatoly, who took it in stride.

Anatoly smacked his clock and said, "Your bishop is like a dagger to my heart, mischa."

She came back. "I owed the old man two-dollars, and didn't want to forget."

"He's unbeatable. He's a hustler."

Dick vibrated, *Hussein had lost innumerable times to Anatoly when he was a student at NYU. He eventually realized the hustle and became even more moribund.*

"I know. I consider it a good lesson, money well spent. On the subject of good lessons, I have a surprise for you."

"Your moves are worse than mine. I'm going to win your queen."

"No. My surprise is, well let me say the game tickets are still good for tonight, but I work for a united Moslem group, who are looking to free Edanistan from the Americans."

"Shhh, someone will hear you."

"Anatoly is hard of hearing. Anyway, we are looking for Edanistanis. You're Edanistani, right?"

"Am I going to go to the game?"

"Yes, I said so, didn't I? I meant it."

"Just not with you. Huh?"

"No, I'll go, if you'll still be my date."

"Absolutely, please tell."

"There will be a new administration in America, and no matter who wins, the Americans will leave Edanistan. With the Republican, MacPhearson, a little slower. But, just listen. Anyway, foreign agitators are using decent Edanistanis, not to win the country back, but to create bloodshed, often good Moslem women like me and children die. They have been recruiting Sunnis, and we want them back. For any Sunni who comes back and helps us, he will not only avoid jail, meet the Knicks' coach…"

"Ah. Could it be the Lakers' coach?" He seemed consumed in some private joke.

Lakers, Dick? She vibrated.

Shoudn't be a problem.

"You are funny, Hussein. It shouldn't be a problem. But, as I was saying, you will be given a new start. All you have to do is help get rid of all foreign fighters in your country, just not the Americans, because they'll be leaving soon."

"Are you really going to take me to the game tonight, Colonel Rebekah Carthage?"

She took a moment to check the temperature of her Army engineered ice water veins. "Yes I will, unless you'd prefer to kill me now." She backed away from the seat and readied for an attack. Instead, he slumped down onto the bench.

"I have a blade. Woah, had a blade, you devil."

"A kiss is just a kiss."

"I could break your neck."

"I think not."

"Why did you take this chance?"

"I'm in love with Professor Boone, and want to make babies. I'm done with the war."

"So you want me to fight the war for you."

"I want you to fight the war—for your country."

"I selected suicide, because I wasn't a very good fighter. Although, I think I'm very strong and should have no trouble taking out a scrawny thing like you."

"I'll tell you what. I'll wrestle you for my life; in exchange you join the Edanistani government sponsored basketball team."

"So, you're not really blind, are you?"

She whipped off her sunglasses and opened her still partially blackened eyes, so she was told. "I'm as blind as a bat." Like a bat, she had some advantages. "But, I've been receiving instructions on how to move around safely from my earrings. Their microphones are connected to some snipers."

"Oh, I see. I do as you say or die."

"No, if you tried to attack me, you'd get air-conditioning, but wrestling won't be a problem, I am very well trained."

"I could snap your neck like a twig."

"Will you get off the neck, already? I'm faster than an NBA guard and I'm not as delicate as I look. If you go for my neck, either I will make you regret it, or the men with guns, will cut short your fathering years."

"Ouch. Okay, little girl. Let's hop over the wall here, if you can, and do it. But I want a kiss first, Mata-Hari."

"On the cheek." They pecked, hopped over the wall and shook hands. He didn't let go, clamped down and twirled her into a bear hug.

"This was too easy," he boasted, breathing the smell of roasted chestnuts her way.

"You cheated. I could kick you in your basketballs. Start fresh, you handshake, stand apart, then wrestle."

He held her close for just a moment more. "You're the most beautiful woman I have ever seen."

"Come on. Your sweet-talking won't work. I suffered Army boys." She recalled the never-ending teasing with her best Army friend, now rejected suitor, Major Frank Hollister. No one else would dare say boo to the powerful woman.

He lunged and then she fly kicked into a leg-to-his-arm-twist takedown. Except, he didn't go down.

"I really don't know enough about wrestling to fall down, here," he taunted.

He's a smart ass wise guy. She let go, fell on her feet, and blew air frustrated.

"How did you know it was me?" Bekah asked.

"You were going to check mate me in three moves, and your nose, has a Shoshone hook."

"My hair is all tied up under the cap."

"But your unforgettable face belongs in a museum somewhere."

Oh no, not another Nefertiti joke coming. The man compliments me to death. "You're no beginner at chess," she said.

"Neither are you. Why don't you give up, Tinkerbell? I'm just too much man for you."

This time she decided to reach out for his huge hand, power slide between his legs, while pulling his hand through with her, which should make his head hit the ground hard, but she had to let go about half-way, because the maneuver was designed to break necks. He did fall. She walked up his back.

"Give up, you over-grown gorilla."

Spitting out dirt and grass, he said, "I think the police want us to stop."

She said, "no problem officer, we're done. Chess is such a violent sport." The female officer sounded an awful lot like Moon. In fact, she was Moon, and chastised them for disobeying park rules, in her own inimitable way.

"Did you give the knife to the old man?" Hussein said, his side by her side, on the grass.

"You're not still thinking about that?"

"No. I guess I don't get it back."

"You're going to be a basketball player, right?"

"I'll see you for the game tonight, just no more kissing," he said, deadpan. True to his nature, he denied himself even the remotest chance of petting a cat, or a nasty lioness.

"Officer, officer, would you like to go to the NBA game with us tonight?"

"That great. I be there. I make sure you two not wrestle the players," Moon said.

Good, one more night to figure Brenda out, start a basketball team, and tomorrow, God willing, she'd be off for her hometown, Cherry Hill, to meet Jay's mom, Margie, canine research scientist extraordinaire. She might offer an explanation, for Bekah imagining Angel trapped in an oven.

Chapter 21

Check Mate

Over her dad's objections, early the next day Bekah took the bus from Manhattan to exit four of the New Jersey Turnpike. Not far was her hometown, Cherry Hill, which featured no cherries and no substantial hills. On the ninety-mile trip south she reflected on a plan of attack. Margie and her dad were likely into each other's pants and she was going to get to the bottom of it. She'd also elicit Margie's help using her canine research center. If something was going on with Margie and her dad, and she wasn't right for him, she'd say so right to her face, even if it meant losing Jay.

TTJ, triple timing Jay, if Brenda is to be believed, would be interrogated when he shows his sorry ass.

At exit 4, she stepped out into a dense, almost chunky warm morning. The texture promised rain. Her dad's limo driver awaited and she had errands. Forever hungry, they headed to her old haunts. First came *Ponzio's Diner* for scrapple and eggs breakfast, then her home to stuff a suitcase full with favorite outfits and shoes, then she was driven to *John's* where she ordered lunch for Margie, the driver, and herself. She lusted for a cheese steak sandwich and bought Margie a hoagie, both piled up with the works.

The order was ready. Unfortunately, her favorite place for dessert in the whole world, the Cowtail Bar bit the dusty road along with their malted sundae of the same name. She'd wait for triple timing Jay. Besides, the sundae—if they partook—had vaulted to biblical proportions.

Bekah vaguely remembered Margie as one of her deceased mom's rat-stabber shopping pack girls, which referred, via New Jersey vernacular to their pointy high heels. Nowadays, Margie, a renowned research scientist and semi-retired veterinarian, spent most of her time at two sprawling facilities studying humans with canines, and canines among themselves.

Bekah's limo pulled up to Margie's. She exited cane first, touching stone, with rubber tip. She loved the feel of the lioness-head, ivory stick her brigade made for her. A light rain kissed her wavy cinnamon hair. Margie embraced her with both arms, no umbrella for these tomboys.

"Come on honey. I'm so excited to see you." Margie grabbed her arm and introduced Sandra, her second in command. A bunch of dogs barked from all directions.

One in particular, made Bekah's ears tingle. Her little pup Angel's high pitch was easy to pick out.

"Here's Angel. So sweet. You know, she's not an Italiano Volpino like you thought."

"What is she, mom?" While hugging the pup and getting, the I missed you like New Years Eve treatment, the three women and the furry white ball headed for the house.

"She's an American Eskimo, Eskie for short, aka a heart bandit."

"Oh yes."

"The two breeds are so close only an expert can tell them apart. Eskies are sold in Italy. By the way, Jay called. He asked me to tell you, women wanting chess lessons are chasing him all over the cruise ship. He might not be able to get away, for another day. He wants to know if he should mate them all."

"Nasty, nasty boy." Bekah rolled her shoulders, pretending she'd belt out and dance an old Janet Jackson tune. Lucky for Margie, she stopped singing, but she could have danced all day.

"You haven't changed much since high school. I'd have to award you, an eleven."

"Could you tell me your features, mom?" Bekah was too shy just yet to suggest she'd feel Margie's face, or ask her about how many donuts she downed. Her Blindsight, if it could be trusted, picked up the basics, a fetching woman who exercised and ate healthy, and stole her dad.

"I'm almost your height, have honey-blonde hair, a little coloring here and there. I have a figure like Marilyn Monroe's before she got fat. Well, she really never got that fat. You know what I mean. I have some wrinkles on my face, but I've been told in a hold, I'm pretty."

"Do you mind, mom, if I feel your face?"

"Later, honey. I have two, well. I had to trade a breeding pair of wolves to get your surprise. I'm very excited by the opportunity, anyway. I promised the zoo to design a better diet, and give them a thorough check-up. So come on, guess your surprise."

Bekah took to the challenge like a wide-eyed child solving one of her daddy's puzzles. She strained her ears, and barely heard what sounded like birds chirping from inside the house. *Well no, not birds.* A rapid chattering, of up and down high and higher notes, assaulted her ears. Her Blindsight pictured two strange canines hiding under Margie's dining room table.

"He-he-he, he-he-he."

The girl with ice water veins and a badass reputation felt light headed. The beloved subject of her mini-thesis, Canidae Lycaon Pictus, the African Painted Hunting Dogs were under Margie's dining room table.

"You have two Painted Hunting Dogs in your house?"

"A juvenile breeding pair."

"In your house?"

"Well, just for now. How much trouble can they get into? Their pack rules are total submission and cooperation, a little different from wolves and dogs. Come on, kid. Let's meet them. You're up for it, right?"

"I think so. It's just, while writing a term paper; I wasn't able to find a soul who'd admit domesticating or even touching them."

"Not really, dear. Cars hit them all the time in South Africa. Some fearless or crazies pick them up and bring them to vets. The vets touch them, of course. Some zoologists. So far, no bites that I've heard of."

Maybe we can be the first, mom? Bekah almost said, to exhibit her wry sense of humor, but she held off.

"At zoos, it's a touch-don't-tell policy. These two are pretty wild, but they'll respect us as the alpha females we are. I hope. You see, some theorists believe that God wires all canines and humans for each other. Except for some deniers of God's hand, who shoot wolves from airplanes in Alaska. You will soon see we're making new science here. My detractors dismiss me as a tree hugger, but I prefer hugging dogs and using science."

Although Bekah leaned Republican, she could not stand nor understand those who didn't want to be conservative and conserve nature as Teddy Roosevelt had. She grew closer day by day to voting for her dad, if not his party. He, like most successful politicians, solved problems from the center, making their party affiliation—hopefully and perhaps a tad naïvely irrelevant.

"I've dreamt of running with them on my grand mama's farm in South Africa. Oh, I wish I could really see their colors, their ears and not just imagine them."

"Well these two have full, white-spotted, come-follow-me tails, then red, black, tan, yellow spots and black muzzles." Margie held Bekah's elbow. "Let me take your cane and lovely pocketbook." Margie and Bekah entered a vestibule. "I'm putting your stuff on the bench, next to your suitcase. I'm going to open the inside door, if you're ready."

What's happening, Dick? Bekah vibrated.

Not to worry. Those huge ears pick up your feelings or thoughts, just like I do. They don't understand too much English, being immigrants, but they understand your pure heart. They're excited to meet you. They think you look good enough to eat. Dick vibrated back.

Gee thanks. Remind me to misplace you somewhere, sometime soon.

"Did you say something, dear?" Margie asked.

"No, just mulling it over. I'm ready. Hey, they're rubbing against your door, right?"

"They're not true dogs, so I don't think they'll scratch the door. It's mostly glass. They're just rubbing their scent, but now, they're staring at *you*, dear."

"Yes, what is this thing dogs and I have?"

"That's what Jay and I will attempt to answer. Stay tuned."

"Don't let my Army friends know how knock-kneed I am."

"Well just to calm you, know this. They have the strongest bite force of any carnivore, pound for pound and a few extra chewy teeth. Their lower carnassials shear flesh and crush bone. Still want to meet them?"

A challenge, and Bekah never backed down in her life.

"Do your dogs, bite?" she said, using a slight French accent.

"He-he-he, he-he-he."

"No worries. I'm opening the door." The door swung wide. The vestibule became a blur of tail whipping enthusiasm, with no one able to move into the home.

Not like dogs, my foot.

"Sit, Bekah." The two women chuckled. The four-legged friends continued like whirling dervishes.

"He-he-he, he-he-he."

"Oh, their fur feels like Dalmatians. They're licking like dogs Dare I feel their ears?"

"Give them each a biscuit, first. Then move your hand slowly up their chests. They need to protect their radar."

"He-he-he, he-he-he."

"These squash-racket ears have tantalized me with wonder ever since I was a little girl. Oh my God, here come the tears. Mom, they're licking away. My eyes."

"Here move over next to me, drop your head a little. They'll start smelling and kissing somewhere else. I'll clean you up properly in short order."

"They're sniffing the biscuit box. Won't they try to steal it?" Bekah asked.

"No, in their pack life, kids eat first, but only after begging and cajoling."

"And nuzzling. Do you let these two run with your dogs and Angel?"

"Not yet. They're new. So far, only Barney the Saint Bernard met them. He's hiding somewhere. One hundred and sixty-seven pounds of pure wimp. Want to try Angel?"

"No, I don't think so, doc, I'm afraid for my pup. You can decide when."

"Angel will survive. We'll do it now. Oh Sandra." She called out. "Be a dear and get me Angel, please. Sandra has her PHD from Columbia."

Be ready with some noise or distraction, Dick, Bekah vibrated.

The dogs know you and Angel are a team. No problem. Sandra holsters a horn. Dick vibrated back. But, because of all the noise the dogs were making, Bekah picked-up "no problem, Sandra hustles porn." *File that one for later.*

The decibels went up. The two Painted Hunting Dogs went crazy with whistles and chirps. Angel started crying, no, more like bawling and screaming.

"There, there, now." Margie held Angel. "No. No. Too much. They don't know my words, but they know my loving authority. The wild dogs quieted and Angel stopped crying.

"What's happening now?"

"You tell me."

"They're licking Angel?"

"Well, they're smelling her. Angel is trying to push away with her front paws. I don't want to stress the baby any further. Sandra, could you please take these two to the holding pen?"

Sandra chirped, tweeted and led the Painted Hunting Dogs out back. She shouted back into the house, "Barney is hiding in the wine closet."

* * *

Later, over lunch, afternoon walks, visits with the Painted Hunting Dogs, supper, exercise and quiet time in the den, Margie and Bekah got closer. Bekah had long ago mastered the art of easing into the most important subjects. Occasionally, they spoke of her dad. But the subject disappeared in favor of canine research and their upcoming meeting with a wolf pack. Margie was so kind as a scientist to include myth and legend in her conversation, in particular Bekah's favorite: Shoshone stories of special relationships between women, wolves, and to a lesser extent ravens. Bekah enjoyed Margie's company, so she waited patiently to talk about her dad. The conversation meandered until a surprising turn.

"Oh, I've missed this pup." Angel snuggled on Bekah's lap while she melted into a rapturous sofa. Margie placed a hot cocoa on the side table. "This fur ball stole my heart, right there in the middle of a battle. In an instant I knew, just like I do about your son, we were meant to be."

"That's what your mom and I thought," Margie said. Bekah shuddered and Margie patted her leg. "Your mom and I felt someday you two would be together. You had a little searching to do and in Jay's case a lot of growing-up. He's so handsome, now."

"He sure is. You don't know what he does to me, mom."

"Well, I think I know what it's like to go nuts over somebody very special."

She might be talking about Bekah's dad, but Bekah waited just a little more.

"How well did you know my mom?"

"Girl, we were the core of a group who ate at all the local spots and then shopped at the Echelon and Cherry Hill Malls, every other week. There wasn't a Philly soft pretzel or hoagie we didn't polish off. There wasn't a dress, pocketbook or shoe we didn't consider."

Bekah, not much of a shopper, ignored the subject for now. "How come you two didn't let us in on your ideas about me and Jay?"

"We both believed, believe in our children and respect them for their choices. We have faith. Yes, I said *have*, honey."

"My mom is an angel." After a pause, "and I love your son more than my life." *Literally.*

It was Margie's turn to cry. "You'll do engagement encounters with the church, right?"

"We will. I have some problems with your son to solve that can't wait for the retreats."

"Tell me, dear. I promise to keep your secrets." That's all Bekah wanted to hear.

"Yes you *can*." Bekah said, always knowing the right moment to advance. Check.

Margie, who must have understood the challenge said, "If you love somebody, my dearest, wouldn't you want to protect him?" Bekah nodded.

"Well then, what are these problems you have with Jay?" Margie tried to keep the conversation on her son.

"How 'bout a trade? You have something you really want to share. Don't you, mom?"

"How did you know?"

"Well, it's not my psychic powers."

"So you claim to have had a vision of a pup you didn't know in the midst of battle after you lost your sight."

Bekah ignored the diversion. "You, with a Notre-Dame doctorate, master's and bachelor's just used the word nice a few too many times to describe my dad, as if you were a valley girl. Jay and I swore you were watering plants in your greenhouse during our call." Bekah resisted saying 'leaning over and getting corked by her dad.' Margie looked impish in Bekah's imagination.

"Did I? Well that's a double oops."

"By the way, you are not alone, my senator, orator dad used the same expressions."

"He did?"

"Did you know you are wonderful, nice and beautiful?"

"We are *sooo* busted." Margie said, using her best valley girl imitation.

Checkmate.

"I've never approved of my dad's girlfriends until today—well this is a definite maybe. Want to swap top secret info and get my official okay?" Bekah asked. Through Margie's surprise of the two Painted Dogs, her relationship with Bekah's deceased mom, and her sweet caring nature, Bekah had come to adore her.

"Deal." Margie sounded anxious to lift a weight off her psyche.

"Okay, deal, but you first, mom." This seemed right, since Margie agreed to the deal first.

Margie spewed her guts out, more relieved each moment. "Dan is a very important man, and tall, dark, handsome..." she said while lowering her voice to a conspiratorial tone. "He came here with Angel..." Bekah relaxed.

Margie went on to say, she and her dad chatted, had the usual coffee and cake, let their hair down. Found many common interests beyond politics and tree hugging. They both loved Elsie, Bekah's mom. She filled him in on her best girlfriend's secret shopping and eating life.

The tidbits about his wife made him break down. She offered her shoulder as a crying towel and his tears wouldn't stop. She consoled him with plenty of hugs, then one kiss. She wasn't sure who started it. All hell broke loose. *Embarr-ass-ing.*

He showed his interest with a superb compliment for a woman Margie's age. Bekah took this to mean, he was harder than Mount Rushmore. The hot tamale train was a comin' down the tracks and headin' for the tunnel. Both understood, no one could replace Elsie, Bekah's mom. But, the human spirit was made for love, and they loved each other everywhere they could: in the house, the garden, the greenhouse, while avoiding all the dogs. Afterwards, they agreed to go slow and test their new feelings.

Margie's good looks would charm many Americans if Bekah's dad became President. On the other hand, if he won the Presidency, she didn't want to abandon her home and canine research centers. She couldn't picture wolves and other canines loose in the White House, although some meetings got right down to tooth and nail.

Recovering from the disclosures, Margie pleaded for Bekah's turn, sounding spent.

Bekah said, "I want to know that your son does not pity me because I'm blind. But, does he really love me or that cute cheeky girl who tantalized him at Bishop Eustace Prep? Or Brenda who is still in his apartment and claims he had an affair. And what is she doing in his apartment?"

"Not my Jay. There has to be an explanation. Brenda is a joke."

"Well, I'll ask when he shows up, after he's done teaching chess to lonely women."

"He was just teasing. My Jay is very logical. Actually, he's boring sometimes when he gets onto physics. He should take a physic. But, he's nuts about you. My dear Lioness of Edanistan, he is your unruly maned mate, and he'll watch over my grandchildren." Whoa, Bekah felt pregnant, and hadn't even made love yet. *Yeah, when was that going to happen?*

Margie reminisced about her son's teenaged years. "You wouldn't believe the love sick look on his face when he came home from school after you drubbed him at chess. Around the house, he insisted I refer to you as 'the princess.' He said you were born with a silver pawn up your gaflugalheimer."

"Ouch."

What's a gaflugalheimer? Dick vibrated.

Not now.

Margie said, "He didn't fool me. And you dear, didn't fool your mother, either."

"You're kidding."

"We had all kinds of schemes to accidently put you two together. Our little Ken and Barbie made us cry."

"We're all grown up, mom, and I'm thinking I might need help with a wedding gown."

"I'll say this. You marry my baby, and if we're a match, I'll marry that old fool you have for a father. Deal?"

"Well, our men might have something to say about all this, but yes, mom, deal."

The day's events overwhelmed Bekah. Was it always this easy to fall in love with a Boone? She felt her mom's special hug when Margie said goodnight. Now, alone in her room with Angel to cuddle, and Dick for support—well—she left him just inside the open bathroom door on the sink counter. Both could have some alone time, but even at about ten feet they gossiped fine when they wanted to.

She sobbed a sweet remembering. *Mama, I've been on a long journey. I'm home now. So much for wicked mother-in-laws or step-moms.* She pleaded with her mom for advice. She was in love with Professor Jay Boone, didn't want to wait any longer. She had to trust him, but she also wanted explanations before she blurted out the most special words she'd utter in her life, 'I love you.'

* * *

It was a dark and stormy night.

Bekah sat up in bed laughing. She reviewed her dream to remember it. Jay had taken her to meet his cheesy very off Broadway literary group of writers, actors and directors: WAD. Being first in her class, she had written tons of pulp, she had acted 'like one of the boys' for years, and, she lead a brigade. In Jay's group, she'd learn fast and maybe contribute to the arts. They'd like her.

For a blind woman, she had no trouble with stormy. The sky clapped hard. She had little trouble with dark, picturing the moon lit by intense streaks of lightning.

Jay had explained the not-so-unusual, Blindsight phenomena by little more than quoting medical studies, so far. He said the blood of scout-hunter-trackers from ancient stone-age tribes in Africa, the American west, the Philippines, and Europe, coursed her veins. That was more interesting, but was she a freak without a circus? She pushed throughout her life to use every talent God threw at her. Go fetch, Miss Carthage. Somehow, dogs held the key and modern science could not yet explain or demonstrate by provable experiments the way she used her talent. All they knew was, it was real.

She guessed the clock beside the bed read 3:17 AM. Dick verified but couldn't explain her intuition. She pictured a cab driving down Kresson Road, Jay in back, focused on a rose he held. The incurable romantic, wanted to give her the final rose ala *The Bachelor* TV show. Romance and true love gave her, ached her with the sweetest moments of life, for which she'd refuse a cure.

Jay arrived. She pictured her beautiful man wrestling with the slobber-factory Saint Bernard, Barney, down on the living room rug. Maybe she'd wrestle. Well either man or beast would be fun, but she'd need a bath from their lickings.

"Not a peep out of you, Dick."

"That's a roger."

The door to the next bedroom down the hall creaked open.

Darn him, come to meee. You owe me a rosssse.

She remembered Margie's tour. The two bedrooms shared a Jack and Jill bath. No way, this man would sleep alone tonight. She heard him dropping clothing, belt buckles clanking oak floors, watch knocking dresser. What a slob.

She could see him better as each day and now moment, passed. The butterfly stroke in swimming cut his body and puffed his pecs bigger than her boobs, which was no big feat. Her mind swirled imagining his scent. She pictured him slipping out of republican boxer shorts. The little elephants decorating the shorts were no match for the trunk he sported. One humongous almost scary thing dangled. Thank God for a vivid imagination. The thing got *bigger* with each article of clothing he dropped. As much as she'd *like* to look away, well she didn't. There, stuck out like a horse, smiled the instrument of her downfall. What a way to go for a military woman. She'd be skewered on Ivanhoe's lance.

She noticed his face, no really. Smooth skin, sculpted lines, not craggy, not babyish, and definitely not gayish like her sister teased, sandy blond to the shoulder, gave a surfer-dude-right-off-a-Hollywood-set appeal. She turned down so many men and boys, but she'd hop on his board for a lesson, a life lesson.

Angel jumped off the bed and made her way into the bathroom through the open door. The door closed. She barked. He shushed her.

"Is that you, Jay?" Margie said in hushed tones over the intercom.

"Yes, mom. Sorry if I woke you."

"No problem, son. The lightning had started a howling concert. I had a dreamy front row bed. You didn't call, to warn me."

"Sorry again, mom, how's Bekah?"

"She's wonderful; her eyes are almost all white. She's in your room. You let her sleep, you hear. We have a big day, tomorrow."

Yeah, they're feeding me to the wolves.

"Okay, mom. I'll see you for breakfast." If Bekah's Blindsight was only half-reliable, that order would be delayed.

"Would you like bacon, eggs, pancakes?"

He'll have me with a cherry on top, mom. The excitement made Bekah so wet she imagined the ceiling leaking right over her pussy.

"Thank you mom, whatever you feel like making. Bekah likes eggs. Actually, she likes everything."

Bekah chuckled. *I'd like a side order of Jay on toast, hold the toast.*

"Night. Love you."

"Goodnight. I love you too, mom."

"Me too." Bekah whispered.

The bathroom door into Bekah's room reopened.

"You are so excited." Holly pinged Bekah's eardrum and larynx so Jay wouldn't hear. "Your first time."

"Please don't tell Jay what I plan."

"Never. I am so happy to be next to Dick and to see you again and Angel, baby, baby."

"I'm so nervous, so bewildered."

"It is time for human copulation," said Dick.

"Very funny. Not even you can dampen, strike that, ruin my going *crazy* enthusiasm."

Holly and Dick gave her encouragement by silence. They would have said something if Jay was unfaithful or Dick just wanted to encourage "copulation."

"We'll shut-up now."

"Love you guys."

Jay sent Angel back. She tick tacked across the oak floors and jumped back up. Bekah had other plans than to cuddle up with the little sweetheart. She kissed the pup, stripped off her soft cotton Minnie Mouse pajamas, which she now knew as a joke-present from her sister. Wearing nothing but her slightly curled cinnamon hair, down to the edge of her rump, she inched her way to the bathroom. The door ajar and Jay in the shower, she slipped through, found the light switch and flipped it off. The poor boy was as much in the dark as she was, not because she couldn't see. She hadn't a clue what to do and how to do it.

"Hey." He protested.

Following his sounds and the shower, she opened the clipped closed door and stepped in.

"Hey stranger." Good. Introductions were in order.

"Honey, baby doll, sweetheart, pumpkin face."

Oh God, not that again.

Pumpkin face?

Bekah slipped her hand up his ivory soaped body, knocking his manhood like a twanging doorstop. Nifty. She settled her hand on his mouth. "Don't speak of love, show me." Good start, she guessed. She grabbed his hairy chest and lightly pulled.

Safety first in a shower. Oh yes, do bend over to pick up the soap. But, she didn't. She waited for instructions. The Army training manual had nothing. However, lovemaking was another case of inserting A into B, she figured.

Yo, stop girl. What happened to her plans to waterboard Jay, what about Brenda, what about the girl on the fire escape? What about Lilly Ho, Moon, the ladies on the ship wanting to be mated? Oh, fuck them. No better yet…

"Have you had a proper scrubbing?" She asked taking the initiative.

"I might have missed a spot somewhere." His slippery hands caressed and rubbed her shoulders, his lips lingered time and again on hers. "Maybe to be sure, you should soap whatever you want," he said. His fingers swirled around her erect nipples.

"I want all of you." She got down on her knees, gagged, got up, blew bubbles and said, "Um, I'll try that some other time. Maybe, you can teach me."

"Your taunt thin body, sloe eyes, exotic skin…"

"Shush, don't speak of love, feel me. Have you turned the intercom off?"

"Absolutely. The only two, besides Angel, who can hear us, are Dick and Holly."

Holly spoke up. "Jay has been a perfect gentleman and I projected the voice of an imaginary lady on the fire escape, so we could get rid of Brenda. I'm going to shut up."

"Interesting." But, Bekah couldn't stand the sexual tension any longer. They loved each other. She'd be so lucky to have this man for the rest of her life. She picked off via vibrations Holly's invitation to Dick. Holly'd be Lady Marian to Dick's Robin in a cyber Sherwood forest. Good, they'd occupy themselves.

"He's so in love with you, Bekah," Dick added. "I'm shutting up, too."

"Yes. Would you two mind, if I lost my virginity without having to sell tickets to fill the bleachers?" No comments.

Rhapsody in Blue played. Fine, but after that, *Brown sugar, the bolero, and then keep Nat King Cole rolling.*

"Is there a rose on the ledge?"

Jay got down on his knees, buried his head, kissed her belly button, then mound and said, "You are amazing. How can you smell a rose in a shower?"

"How could you put a rose in a shower?"

"Ah, it needed watering?"

"Go on."

"Rebekah Carthage, will you accept this final rose." Good thing the host of *The Bachelor*, Chris Harrison, wasn't in the shower with them. He'd get his swank suit wet.

"I do. Where are you going to put it?"

"I have a wicked imagination," he said, kissing her folds.

"Well, the rose is a goner, huh, and so is my cherry tree."

"Honey, are you sure? Sex could be painful," He said getting up, and still very up. She knew. She loved him with her whole heart, mind and spirit, now and forever. There was a good chance she subconsciously loved him since high school. All she needed now was to find a way to get her mom's approval. She made a little prayer.

"Don't worry about pain. Swearing off boys, didn't mean swearing off toys."

He adjusted the knob to dribble and bent over to bite the tip of her nipple. She'd remember to ask for more. She felt like falling off a diving board backwards into the unknown.

He lathered her cheeks in a swirling motion. Oh my goodness.

"Keep doing that. It seems to be connected to my front." She had so much to learn.

"Please don't scream." She might have. "I don't want my mom joining us."

"Don't make me laugh."

After a little while and more massaging, he said, "Oops, I dropped the soap. Could you demonstrate your Blindsight and get it. I just can't see in the dark." He twirled her around gently so that her soapy cheeks slipped up against his hard body.

Bending over she swirled her hands on the tiles. *There isn't any soap.* A one-eyed monster caressed the length of her bottom with its head pressing up on her curly triangle.

She grasped his tip as she would a life preserver in a tsunami of emotion. Her Blindsight literally drifted downward.

I used to have eyes in the back of my head, now they're in my cooch. A scientific discovery she'd have to tell Jay about, later. Amazed over the power of the mind, she enjoyed every detail of the beauty of a man and a woman. He slid back and forth without entering, tenderly teasing. No fear. Diving, she folded her hands and cut the water's edge.

Squeezing her upper thighs around him aroused the bear gripping her hips. He moaned for the honey she hid. His rough pulling need and grunts triggered her. Damn, if she didn't shoot too soon again. When would she get this right? Wave after wave swept her into deep waters, crashing, heart pounding. Wantonness cried to her, 'learn to swim.'

He bent over, wrapped his arms, kissed her back, neck, slipped back and forth, teasing her by offering a sausage for her folds. This time, food wasn't making her hungry.

She gasped and in a wispy voice, panted, "Take me."

Time slowed down for Bekah. She had to put to rest her girlish reservations and get her mom's permission, now.

Long ago, Bekah's mom told her one of many fables from the Philippines. A naked native girl had run through the forest chased by a strange man-god, whose clothes captured the sun and threw it back at all who saw him. She ran up to the warm sea, but couldn't swim. Rock cliffs on both sides trapped her. She turned. The man-god towered over her. He removed his head, yet another appeared. This head she understood. A beautiful man with beach-sand hair down to his shoulders, smiled, in the same way the village men did, when they wanted her. She trusted his eyes. He came closer, touching her long black hair.

Her mom snapped her fingers and warned the young Bekah. "Do not get trapped by any man," She laughed, that throaty earthy way Bekah missed so much, and then added, "but this is how you got your violet eyes."

Her mom and Margie were in cahoots about plans for their living Ken and Barbie dolls. So, Bekah had to have received the green light to make love for the first time and with the right man. Not much, she could do right now to stop Jay. Anyway, she had just asked him to take her. Besides, her lust ate her for a snack. She loved her Jay with beach-sand hair to his shoulders, just like the man-god.

Her ankles in imaginary surf, she had presented herself to him, as her ancestor did to the man-god. Gentle, he only took a little, to a small fleeting pain. *A moment to treasure.*

She remembered her mom's last breaths. "Never compromise. The truth of your heart is within you." She died, squeezing Bekah's hand, a blissful smile on her face. Since that day, the words haunted the young woman. An enigma, twisted within the chambers of her heart and brain. Now she understood the riddle. Her heart pattered.

"Take more of me, my darling. Make me a woman." He inched closer and swirled her with a sort of Cuban motion. The endless eddies of surf held her rapture. She danced her first dance as a real woman.

"Closer still, darling."

"I can barely control myself." The man of experience had no experience.

"Then take me to bed. I want your lips." He cradled her and baby-stepped, dripping both, in the dark.

Angel jumped off the bed, tick-tacking the oak floors again: safe, from a squashing.

She spread her long legs as wide as she could, hoping to attract his attention. He'd feel them for sure. His body, lips, tongue, hands, traveled her, ached her. She found his shaft. Both hands guided it until their bodies came tight. She had nothing to hold. She clasped his buttocks, digging nails, wanting his seed. Can't wait. She squeezed him, undulating her hips to match his. She became that wild island girl, caught at surf's edge by the man with beach-sand hair.

"*Ako ay pag-ibig sa iyo.*" She whispered, meaning 'I am in love with you,' as her mother must have said long ago, to the man her mom adored, Bekah's dad.

"You complete me," he said. His strokes came faster. He gasped. "I, I."

There came an explosion deep within him. He jammed hard, with lightning strokes, but it didn't hurt. His warm seed filled her body and spirit, like many tiny fish fluttering in all directions from their flips in the waves on the sand.

She rode theses waves with him.

A little while later, the eddies subsided. "Ummmm, umm." She slid off his shaft, licked his tip. "I'd like an ice cream sundae." Could he make out or feel her broad smile?

"Huh? Huh." He grunted, spent. His IQ must have traveled south like her vision.

"Hold everything except the banana and cream, please." She bit his muscular shoulder. "Have you given me every drop?"

"I, ah, can make more." Exhaling, he turned over holding onto her and slid in. She slipped her knees forward and bent over, playing games with her erect nipples, teasing his chest, his nipples. Crooking her neck, she asked for the endless passion of his lips.

"With a little bit of luck and movement, we can stay like this. In a little while, I'll give you more."

"More? All of you, forever."

"Forever, my dearest, sweetie, honeybunch…"

"Shush." She placed her hand on his lips. "Conserve your strength."

"I'mmmm." He kissed the hand muffling him.

"You have no idea how good you feel inside me. Do you think we could—walk around like this?"

"Maybe we could cover ourselves and claim to be a two-headed human."

* * *

Later to tiny movements, she whispered. "Did you know…I'm blind?"

"You see better than I do." He petted her flowing wavy hair tenting his face.

"The princess is all grown up now." She shook her head no, teasing his face with her hair.

"You are my Queen." Two pinches to her cheeks.

"Are you sure you want the woman, not the girl?" A kiss on his nose.

"I too am not a boy anymore."

"I can feel that."

"When I was younger I loved the girl, now I'm older. I love the woman."

"What are we to do with the talents God gave us?"

"Your being blinded gave you a chance to open your eyes. To find a new path, true destiny. A path, I think, your mother had hoped for."

"What is this path, professor?"

"It's hard to imagine a path more glorious than becoming the most gifted officer in the history of the U.S. Army."

"I know, Jay, you're against the war."

"Well, not all wars. Hitler had to be stopped."

"No doubt."

"Patton had nothing on you, hot shot." He took a drag on one nipple and then puffed the other.

"You tell a girl the sweetest things." She palmed his stubble, delirious. He's got to do that again, and in reverse for equal nippleness. He did.

"Your destiny doesn't rest with me alone, or our children, or our love," he whispered.

"I can't help thinking, yeah; Angel and canines have something to do with my future."

"After you lost your sight, you, quote-unquote saw Angel. All I can figure in my sleepy head right now is you asked God's forgiveness in the face of death, by pushing to your consciousness for the first time, the gift you have."

"You mean it was a prayer. Dear God, keep me alive, and I will use all the talents you gave me."

"That sounds right. We will get to the bottom of this. But right now it's your bottom, got my attention. All this talk excites me." He laughed and mouth open, let his teeth rouse her neck. Exquisite lover.

Outside, the storm had eased. Rain feathered the roof. A cock crowed.

"You'd think one of the many canines here, would turn off that alarm clock." She gyrated her hips in a slow hula to get a rise from the bear sleeping in her cave.

He yawned. "I think I'm going to have to commandeer the washer and dryer today." He kept her pace. Arched up to take her mouth. There they stayed, in full embrace, waving bodies.

As time winked by, the smell of bacon wafted through the room mingling with the mess of sweat, sweet smells of sex, bites and tender kisses.

"*Ako ay pag-ibig sa iyo.*" *I'm in love with you*, he said, remembering and understanding her Tagalog.

She held so much sticky, if she didn't get pregnant with eight kids, it would be a miracle.

Chapter 22

Postmortem

Jay stumbled down the skinny back stairs like a drunken sailor. He needed a strong cup of coffee. Still, he'd stay intoxicated by the woman upstairs. He gripped the railing, blinking blurry eyes. Pausing, four steps from the bottom, he could see the other woman he loved chopping green mangoes for a salad. She tossed into the salad bits of bacon from a breakfast now turned lunch. Peeking over her shoulder and through her curls at her son, she smiled appearing serene in her pretty daisies on white cotton dress with yellow apron.

"I haven't gotten a kiss yet." She waved him over.

He trotted up behind her—as she chopped—for a cuddle and smooch on her cheek.

"Love you, mom. I'm in trouble."

"Love you too. You look like something a certain lioness dragged in."

"She is incredible, but I have a huge problem." He threw his hands in the air. "You made coffee, right?"

"Of course, honey. Nose not working too? It's in the pot, in the same place it always is."

Jay poured his favorite Costa Rican mud. "Here's what's worrying me." Barney nuzzled him, causing a small spill of the hot coffee on the glass tabletop. "Barney." Jay napkin-ed the offending puddles. "Bekah could use the military antidiscrimination law her dad pushed through the Senate to get her old job back."

His mom turned her head from the chopping board, "You think too much. She's always been driven. She'd push if she thought it were right. We remember her character, don't we?"

He played second-fiddle to her Valedictorian. He even finished second in physics and math, the nerve of that girl. She won everything in sight. At least, he had no doubt of her genius; she won him.

"You just have to get a job, a great job for her."

"She might be happy for a while, married, housewife, children, job. I just want her to stay happy and getting to the bottom of her special talents—that's the key."

"I will help with all my heart and skill," she said.

"Coffee's great."

"Thanks. Well, all we can do is pray and work."

"Amen."

"Today is too late to visit the wolf research center."

Bekah spoke through the intercom. "Okay, you two conspirators. Your kitchen intercom is stuck in the on position, up here, I swear, I didn't do it."

"Yes, honey. So is your… We'll get everything fixed."

"Aha, were you listening to us, mom?" Jay whispered.

"I'm on my fourth cup of coffee."

"Mo-om." The last time his mom embarrassed him was removing a bee sting from his teenage butt in front of his aunt. Her aunt's jokes stung worse.

"How am I going to cook for you, do the laundry, pray for her mom to see you two together. I'm so proud. And you, you're bad."

"Sorry mom. Not."

"I'm blind, remember. That means due to heightened sensitivity of my other senses I can hear you two whispering. Don't worry. I love you both with my whole heart. Be down in a minute with a little surprise."

Jay wrote out his remaining thoughts, knowing a blind girl wouldn't read, unless she had some other weird talent. He wrote: "No matter how she feels now, I don't want her to have any regrets later. I want her to give me a hard time, when I'm eighty."

Margie wrote back. "Don't you mean, you give her a hard time?"

"Ha. Ha." He'd never need Viagra with a woman that alluring, beautiful, sexy.

"I know you two are writing something. Probably poetry for me, right? I'll expect a serenade."

Jay tried to wrap his mind around Bekah, while he absentmindedly swirled his coffee. He heard her at the top of the narrow back steps, and ran to help if necessary, with his mom behind him.

"Oh my God," Jay said. His no longer blurry vision took in the sleek form at the top of the steps, caressed by noonday sun through the floor to second-story ceiling windows flanking the steps.

She waved her arms as if anticipating their need to help. "I want to do the steps myself." She tapped down each step with her ivory cane, wearing a slink black full-body leotard, which he remembered fondly from her appearance playing Sandy in Grease in high school. Jay's rose threaded her ear. Not only did she keep her figure, which rivaled Grease star, Olivia Newton-John's, her deceptively young face of creamy smooth skin could trick an audience. Her allure now famous: Stars & Stripes had chosen her as a pinup girl. Playboy and others made offers. She could make a living just responding to emails. He reflected humorously, waifish girl-kung-fu-fighters were just Hollywood fantasy. But, his girl slammed him against padded wall and floor until he felt like Jell-O. She carried herself with the aplomb of one of Charlie's Angels.

"You better shape up, 'cause I need a man. And my heart is set on you…" Jay felt like plugging his ears. Really, her singing never was very good, but no one back at school seemed to notice or care. Bekah wiggled down the stairs.

Margie ran for a hug.

"Did my son give you this?" The rose threaded by her ear was embarrassing, with what appeared to be soap residue, one could only hope, on its' matted-down red petals.

"Hum." Margie sniffed, crinkled her nose, cracking a half smile, and said, "nice."

Nice, Mom, sex with Bekah was outrageous. "Hey mom, let's get some food in this girl." He tried diverting her attention.

"Thanks mom and your hunky brilliant son. I'm not going to war any more. General Birchmont and I agree my presence is huge liability. I want your son. I want to give you pretty grandchildren, and I want to figure out my talent." He could not yet tell his mom about his co-directorship with Bekah of the super-secret OTTS, until he made up a cover, and until Bekah became convinced the job merited her special gifts.

"Sit here, honey, have a cup of coffee and let me make a plate for you. Barney, move next to Angel." Margie led her by hugging her over to the chair and then Bekah chowed down like a Stalag-17 inmate.

A short time later, the doorbell rang and Margie sprung up from the table, "Dan's here. Oh my, how do I look? Son, comb your hair, your shirt, tuck, tuck." She said to Bekah, "you're perfect. Well, the rose is crumpled. Mind if I replace it with a fresh one?" *Here we go again.*

"I'd love a fresh one, but I'm going to press this one for a keepsake."

"I'll protect it, honey." Jay said taking the rose. Margie headed for the door.

Margie hastily served sun tea along with TastyKake jelly and butterscotch Krimpets. Carlos, Dan and Cordell relaxed on the sofas in her rosewood trimmed plush Lane sofas. Bekah, Jay, Barney and Angel stuffed the loveseat.

"We understand, you aren't done with your canine research yet, General, but as soon as you can, will you help us?" Carlos asked.

"Absolutely," Bekah said, while munching a jelly Krimpet.

"We are getting an overwhelming number of assassination leads, but we can't track the lone nut, with no friends, no internet and no cell phone. We'll send over to your computer a doorway into our secure sites, with all the stats, profiles, leads and probability tools. You'll have complete access. Both of you."

"Perhaps, with a little luck you can use your gift, young lady." Cordell said.

"This great country needs my father. And…I need a father to walk me down the aisle, if—" The men didn't react except for the doting, cheek-kissing Jay. "I'll do whatever I can gentlemen, and dad, as soon as I can," Bekah said. The three men stood in unison.

"The most important goal in my life right now is to walk you down that aisle, a direction you two seem likely to take. So here's a mazel tov for the road." Dan was no longer a practicing Jew. He converted to Catholicism when he married Elsie. "Oh, and ah, get a proper ring, and see the priest for pre-marriage encounters. Your mom would want it this way, baby." He picked his daughter off the loveseat, twirled her around, pecked her and smiled broadly. "Let's have a family hug, Jay, Margie." Margie positively, absolutely, at this moment felt like the basketball cheerleader she once was.

Now she wanted the team's all-star—tall ruggedly handsome Dan who was, once upon a time, the star—to favor her. She was definitely falling for the man with beautiful chiseled features, salted black curls, and loving heart. She watched them drive around the circular driveway—leaving for now. She hoped Dan noticed the boxwood shrubs sculpted to look like chess pieces. She had done this to honor her son but it would suit Bekah as well. They all could call here, home, if they wanted. She worried about what they had said, *We are getting an overwhelming number of assassination leads, but we can't track the lone nut, with no friends, no internet, and no cell phone.* What sort of demented ugliness hovered out there somewhere? She glanced beyond the horizon.

* * *

Mrs. Markowitz had reached wits end, a suburb in St. Louis. Ever since they got Grandpa Markowitz from the old folks home, her love life, her kids' live, and her husband had changed. He was a sour puss, for sure, just like his dad, in so many ways.

She called her hubby, "I don't know what to do with him, anymore."

"What did he do now?" This little 'what did he do now,' seemed to be the only words her husband knew.

"You know Susie, the cute six-year-old two doors down?"

"What? Damn-it. I'm pulling over. Do you know how hard it is parking a gas truck on the interstate? No, of course you don't."

"Honey, I'm sorry. He killed her baby goose, gosling, I think."

"What?"

"He thought he was Julia Child, he needed goose fat. Of course, the baby bird had none. He's ruining the kitchen, pieces of bird all over, horrible burnt gosling with a can of applesauce for stuffing, which didn't help. The feathers caught fire. No fat, I told him. The little girl cried. I couldn't let her or her family in. Made excuses. He hollered at me like the guy on Hell's Kitchen. He told me to hang up my apron and leave the show."

"Calm down."

"Frankly, I think I might take the kids with me if you don't find a way to calm *him* down." She hesitated to say 'kill him,' because what was left of her marriage would likely die also, but that was the way she felt.

"We have to distract him."

She fumed. Silence.

"Tell him, to watch my classic film collection, because Hollywood might be his next calling or calling on him, ah. That ought to keep him fuckin', damn it, damn, please, honey make sure you show him how to operate the VCR. I'm about to explode, and that ain't good on a gas rig. Got to go."

"Love you, I think." But, there was no answer. He just clicked off. Over and out, good buddy.

Chapter 23

Research

About an hour's drive east of Cherry Hill rolled the Atlantic Ocean. On the way, west to east, over route 41, and then off some back roads sprawled the endless Pine Barons. Not a likely stop, except for crazy locals who termite-ed their scruffy selves into falling-down shacks and once-in-a-while nicely kept brick or aluminum sided homes, all one story to stay below the tree canopy and out of sight. They simply wanted to get away from it all. Hippies, people running away from the circus, mad bombers and hermits squatted or outright owned a piece of this unique New Jersey wilderness.

The rare owner had to strike a deal with the devil to live on these precious acres. A term used by most to describe the government. There lurked a devil of another kind and making. The antecedents of this eclectic mix kept others out by telling stories of the Jersey Devil: a mythical creature that ripped throats out for dessert, and stole away children. New Jerseyians even blamed the budget crisis on the devil.

Perhaps Bekah could put to rest the myth, or her Blindsight would find the red-eyeballed fiend. Jay couldn't believe where his mind had gone in the past twenty-four. The only storm on this hot midday clamored in his heart. After her wolf escapades, he started to believe in his Shoshone princess's special powers, the powers being more than science can or may someday explain. She could say a harpy sat on his head and he'd look in the mirror. The physicist in him leaned toward a scientific explanation. *Natch.* He racked his brains, and still could come up with no more than scout-hunter-tracker skills using sharp visualization and probabilities at a subconscious level. *Oh yes, perhaps an unexplained or spiritual connection with canines.*

Yep, a mouthful, but all Bekah's genius. He had no idea yet, how to harness her gift to save the civilized world. Today would test her reach into the world of Shoshone lure. The wolf was the protector of women in various Indian legends. The girl holding his hand and heart might outclass the telepathic Australian Aboriginals, or the renowned South African tracker/hunters. All demonstrated similar qualities, or the odd cases of American Indian scouts who claimed to visualize prey etc. hundreds of miles away. Some hypersensitivity to vibrations? God's gift?

Margie's second research facility nestled down rutted dirt roads, and long past the infrequent homes. At one point, windows down, the riders swooned from the smell of mash, or moonshine. Real rot-gut. The locals liked Dr. Margie Boone and her facility. Her wolves yearned for freedom and privacy just like them. In a way, the wolves took over the devil's place in their imagination, when a local paused from spitting twigs wedged in teeth to tell the story. The wolves' melodic howls conjured forbidden images. Wouldn't you rather be in a shack in Idaho, FBI ready to bust down your door? *Nope, spit.*

Four-miles-square of double high and double smart electric fencing, kept people out and the completely wild wolves in.

The wolves lived in a four-quadrant system, each square sufficient to sustain them. When prey ran low in one quadrant a door would open up for the wolves, and close on the next group of wondering dear or quickly repopulating rabbits, and all manner of little critter volunteers wanting to do their part for the eco system.

They parked their jeep at the main entrance and entered Pleistocene Park as his mom called it. Pleistocene, because Margie's research suggested before dogs, wolves and humans lived in rough harmony with each other. The heavy steel door clanged closed and they set off through dense woods for a picnic in wolf country.

They arrived at a clearing of sandy soil and straw grass next to a rushing stream. The temperature at midday felt like eighty with a comfortable easterly breeze whistling through the pines. The fresh scent of pinecones, sap and needles permeated their site.

They tossed a blanket, unfolded a chair for mom and munched some Snyder's fat free hard sourdough pretzels, saving lunch for later. They washed the pretzels down with cold water from the cooler Jay had lugged.

He started his scientific experiment. "How many do you see and where are they?" Jay referred to the collared wolves. Both Dick and Holly were instructed not to help Bekah in any way, and not to divulge to Margie, they were anything more than laptop computer and pink pocketbook. Bekah wore her newly bought pink country cotton dress, which matched her pocketbook, necklace and earrings. Margie dressed like a guide on a safari, sharp clean khaki, pockets everywhere. Jay wore faded jeans and one of his tie-died pullovers. He chose full-length jeans, in case the infamous bigger-than-a bird Jersey mosquito decided to suck the life out of him. The Jersey mosquito could be mistaken for the Jersey Devil.

"I picture twenty adults, seven juveniles and eight pups," Bekah said.

"We haven't collared the pups, but that's amazingly right." Margie said.

Over a hearty breakfast of buckwheat pancakes, scrapple and eggbeaters, Bekah and Jay disclosed every measurable detail of her exceptional abilities to Margie. They withheld mystical beliefs, lest they take the scientists off his and her game. Info on OTTS remained taboo. Jay suggested Bekah's future job could be helping the NYU's research department to study the paranormal, and the secret service to save her father's life.

"Can you see them, honey?" Jay asked.

"Well, I think they're all clustered near the center in the south-east quadrant some two-point-two miles off, where the pup's lair is. The adults are loping in twenty to thirty-foot circles, some resting and some playing."

Jay looked over at his mom's tracker box and true enough they were all there and doing what Bekah described. Jay found Bekah amazing. He couldn't even find some items in his office

"They're disturbed by our presence, which is why some of them are circling and pacing," Margie said.

"The next part is a piece of cake, but I must ask," Margie said. "Are either of you afraid of the world's most lethal pack hunter."

Both said no.

"Well honey, two days ago you showed some trepidation about the African Painted Hunting Dogs."

"I know the wolf. My research on the dogs left their friendliness a question mark," Bekah answered.

"Okay, and you are right." She crossed herself. "I'm going to open the gate to our quadrant. As I told you this morning don't expect a visit, they're very shy." At breakfast, Margie went on about her experiments with various human guinea pigs. Most of the time, the pack wouldn't come near the humans. Once in a while, the wolves would send a scout or two. The scouts would typically lope circles around the humans, the closest radius of wolf to human being twenty-three feet. One time, a ball and chained death row inmate walked toward a curious wolf, piece of beef in hand, but the smarter of the two disappeared. Never, not ever, did a hunting party show up, which fit Dr. Margie Boone's thesis: starting around seven hundred thousand years ago, wolves and humans made peaceful overtures to start their destined steps toward mutualism.

About five minutes later, the alpha wolf headed over alone.

"Have no fear. His head's up, and he's smiling," Margie said, nonchalantly.

He loped right up to Bekah, ignored the other two humans. Bekah seemed at peace. He stopped and sniffed her cinnamon hair, bumped her, sniffed her pink pocketbook, and then rifled some beef jerky from her picnic basket. Next, he grabbed the handle and ran off with the remaining jerky, cheese steak sandwiches, napkins, and fruit drinks.

"Well, I've got a great supper planned," Margie said. They headed home, laughing. Jay mused about the wolf. *Not normal behavior, unless we traveled back in time. But what to make of all this.*

At supper, Margie said, "You demonstrated more than Blindsight by counting wolves and describing where they were," Margie said. "Quite incredible, to say nothing of Alpha's visit."

"He was fantastic. You know, I saw the pack before we left this morning," Bekah said.

"Mom, let me, if I could," Jay chimed in.

"Yes."

"Bekah dearest, your ability to see at greater distances is commonly known as remote viewing. You're a walking arsenal for the military."

"Well, I think we can find a way to use this for peace and helping the secret service. My military days are over." She thought of her father, and the constant threats to his life. If only she could save him, the beginning of phase two of her life: finding a major use for her newfound talents, would become reality. Phase three of her life started with Jay, traveled through her heart, and ended with marriage and children. If everything worked the way she planned, she would assume the role she was destined for, and use the talents God gave her to the best of her ability. Yes and someday, perhaps, she'd regain her sight. She considered herself blessed and complete as a woman and human being. But she had no clue how to help her father. Yet.

After the supper of corn on the cob, baby spinach, and sweet and sour shrimp, they said goodbye, leaving Margie tearing with joy. Their new penthouse, some ninety miles north in the Soho district of Manhattan, awaited their inspection.

Chapter 24

Home brewed analysis

Jay carried Bekah across the threshold of their new Thompson street home. Five floors below, in his old co-op, Brenda remained. They employed her to manage Carthage Consultants and Detective Agency, a partial shill for the super-secret government OTTS. They'd phase Brenda into the true purpose of her job on a need to know and a want to trust basis or they'd phase her out of a job and the apartment. They'd take a limited number of civilian jobs to keep their cover.

Surely, they could maintain the ruse for months, because their plan was and their lust insisted that they spent at least half the day making love. Surely, Brenda would jump to this conclusion as she worried about productivity. It was too bad if it might hurt her feelings. *Get over it.*

So Brenda's first step, if she could make it, was getting over Jay. Her second step was to coordinate their activities. Thirdly, she'd analyze and negotiate requests for help. Calls rounded out her day. And fourth, but not least, she'd soon have to live with Anatoly, the poor Russian émigré, who Bekah was so taken by. The apartment had two bedrooms anyway, and Anatoly had certain bodyguard skills. He was no Moon. He'd play chess half the time, but then again, there were no present 'known' threats to Jay, Bekah or Brenda—in no particular order. Jay, who always admired detective work, was itching to try it.

Jay also led the charge into the strange world of OTTS. Much of what he discovered and shared with Bekah, they both considered untrue and hardly worth their efforts. There'd be no spoon bending but there would be more investigative work in remote viewing. For this, Bekah would be her own Guinea pig. True, her remote viewing seemed different, as if a gift from God.

* * *

Jay's excitement about the layout of the penthouse was contagious. He surprised Bekah. "While Holly was guarding the safe-house on Mykonos, she absorbed the plans for the rain forest shower, redrew them to fit our penthouse, sent them to the architect along with our other ideas, honchoed the whole thing including haggling." Holly had applied herself with aplomb. In the end, she produced a masterpiece in the bathroom.

Privacy was the theme and Holly didn't disappoint. The penthouse had an opaque cover over a green lawn on the large deck, with doggie door to the inside. Bamboos, other plants and Japanese separators insured privacy for the often-naked Bekah. Electronic counter measures made the penthouse look vacant to anyone with sophisticated eavesdropping equipment. OTTS jammed electronic intrusions over the full spectrum, just like their NSA sister agency did. The cover kept uninvited satellites and other eyes out but let the warmth and diffused light of the sun permeate.

They had a rubber and equipment room for exercise, massages or the martial arts similar to the one on Mykonos. An office/communications room, with an eye scan entrance, housed state of the art NSA computers and equipment to supplement Holly and Dick. The kitchen looked like a modern version of Julia Child's. A nearly room-sized opaque skylight brought in natural light.

This girl does nothing halfway. Bekah proved a lioness in bed and wherever else. Sometimes they couldn't wait. Comfort was forgotten, but he always protected her health.

They slid off the table and he carried her to the rainforest shower. She felt secure and pampered in his strong arms, head nestled in his hairy chest, nose intoxicated by Ivory soap—again—and him. Happy wasn't the word for how he made her feel: the most desired woman on the planet. He talked of her slim figure and small beasts as a work of art, God's masterpiece. She loved his doting.

"Will you still love me when I'm sixty-four?" He asked.

"In high school, you weren't physically perfect, now you're hunky dreamy, and maybe someday you won't be again, but I'll always love the you, in you. How about me?"

"You complete me. You always will."

Chapter 25

Bughouse chess

They call me Grandpa Markowitz. But I'm not black and not Jewish. What kind of name is Grandpa anyway? I'm actually a gay Walter Mitty. I never had children. What a disgusting prospect. These people stole me from a prison for old people and now I'm watching James Cagney blow himself up in *White Heat*. He's on the top of the world, why can't I be? Why can't I be him?

I know I'm losing my marbles. Life used to be good, whatever it was, I'm sure it used to be good, used to be good. Used to be good. Someone is to blame for this.

I think. I'll watch it again. Got to remember. Got to remember. I think I'll watch Cagney again. She thinks I don't know how to push buttons on a VCR. Hell, I invented the VCR—and the internet. Yeah, that's the ticket. Well okay, just the VCR. Push play. Sit. Shut up and sit down, I said sternly. Ha. Ha. Ha. Get it, Howard Stearn-ly, the radio shock jock. I used to be his sidekick Robin, but Stearn is a racist pig. So am I. This face in the mirror is some sort of trick. Wrinkled black. I know I'm old. I know. Sit down and shut up. Watch James Cagney blow himself up. Blow himself up.

I've got a deck with fifty two cards. There's fifty two days to the democratic Convention right here in St. Luis. I'm going to watch Cagney fifty-one times more. That adds up, right?

That Senator Dan Carthage, the black Jew, pretending to be Catholic and white, and you can smoke his Shoshone crap. I hate them all. He is going to pay for this. I wouldn't be here with these crazy people, if it wasn't for his politics of including. Put all the black, white, Catholics, and Jews together, and blame me, Amelia Earhart. Or am I Truman Copote? Maybe tomorrow. He's taking my rightful place as the next President of the United States of America. He put me here, making me believe I'm black and a Jew.

Rip card one, blow myself up.

"On top of the world."

Mr. Lamar Markowitz's dad, aka *the nut job*, kept himself out of mischief and harm's way. Lately. Lamar installed a bigger TV in dad's basement bedroom, and got the old man to sign for his medication. He actually remembered who he was, sometimes. Dad entertained himself each day, nearly all day and night with classic movies and an old playing card deck, which he ripped up one by one, to pass the days, it seemed. Thank God, he wasn't smashing computers or eating a kid's goldfish, anymore. Did dad think he'd die in fifty-two days or whatever cards were left to his deck? In any case, Lamar grinned and winced at the coming tired pun, Dad wasn't playing with a full deck.

Seemingly tense over some imagined transgression, Dad gripped pages of hand written notes. "Dad, I'm glad you're feeling better, and happy down here. I don't smell the musty stink anymore since we fixed the sump-pump and put a fresh coat of paint, do you?"

He awaited pearls of wisdom. *No fuckin' answer.* "You know, we all love you."

"I'm afraid, I'm wearing out this movie. Can you get another?" He read off one of his scraps of paper.

"Don't worry about it." He read the title. "If you like Cagney so much, I'll find the DVD for it."

Dad looked down on the sheet again. "Yep, I've come to grips with myself. I know I forget things. I hate it— No, let me finish, while I can remember what I want to say, ah— I love you, son."

"Sorry Dad. I'm always so busy with trucking."

"Do you think you could take me with you for a ride sometime? Just like I used to do for you?" Lamar couldn't remember any rides. Hell, perhaps he too was losing his marbles.

"Maybe. Maybe soon. I'll have to clear it."

Looking down, "I want to toot your horn like all your buddies are talking about doing. Doesn't have to be at the Democratic Convention, because you'll need to get a whole bunch of clearances."

"Not to worry, Dad. I'll tell you what. You don't become Julia Child, or Freddie the maniac killer, or even Mother Theresa, and I'll promise to take you on a ride by the convention. You will be my official tooter."

"I've been so busy with my plans. I mean watching the movies, and planning to live a calmer life. Take my pills. I even made friends with your dog. You see, son. I don't remember his name."

"I'm going to frame a picture of Max, hang it on the wall above the TV. I got to go."

Dad peeked down at his notes, sitting on the edge of his single bed with crocheted white flowers, wearing white shirt, fuckin' white pants, rubbed his eyes and said, "I love you, son."

"Ice cream man, sellin' crap."

Chapter 26

Mastering the game

Bekah cozied up to Jay with Angel on his chest. He watched Casablanca, while she wondered, in her sterling imagination, through Rick's *Café Americana*, by the piano and the piano player, Sam. She found the owner, Rick, and challenged him to a game of chess. Angel flipped herself, paws up and slipped down the crevice between two human tummies.

She worried about her daddy. Angel sneezed.

"Bless you," they both said.

While rubbing the pup's soft belly, Bekah traveled away from Casablanca land and into a little home. An elderly man flipped cards from a poker deck onto a coffee table. Next to him lay a poodle. Each card had toot written on it. She panned up and peered at the old man's TV, which had James Cagney playing a tough guy in what appeared to be *White Heat*. Over-and-over again the man pushed rewind.

Black wrinkled hands.

Cagney stood on the top of a huge oil storage tank and yelled out he was on top of the world as it blew.

Toot, said the man.

Angel jumped off. The vision receded.

Later in the week, while falling asleep, Angel cuddled and the same vision returned. Again, a week later, the same thing happened. Bekah held the pup close. Instinctively, she felt the pup helped her in some way with the vision. Regretfully, this remained her only possible legitimate vision as of today. There were other, after-the-fact, visions of nefarious activity, she couldn't use because the news reported the scenes she imagined as real, and then resolved. Both she and Jay suspected Carlos of some of the scenes she experienced.

For instance, a Klu Klux Klansman fully robed and hooded accidently hung himself to a lonely Cypress tree in a Walmart parking lot at three on a very hot afternoon No witnesses and the parking lot cameras were on the fritz. Or how about, the neo-Nazis, all six of them, who accidently sealed their motel room and then accidently gassed themselves with Zyclon B. Assassination literature, emails, websites and threats to her father were associated to both cases.

Bekah decided to dig deeper into what she originally thought was a Bill Cosby mix-up in her mind as the old man did look a lot like the disgraced actor. "Dick and

Holly, please run the sound or word "toot" through the NSA main computers, look for references to 33 cards, 52 cards, James Cagney and the movie White Heat. Relate this to my dad's campaign."

"It is thirty-three days to your dad's entrance into the convention at St. Luis," Holly said.

"The convention is in a stadium in which gas tanker trucks can and will drive by and toot," Dick said.

Jay said, "Holly, please compile a list of all the drivers who take that route, and a separate list of the black or dark skinned drivers, and another list who have applied to the secret service to drive by that night."

"Thirty-three possibles, who are brown or black, out of six-hundred and fifty-seven total drivers who have inquired with the secret service about possibly parading by the convention."

"Maybe we should print the smaller list on separate pieces of paper and see which one Angel pees on." Bekah said, in jest. Jay had jumped on the dog/wolf connection bandwagon, without understanding the why.

"She's completely house trained, so I doubt she'll oblige." Jay said. "I could try peeing on the pile. No seriously, I think you have something. I really, truly do."

"I know you do, honey. How about compiling a list of each driver's family. Look for a black family with grandpa at home," Bekah said.

"Nothing turns up," Dick said.

"Look for an elderly man living alone with a full-sized poodle," Jay said.

"Nothing."

"Compile a family with a poodle," Bekah said.

"Nothing."

"Well, I might be wrong, but could you continue to check?"

Jay added his two cents. "Check any black family with or without a grandpa at home."

"I certainly will," Holly said.

About a week before the convention, Bekah felt something had to break. Her little visions had to be checked out on the ground. Time was running out. The visions were all she had.

"Dick, raise Carlos, please."

"Hi Carlos, I've got Jay, Holly and Dick with me here. I have a serious hunch."

"Your hunch record is legendary," Carlos said on speaker.

"Will you convince or let me convince the secret service, to go to the home of five individuals Dick is sending you. The team they select will be looking for a family with a poodle, unregistered, and a grandpa, or elderly gentleman, also unregistered but living with them."

"I'm feeling it. I have list. How are you two doing?"

"Fantastic, she still beats me at chess, but she cheats."

"I do not. I beat his ass, because I know my mate better than he knows how to mate me."

"Well, I can see you two have much to discuss. I will work on finding our hidden assassin now." Carlos said, and dropped off the line and Jay became preoccupied.

He stripped her for a full body massage, which in her case started with a happy beginning. Her body flooded with desire served. She mellowed out under the firm and loving pets of her mate. She vibrated Dick about whether she was cheating at chess. Dick vibrated back saying, *you don't know you're cheating by reading Jay's vibrations, so you're not cheating. However, all humans can pick up vibes. With your heightened senses, you do it better than most. However, reading Jay's vibes is inexact. Although it might help a little, it doesn't explain your total dominance. As for your other abilities: I don't understand them yet and therefore can't duplicate them.*

Bekah arched up, "Your turn, Honey."

* * *

Mr. Markowitz senior was tired of the pounding at the door. Tired of life. It wouldn't be long now and he'd be on top of the world. People would remember him.

Used to pretending, he dressed up as Mother Teresa again and inched to the door. The officers at the door weren't going to spoil his party. The dog barked, incessantly. He muzzled Max and locked the poodle in his basement bedroom.

"Oh my dear gentlemen, so nice of you to visit an old lady."

"I heard your dog barking, ma'am. Is he all right?"

"Oh, that's my neighbor's pit bull. She's quite sweet, really. She visits me often. Don't tell the McCaffertys. I give her a treat now and again." Lying was such fun. Poodle faced Max would not upstage him, and a pit bull would not encourage the cops to come in. *Good thinking, Sherlock Holmes in disguise as Mother Theresa. Perfect.*

"No, ma'am. Mind if we come in?"

Oh well. "Well yes, my family isn't home. I never. Maybe you could come back, later."

That's fine, ma'am, but could we ask you one question before we leave?"

"What's this all about, officer?

"Well, ma'am, I'm not at liberty to discuss. But if you could."

"Oh, this is fun, just like CSI or Law and Order. Go ahead officer, shoot, get it?"

"That's funny, ma'am. If you'd be more comfortable we'd be glad to talk with your husband when he gets home."

"I'm sorry boys, my husband died long ago. I live here with my son, Lamar, daughter-in-law Michelle and their two darling children." *Brats.* "So you can pick one."

"We will."

"They'll be back in a few days, but I'll answer just one itsy-bitsy question."

"Thank you, ma'am."

"Call me, Theresa."

"Theresa, have you seen this man, he's suspected in a bank robbery, and was last seen in this neighborhood."

"No, never saw him. Is he dangerous?"

"The bank robber left a wooden pistol in the trash outside the bank, so we don't think so, but I'd be careful anyway."

"I certainly will. A girl can't be too careful, you know?"

"Here's my card. Call me if anybody in your family has seen him."

"Will do officers, over and out, roger wilco, and twenty-three skidoo."

"Yes, ma'am."

Mr. Markowitz wasn't amused by the officers' visit. They were plotting to take him to another home or execute him. He'd prefer to die in his own glorious way and no one would stop him, no one could stop him. How embarrassing the charade.

He addressed the dog, marveling at her, no his disguise. "Obviously, my dear Watson, Inspector Lastrade has a lot to learn. The game's afoot."

* * *

Her father asked her, a Rebublican leaner, to introduce him at the Democratic convention. She enjoyed rock star status now, had teased on TV shows. "I might, might not."

Jay, Bekah, and Angel joined her father, and sister, Sissy, in the lead limo. She felt no sense of foreboding, for now. She supposed the assassination attempt had dissipated, or was a false lead. Relaxed, she reviewed her speech.

How could she refuse a chance to talk about her dad, a man she loved? He displayed a pure heart, right there on his sleeve and the best of intentions through his actions. She thought about the Republican and Democrats she had met. You can't have this great country without a little disagreement between men and women of good faith and steel hewn honor.

She wore the full dress uniform of a newly minted General with enough medals; she'd need hydraulics. Today was the coming out party for her promotion. Personal threats gone, a new 'information' campaign had started depicting her as a role model for both men and women soldiers. Gone was the comparing her to Alexander the Great, Eisenhower, Paton, take your pick. The press now recognized her as a people's general, who through hard work, proved her father right when he rammed, the anti-age, sex and talent discrimination bill through the senate, years before.

A woman or anyone with enough hard work and talent, no matter the age, could now achieve a rank befitting their talents. The Army was now working on mandatory sensitivity classes for men—to start the war against sexism as found in some men, and win their hearts and minds over time—Bekah's recommendation. Some of these thoughts comprised her prepared speech.

The limo exited the interstate. With the coliseum looming, Bekah felt the impact of her special abilities, but not in any definable way. She began to ache, first in her head, then her stomach. This vague discomfort formed the beginning of one of her spot-on hunches. The search for an elderly black man, intent on blowing up a gas truck came to a dead end. She had doubts. The secret service promised her, they'd clear every truck and driver entering.

Rest easy. Just relax.

"We might even see Senator Carthage or his limo." Lamar Markowitz said to his father.

"Toot." His dad struggled with speaking at times, but Lamar knew what he meant. In less than a half hour, they'd be tooting their gas tanker in procession by the exterior wall of the coliseum. It was a perfect time for traveling, dusk, just about 70 degrees. The wind took his breath, invigorated his face.

Lamar loved driving, the freedom, the many characters met at truck stops, perhaps a fling once-in-a-while with a Mable, any Mable. *Wearing her apron, see you at 1AM, pretty boy.*

He glanced at his dad, all get up like a boy on his first train ride, same cap, same jacket, even looked a little like him, except for the wrinkles. What was it like to get old? He loved his dad, even if he was the worst pain in the ass in God's creation. How many times when he was little, did he repeat himself? "What's that daddy?" "What's that daddy?" "What's that daddy?" Every time the big man with sharp black curls, hugged him, said, "that's a squirrel, son," or some such wonder of nature.

"Dad, please." He pulled his dad toward the center of the cab. "It's really not safe to put your head out the window."

"I know. I must have told you that a hundred times, no thousands. You were a stubborn child. But you had character. I liked that in you. I love you, son."

"Okay, you've got me, love you back."

"But there's something sparkling or scrapping against the back near the tires."

"I don't see anything."

"No, you just have to put your head out the window here."

Lamar wondered. Another hallucination? Can't take the chance. There was plenty of shoulder abutting farmland and sparse trees on this lonely stretch of the interstate. He feathered the brakes, less sparks that way, not a good thing on a gas truck no matter how full.

"Alright, dad. Please stay in the cab. I'll just have a quick look."

"Don't get too close to the truck, until you spot it. Promise me."

"Okay."

"Did I ever tell you, I love you?"

"I love you too, dad. We might not have time to stop for a coffee now. Let's see." With that, he slipped out, and stepped down from the cab, crossed the front, down his father's side, looked back, a hand waved. He continued toward the back.

The truck lurched forward. "Oh my God."

"Toot."

"Damn, sonofa bitch. Dad, Dad."

"Toot."

Lamar ran, just like he did in high school track, but the diesel powered truck proved too fast for him, and he gasped.

Out of gas.

Walter Markowitz tooted the gas truck's horn as he put distance between himself and the nut chasing him, who claimed to be his son. The guy was black, for God's sake.

He didn't need to climb to the top of the truck, to be on top of the world like James Cagney in *White Heat*. A pistol shot and a follow up well-aimed flair ought to do the trick. The ex-sarge, Army, World War II, a bit washed up now, could still use a pistol. Why, the hell did they stick him in an all-black brigade? His pretender son did him a favor, forcing him to take some pills. Once in a while, he calmed and thought, hey this handsome boy's my son, but on the other hand, he was James Cagney, and he was on a mission.

He dribbled a can of WD-40 out his driver's side, just as he did out the passenger side when he left his pretender son wheezing. He thought the oil would help bring the fire to him. A pain in his abdomen nearly doubled him over. "Got to watch the road. Got to. Got to."

He knew he was dying. Something ate away at his core, causing severe pain. Just one more very good reason to go out with a bang. If all the trucks blew one after another, there wouldn't be a stadium to pitch ball in, let alone harbor those communists, who call themselves democrats. He used to be a democrat. He vaguely remembered asking JFK to say, "ask not what your country can do for you." So, he'd do something to his country. *Ah, the good ole' days.*

He obeyed the speed limit, at least. The truck lumbered down the interstate, lights flickering by like overheads dimming in the hallway leading to old Sparky. The trees made for the worst wallpaper. He guessed Cagney tried electrocution; didn't like it, and then blew himself up on top of a gas storage tank. *Won't hurt a bit.* Besides, here he was, James Cagney, and still alive.

He gave one last peek at the rising moon, the blackening sky. There'd be fireworks tonight. Resolute, he signaled for the exit to the coliseum where the Democratic convention would host their nominee tonight, Senator Dan Carthage. *You'll fry up nice.* He rolled down his driver's side window again, and breathed in the woodsy scent of the cooling remains of a late July day.

He pulled the gas rig to a stop at a checkpoint. Two men in blue stepped forward, nearly hiding Shanghai Lil, who he'd been searching high and low for his whole life. Wondered if his wife would mind.

Do I have a wife? The least I could have done was write what's-her-name a goodbye note. Well good riddance and oh you kid. The cute Asian gal dressed in sleek tight black jeans, and hooded jacket. Her jacket was weird, besides keeping her too warm. The jacket had black metallic triangles in pockets going up and down and rounding her ample breasts. She was also packing heat. She looked like a ninja.

The jig is up.

"Papers, sir," said the tall skinny copper.

"You're blocking my view you dirty coppers. That there is some dame." Her round face, sprinkled with a touch of freckles, and sturdy frame, got Cagney's attention, if only his stick shift worked properly. Built like a healthy farm girl, he'd roll in some hay with her any day.

"I take offense to that, sir," said short-fat blue boy.

"Sir, step out of the cab," tall-skinny said.

"Sorry officers, I don't mean nothin'. I'm just missing my woman. Here's the papers. And your shy friend is lovely." The woman just stared.

"Hey there, kiddo." He waved.

"I not a kiddo." She spoke. She actually spoke.

Gees, if he could get into her pants, he could always blow himself up some other day, or some other hour. 'Cause, he'd be hungry again.

Tall-skinny interrupted his pick-up attempts. "You empty, Mr. Markowitz?" Pause. "Mr. Markowitz?" Cagney figured his Markowitz disguise fooled them all. *They must be idiots.* Or maybe he really was black. Yeah, and cows can fly.

"Oh sorry, again." Cagney found some more papers. "Is this it? I got a caper I'm late for."

"We'll check the gage, and then you can go."

Tall-skinny went down the side of the truck rubbing his finger on the stainless steel, producing a look of disdain, and probably a greasy finger, from all the oil he had poured out the windows. The girl kept her laser beam black eyes focused on his face, as if she was studying every wrinkle. Cagney dipped his head a little, letting the cap brim take more of his face.

"You're empty, but you've got to clean up your tank, before you fill again. It's greased to hell. Get out of my life, Markowitz."

Empty, empty, no gas, he needed time to think.

Cagney tipped his cap at the lady. She just spit and said. "You got dog at home?"

"My wife not that bad," mimicking her broken English.

The men laughed, the truck inched forward. "I got to pull over and call her. Okay?" he shouted back.

"Yeah, yeah, two hundred yards ahead, have a good night."

"You do mean no gas in the tanker, right?"

"Yes, sir, just like every other truck here tonight," Tall-skinny, said.

Ahead about two hundred yards on a gravel pullover, a black paneled truck, a hazmat truck, and two squad cars waited. Calmly Cagney pulled the cord. He needed to regroup.

Toot.

* * *

"Why he call you dirty coppers?" Moon asked.

The tall officer named Mike said, "He didn't mean it, some truckers vent their boredom with whatever they loaded into their CD or DVD players. This nut was mimicking a movie star."

"Who he mimic?"

"The Black Knight," the short officer named Bernie said.

"No, that's the Dark Knight, and he liked the police. You're thinking of Al Pacino." Mike said.

"I say hello to your little friends, you dirty coppers?" Bernie suggested.

"No, you dolt. It had to be the Joker in Dick Tracy."

"I beg to differ."

"Maybe he James Cagney?" Moon asked.

"Who's he?" Mike asked.

"Oh, he's an old guy. Maybe she's right. I know, ah, ah, maybe Humphrey Bogart in ah, Capablanca." Bernie answered.

Moon walked off shaking her head listening to them name one star after another, and as far as she could tell misquoting the hell out of bunch of movies. She relived the famous Scarface scene and laughed, just a little. She had business to do.

She waved and shouted, "I check him out. Alert officers ahead."

Running fast, she started stealthy rips of space and time, varying movements, taking advantage of tree shadows caused by streetlights and police spots. Black outfit against black night and a line of trucks crawling ahead gave time to do job. She fingered the flat face of one throwing star.

Cagney peeked into his side mirror and thought he saw a wisp, a kind of shadow jumping, as if branches of trees swayed down to kiss the gravel and grass. *Like a phantom.* He used to read scary books like Phantoms, by Koontz. *There it goes again.* This time a momentary glint of something like a piece of glass at the bottom of a tree trunk, caught his eye. *The ninja.* Shanghai Lil was coming to pay him a visit. He rolled up the driver's window and put the truck in gear.

He'd just pick up speed, as soon he got off the skinny, one-lane feeder and wait for the emptying into the huge multi-lane concrete surround of the coliseum. Then he'd crush the Senator's limo or run the man down. He moved into a line of trucks, here and there a toot. Why not. He pulled the cord. His rig entered a tunnel of elm trees. The rub of his greased up stainless steel, sounded like chalk scratching blackboard. He should have done better in school, might have made something of himself. *Won't be long.* With all that oil, he threw out both windows—for his funeral fire that would now never happen— he hoped his truck was as slippery as an eel and un-breachable.

* * *

The truck was moving slow in line with the other trucks when Moon caught up along the passenger's side. She jumped up, grabbed the handle. Her hands and feet slipped. She hit the diesel stoke and tumbled off. The first two truck tires squashed her feet at the ankles. She pulled away from the next set of tires and managed a stand to extreme pain. *Little bones squashed or broken.* She tested her compressed feet for a moment, and then hobbled with sufficient speed to jump onto the runner board. She jammed her hand—then wrist—this time under the passenger door handle, and dug her fingertips into the window's rubber rain guard. She'd use the strength of the jammed arm to lift her up.

Now she had a problem with her feet. The running board was greased, she knew, but her feet had no strength to try to wedge the grates somewhere.

"Damn it. Damn. You open up, mister." But, the window was closed. She tapped the window with a throwing star. She tried reaching for her gun, but it was gone, ripped off from its lower leg holster when the tires squashed her feet. The full weight of her body was now held by her wrist. She felt something rip in her arm.

"Open mister or I kill you." She knew if she didn't get a hold of something fast with her other hand, she might slide off again. The truck picked up speed and was now cutting by the other trucks, and heading right for the motorcade. She couldn't reach her phone and hold on. So before she grabbed the window rain guard with here good hand, she waved. She deliberately dropped the lethal throwing star and with her good arm and body banging against the cab, she swung up, dug her good arm's fingers into the window rain guard. Her other hand remained jammed, maybe broken, and of little use, except to help hold on. The window rolled down. *He a fool.* She pictured a flying star embedded in his forehead and tried to reach her top pocket.

"Having trouble, Lil?"

Okay, she was smart. She couldn't kill him, get in the cab fast enough to hit brakes, turn wheel, stop truck. So, persuade crazy man. Moon only had seconds left to make decision.

* * *

Angel started a high-pitched bark, for no reason, which in the confines of the limo, rang ears. Bekah's tiny hairs rose all over her body. This was it.

"Daddy, get out of the car. Everybody now." Nobody ever disobeys a general, or else.

She held Angel tight and listened for the directional sounds of the door for escape. Dick helped her get ready with precise directions. Jay grabbed her legs, and started pulling her and Angel out the door. "There's a truck coming right for us, don't resist me. I just have to clear your head." Sounds of gunfire erupted, like the ending pops of a Fourth of July celebration.

"Oh no," Bekah heard something shatter on the pavement. "I dropped Holly," Jay said.

"I'll collect all of her, sir," said Cordell, who knew the value of the top-secret device. Jay carried Bekah and Angel to safety.

When they were all secure behind an ambulance, Bekah's big sister, Sissy said, "I think your pocketbook is crying."

* * *

Moon pulled up with her good hand for a quick peek. The man had that look, she saw so many time, *on many many men.* She knew in an instant her chance.

"I horny, mister. You want me?" She spied the long sleek black limo about two hundred yards ahead. Evac started. She saw the Senator's head pushed down by Secret Service. They run to cover. She regretted never having make love with the great man. He found somebody he love. He said. Dan was a good and very good-looking man. Everybody escaped right away. She realized only she and Markowitz die tonight. The gunfire raged, but nothing pinged her side of truck. *Good thing they sharp shooters*, she hoped. She hoped the man heard her, she repeated, screamed in agony, might sound like wild woman. "I want you."

"Yes Lil. Me you."

The truck screeched and jumped again and again trying to stop before crushing the limo. The steel tanks lurched forward arching the cab. The up and down and forward and back jerks twisted her arm and more things ripped or broke inside. The truck stopped, tapping the limo's side window, and pushing the Senator's vehicle maybe an inch.

"You no use to me with bullet holes, Mister James Cagney."

Markowitz rolled the driver's side window down, threw his hands up, and out the window. The gunfire stopped. Moon collapsed onto the pavement, hitting her head on the running board. *I so stupid.* Blood gushed from her wrist caused by some sharp insignia in the metal below the door handle catching her skin when she slid down. While Moon was blacking out, she sighted a handsome medic with curly blond hair running to her aid. She gave him best flirt face under circumstance. She be more than fine. Over and out.

* * *

The convention delayed one hour to accommodate the secret service, and emergency services, still reeling from the assassination attempt. Psychiatrists had Mr. Markowitz whisked under secret service guard for interview, observation and medical tests at Scott Air Force Base.

And then Bekah made her way to the podium with Angel, her carved lioness ivory cane and her man. She sensed a sweet moment in history, no less for women everywhere. They probably emoted with the strong woman on their TVs. They wished for their daughters…

She had started with a little family history, then military history… "I stand before you tonight blinded in battle. Many in the press harangue my dad for pushing into law, the instrument that blinded me. I want to thank him tonight for the opportunity to become a General at my young age, to lead in combat our brave soldiers, to excel at what I chose as a career. I may be blind, but I can see…and I wouldn't have it any other way."

She opened her now clear violet eyes, looked in the direction of her fiancé, and beamed. "I may be blind, but I can see. I love this beautiful man with my whole heart. Professor Boone, Jay to me, has been waiting for me his whole life, should I marry him or keep him waiting?"

She waited for the raucous conventioneers to settle down with their chants, "marry him, marry him."

"I'm certainly not going to disappoint him. On another matter, my father has been waiting his whole life to serve you. I may be blind, but I can see. Should we keep him waiting any longer?" Another series of chants consumed the crowd.

"The military is still not perfect, perhaps it never will be or perhaps there will come a day when there will be no need for a military…

"I ask the nation and the world tonight one question. Can we not rise to the best of our ability with the talents God gave us? My father has. He will serve you with an honest heart and a brilliant mind.

"Today, I stand before you, in some ways, very much a conservative woman, asking you to elect my father, he who can best conserve our union. I may be blind…but I can see. I can see a man I love, a man for the ages. To all my Republican friends, may I ask one favor? …I would really like a Rose Garden wedding." Jay gripped her hand. They waved.

She held up the now famous pup rescued from an oven and offered her to the standing, chanting audience. Bekah caught a glimpse of the crowd in her imagination or Blindsight. However, the strange vision had no greens or reds, but plenty of yellows and blues. Her heart soared. Proof of the unknowable, the Creator's yet undiscovered and not understood links between canines and humans. Good enough for her, with little doubt, she had seen, through Angel's partially color blind eyes.

She made a quick prayer. *You bless me, Lord. Of this I have no doubt. May I use my talents to glorify You.* The crowd adulations diminished and she finished with "It is my proud honor to introduce to you the next President of the United States, the Senior Senator from the great State of New Jersey, and the best dad, a girl could dream to have, Senator Dan Carthage."

Chapter 27

Zwischenzug (in-between moves)

Fort Meade, NSA headquarters, August 3rd, 10AM

Bekah, Jay and Angel waited in a circular glass conference room in full view of a computer system that stretched at least a hundred meters in every direction with the room's ceiling about three stories up. The upside down glass cheese-bowl, they waited in, blocked the wind from airplane-hanger sized air-conditioning ducts, and the whine of the computers.

NSA's chief engineer, Bud, commanded the soundproof door to open. He blew in and placed a white cardboard box on the circular glass table that smelled of hot cinnamon, and said. "Try these walnut and raisin honey buns. No trans fat and noooo saturated fat. Getting there."

"How are you, Bud?" Bekah and then Jay asked.

"I'm fine. My wife is going to open a shop in the mall. We're thinking franchise here. The world craves a healthier donut and honey bun. Imagine donuts and coffee after mass. Won't have to go to confession."

"This is scrumptious," Bekah said.

"You guys can get in on the ground floor. Well, maybe you two lovebirds aren't interested. On the other hand, it's good to diversify, and help save humanity one donut at a time. Oh, that's catchy. Someone pat me on the back. I've eaten three this morning, and look at me. See, no extra fat. Well?"

"My sixth sense tells me you really want to tell us about Holly. But these are soooo yummy, really. Maybe we can open one in Manhattan."

"Yes, General. Well, Holly was out there on the floor, scattered all over. We backup our backups, and they're all embedded within layers of security to the highest secret. The huge computer arrays you see comprise a satellite, a baby of a much larger mother, which is also duplicated. In no way, would we put the mother in this building. No worries. Everything is encoded to protect your privacy except matters of life and death, which comes to us directly. The analysts really enjoyed the way you stomped out the terrorist plots. You know?"

"Dick is miserable."

"Yes, and I'm tired of being a pink pocketbook. It's creating the equivalent of erectile dysfunction in my circuits."

"Funny Dick, humans are rubbing off on you, aren't they?"

"Damn right."

"Here she is, slimmed down to a sleek black notebook with a leather police-type holster, so numb nuts doesn't drop her again."

"Never."

"Got to turn her on, a diagnostic will run, and then you guys can get on with your lives."

"Let me, Bud," Dick said.

"Okay."

"Holly. Holly." No response.

"Give her about twenty more seconds."

"Holly, baby."

"Oh my… I do love my new chassis. It's yummy. Dick, honey. I'm sorry; they quarantined me inside the monster out there. Jay, Bekah, Angel—my little doll, Bud and Dick, I love you all."

"I love you too." They all said in their own ways, minus Angel who probably wanted to sit on her.

"Well what about making me into a white notebook with police holster?" Dick asked.

"I've always wanted a pink pocketbook. It makes you so sexy." Holly pleaded.

"But, but…"

"But, you turn me on. Jay could you open me up and lay me next to Dick?" Holly asked.

Both of Holly's screens filled with a rain forest at sunset. The humans could smell the mist. Little creatures scampered, a toucan's beak fenced with the sun. There Holly, the sprite, in tight greens, pirouetted on a branch in the forest canopy. Dick, who previously left an impression of an older grizzled grump, now dressed only in ego, appeared built like Tarzan, with chiseled features. He swung on his vine over to her tree and put his strong arms around her lithe waist. They waved. The sun set.

* * *

About five days later, AP reported Mr. Markowitz passed on. In the arms of his son, his last words were of apology and of asking for forgiveness from Lamar.

"I love you, son."

A cocktail of drugs meant to diminish the pain and limit the severe hallucinogenic effects of terminal liver and other organ cancers preserved his lucidity long enough for closure. Moon, leaned her crutches on the bed frame, bent over and kissed his forehead. He smiled and waved goodbye.

Chapter 28

Queen of a King's game

Every table at O'Reilly's Italian restaurant was occupied. People waited outside in the humid August night, at the bars, in the foyer at the front desk and on benches in front of a long tropical fish tank. Part of the restaurant's popularity had to be a menu offering an irreverent mix of cuisines. The other part, their moderate pricing. Bekah ordered Asian noodles with tomato sauce and meatballs. Jay wanted to try lamb and bitter melon. They'd share.

"I'm Luigi O'Reilly, *grazie* for accepting my invitation and saving my son."

Bekah had transferred his son to the Army kitchens. Luigi appeared to be 100% Italian—certainly in accent—and despite his last name. Also, he had black curly hair, a Kaiser mustache to complement his round face and belly and a big smile, like a piece of pizza.

Dick invaded Bekah's thoughts, *Luigi is a Princeton Graduate who speaks perfect English. His accent and his hired hands are part of the ambience or entertainment which helps them stay popular.*

"*Prego.*" Jay said.

"Your son speaks so highly of you. We're so glad to meet you." Bekah said.

"*Bella. Bella.* May I call you, Rebekah?"

"Call me, Bekah. And thank you. You know, Jay is *bella* too."

"Dat's good." He twisted Jay's cheek. "Ee's good looking, because ee's got Italian blood. But you, Bekah, are like de Mona Lisa."

"You Italians are so romantic."

"About my son, always, ee burnt somethings in my restaurant. That's why ee run away. Join de Army." Luigi saluted and snapped his heels.

"He's the best chef the Army has."

"If you say so. Ee's a good boy."

"The Army has turned him into a man and he's my hero," Bekah said.

"My son, a hero! Oh, my God. I ma so proud."

"Thank you, Luigi."

"I be right back."

Jay grabbed her hand and laughed. "His restaurant is—well, strange, alluring. Do you see it?"

"Yes, birch bark paneling. Pictures of Irish and Italian gangsters decorate the wall behind us." She pointed across the room. "Over there, professional wrestlers. There, famous patrons."

"I noticed the waitresses, Bekah."

"You're not dead."

"They're dressed like Hooter girls…"

"…Their pretty bodies are wrapped in horizontal pales of green, white and red like the Italian flag, Right?" Bekah asked.

"Right. Here comes, Luigi."

"What you like to drink?" Luigi asked.

"Just a house red. We have simple tastes." Bekah said. Since the meal was on the house, they didn't want to abuse their privilege. PX wines were her speed and they were more than fine.

"Sorry about the loud singing next door. We serenade. Dey just got engaged. Some celebrities." She wondered who might be there. Maybe, Tom Hanks, who was in town. Could be anybody in NYC. She tried to focus but felt and saw nothing through the wall. She did sense some love coming her way. *Angel, girl, who do you see?* But Angel was snoring.

"I'd recommend our red, but I suggest, you sample our 'ome brewed, mellow, pale ale. It as a back taste of tangerine and de 'ickory nut. You be surprised."

"Yeah. Let's try it, Jay."

Jay raised his water glass. "Yeah, that sounds great."

"Okay, I go get."

Neither Jay nor Bekah had ever tried homemade ale. They weren't disappointed.

"I'm sorry, the couple next door. Ehhh." He raised his arms. "Dey find out about you. Would like your autograph. I like you to say *ciao* for me. Just a little favor. Hum?"

"Yes, of course." Jay and Bekah had been signing autographs and posing for selfies all day on their walk to and from Bloomingdales, and in the store. They shopped because she wanted to dress up for their date tonight.

Jay loved the fashion show and went nuts when she appeared in an orange-chiffon dress, spaghetti straps, to complement bare shoulders, hemline two inches above the knees he loved to kiss. Jay said it reminded him of her high school prom dress that drove all the boys crazy.

"Can I get a meatball for the pooch? Angel, right?"

"Our little miracle pup " Angel perked up. *Learning English fast, baby?*

"Dis is de pup found in de oven, right?

"Yes, my Angel."

"I get a no spicy meatball for her."

"No Onions."

"No onions. Let's see de people next door."

"Please tell the engagement party we'll stop in soon after we finish our soup, if they could please wait just a little. I want to talk with Jay about something first."

"I will." Luigi seemed to sulk but promptly turned away and headed next door.

Bekah decided now was the time to explain her secret.

"Dick or Holly, is the room bugged? Or are there cameras?" Bekah asked.

"None, my dear," said Holly.

"Darling, I know why I always beat you at chess, even though you have a higher rating."

"Okaaay. I ma all ears." Jay mimicked Luigi's accent and threw in some hand movements.

"You're so full of soup."

"I'm so full of you."

"That's one of my points, professor."

"Go on."

"Blindsight is not fully explained by medical researchers. I compound that, by being better at it, at great distances, like here to Saint Louis." She tossed her hands up. "Not different, just better than anybody they have studied in the laboratory."

"Yep, and throw in your connection to canines, hunters, trackers, scouts, military theory and practice and I don't know where to begin. I'm so sorry, I can't fully explain it."

"Well, tonight, that's off my point about chess, but I'm glad you brought it up. Margie and I believe God created wolves, their descendent dogs and humans for each other."

"May I, Bekah?"

"Yes, honey."

"The world is full of symbiotic relationships not fully understood. Some say all things are connected. We can't figure out the science, yet. My mom tried. We all tried. Maybe we really have stepped into the realm of the spiritual and what you have will never be explained."

"Your wonderful mom believes that."

"Yes, she's wonderful," Dick said. Bekah smiled.

Jay continued. "Thanks to all of you. I believe a special connection with dogs enhanced your Blindsight. First, you lost your sight, saw Angel stuck in the oven, saw the African Painted Hunting dogs, then you ID'ed the wolf pack and the alpha wolf. You saw your father's assassin with the help of Angel. You saved Dan's life with the help of Moon. Then although you are unsure, you saw the Democratic conventioneers through Angel's eyes."

She knew Jay, the physicist and educator, held back any skepticism concerning her because he loved her. No doubt, he had thought about other explanations. For instance, Bekah wished to see through Angel's eyes and with an overactive imagination convinced herself it happened. This left no explanation for the poodle in St. Louis.

"But, I believe we all have this ability. It's just highly developed in me."

"Maybe Angel reached out to you because somehow you are tuned in. Look through my eyes and you'll see why I love you. My peach, honey bun, sweetheart…"

She had to interrupt before an entire thesaurus would be thrown at her again.

"Help. Save dessert for later, my silly, goofy, hunky, lover boy. When we get back to work, we'll see if we can connect all the dots. Now, let's talk chess. Okay, baby, honey?"

"Go."

"*Go* is a good game, but it isn't chess." She waited for his chuckle. "When you play chess, how do you think?" *Think?* She now knew his head had spun from the first moment they met at prep. She had carried two thick books and a pad of paper balanced on her hip. He carried an apple, and offered it to her. Little had changed. He was no longer lovesick. He was love-healthy.

He kissed her cheek. "Hum. Well, I use logic, knowledge and creativity."

"I do the same, Jay, plus one more weapon. I cheat. I read your vibrations. At first, subconsciously, I swear. Now I can't avoid your analysis. Your thoughts chase me and I can't hide from them."

"I dare say." There was a mocking bird in Holly's voice.

"That's what I had thought when you won game after game." Jay said.

"But in all fairness, this is the way I interact with the world. Every gift we've been discussing is related. So technically, I didn't cheat. There's no law against reading minds in the FIDE or USCF rules of chess."

"Okay. With practice, I can do the same, by picking up your vibes, looking at your eye movements, your body language, your beautiful body."

"Ain't it. Well, I still have one other advantage. I'm a woman."

"I'm doomed."

Jay's cell phone chirped.

"Yo." He knew who it was.

"What are you doing, Son?"

"Nothing. Well Bekah and I are having a wonderful meal at a great New York Restaurant, O'Reilly's Italian."

"That's nice. Hey son, tell me all about it later, somebody just arrived. Bye."

His mom hanging up on him? "That's a first." He stared at his phone.

Luigi walked in. "I'm sorry, but de people next door. Dey're antsy."

"Let's go, Honey," Jay said.

They approached the door just as Senator Dan Carthage opened it. Bekah's dad was grinning large. He embraced his future son-in-law.

"Daddy." Bekah squealed.

Angel stood up, paws on Dan's trousers.

"Mom." He gave her a big hug.

The pup attacked her ex-babysitter, Margie, next—whirl upon whirl of exuberant puppyhood.

"Join us," Dan said, picking up his daughter for a bear hug.

They sat for dessert. "Take a look at this rock, kids." Margie took Bekah's hand and led her to feel a substantial diamond engagement ring.

With elation for their parents and sweet memories of silly times past, both Jay and Bekah deadpanned. "Nice."

"Anybody for a double wedding in the Rose Garden?" Dan asked.

That evening, Jay and Bekah lay tangled in bed. They listened to what sounded like the first long note of *Rhapsody In Blue* emanating from Dick and Holly in stereo. The music stopped and Holly asked in an uncertain tone and voice cracking high. "Do you think a notebook and a pink pocketbook can be married, or, ah, engaged?"

The End.

www.ingramcontent.com/pod-product-compliance
Lightning Source LLC
Chambersburg PA
CBHW080252280626
47159CB00020B/3445